12/31
LAS VEGAS

12/31
LAS VEGAS

MAELYN BJORK

To order additional copies of this book, contact:
Xlibris
1-888-795-4274
www.Xlibris.com
Orders@Xlibris.com
796557

CHAPTER ONE

———— ✦✦✦✦✦ ————

THE SPECIAL OPS team assembled at the field office of the FBI, Southern Los Angeles County. One by one the four men and two women arrived, all dressed in black Kevlar jackets, caps, and each carrying a side arm. The plan was to be a surprise attack. The information they had gleaned spoke of a cell calling themselves soldiers, Sons of Allah. They were supposed to be embedded, but they had been seen in an out of an out of an abandoned warehouse near the Port of San Pedro.

One of the team's last members walked in pulling down a black, ball cap over his bright, copper colored hair. This was the official 'computer geek', Mac. aka Dexter MacCandlass, though he answered to either name. He had gone through the training at Langley to be a field agent. Yet his preferred talent leaned to cracking computer codes, rather than the heads of bad guys, breaking down firewalls, rather than the doors of suspected criminals. Because of his red hair and his Kansas farm boy background, he took much good-natured teasing from his fellow agents.

Chief of the South L.A. field office, Thomas Velois called the group to silence. This man was well into his fifties, with thinning hair and a thickening waist. Yet any of the field agents would trust Tom V. with his life. He quickly reminded each member of the group of his or her particular assignment. "We are going into an area near the ocean docks of San Pedro. We've had tips of squatters in the area, and a New

York field office has listened to phone calls between this group and the recently arrested members of a terrorist cell, and those still free in the UK. The locals have been seen going in and out of an old warehouse. MacCandlass, tell them about the Email you intercepted."

"I managed to find an Email meant for somewhere in Syria. It was, I believe, in Arabic. After having it translated, it spoke of the 'whore of the 'desert'. It promised about many things dear to Americans would be destroyed. As far as was possible, it was traced back to this warehouse location."

"So when you guys get in there, MacCandlass will find their computer and pull off as much information as possible. The rest of you will search, arrest and secure the area." Let's get going."

The team left in two dark colored, unmarked vans. Mac's partner, Theodore Kastanis rode in front, Jeri Fox, and Velois rode in the back and Mac at the wheel.

Theo, who usually seemed laid back and calm, was strangely nervous. Normally, he was an easy going, good natured guy. Tonight he fidgeted, continually shifting in his seat as much as his seat belt would allow. He ran his hands through his black curly hair, and kept careful watch on the clock on the dashboard. Sometimes he turned his head to wordlessly stare out the window. "Hey, Mac, I thought we were supposed to reach the target at 11:30 p.m. We're early. You'd better slow down a little." Theo Kastanis said.

"Don't worry about it, Theo. It's okay if we're a little early, because it will give us time to get into position, hide the van if necessary." Mac glanced at his partner. "Stop fidgeting. What's the problem? Did you eat too much of that spicy Greek food you love for dinner?"

Theo blew out a breath; his gaze directed at the floor. "Yeah, I must'a overdone the food."

Mac shook his head. He had never seen Theo so anxious. Even though they had been partners for nearly a year, he hadn't a clue about his friend's anxiety.

"Hey Kastanis, you and your 'old lady' have a tiff?' Jeri asked.

"Nah, we're fine. Maybe I'm coming down with something?"

2

Mac took the freeway off ramp, then a right and turned down a dark street heading toward the waterfront. In the distance they could see the abandoned hulks of ancient warehouses, rows and rows of them. He slowed the van and cut the headlights. In his rear view mirror he could see the other van less than a block behind.

The targeted warehouse loomed directly ahead. High on the wall of the building facing the ocean showed at least three levels of small paned windows. Mac eased the van around the west side of the building. The other dark van followed. He could see a streetlevel door, and parked the van close to it. He and Theo got out and eased toward the entrance. The members of the team in the other van began to spill out, and leaned against the wall as Mac began to pick the lock.

A car screamed around the corner, shots were fired from the car, aiming mainly at the vans. Mac dropped and rolled and came up, weapon in hand. The other members of the team did much the same. He aimed at the car and fired at the retreating taillights. He watched left taillight explode.

"Theo, Jeri you guys all right?" Velois asked.

"Yeah, where did that come from?" Theo asked.

"One of those shots about gave me a new hair do." Jeri squeaked.

"Did any of you get a good look at the car?"

"Yeah, I think it was a Mercedes, an old one." Jeri answered.

"Let's get in there." Velois came up to the door. "Maybe they left a cell member behind."

"You sure you want to go in there?" Kastanis laughed nervously.

"Sure Theo, That's why we came here." Velois said

Theo swallowed, and took a breath. "Ok, let's do it."

Mac picked the lock, and tried the door. It stuck. Theo gave the door a mighty kick and it gave in. They moved in with weapons drawn. Dust motes floated up, and for a moment, only light came from the moon shining through dirty windows.

Mac located stairs along the wall leading to an upstairs office. Flashlight in hand he raced up to the top. He found the door to the office unlocked. He yanked open the door and saw the soft blue glow of a computer screen. Pulling on latex gloves, he yanked a disk from his pocket and slid it into the computer slot. Even though he found the computer files set on DELETE, he began to download whatever files still remained on the computer.

Two of the other six agents began searching the cavernous warehouse for any useable evidence left by the 'cell'. Velois galloped up the stairway, and burst into the office. "Anything left on that computer?"

"They set it to the delete mode, but maybe if we take it with us we can get as much as possible from it." Mac didn't mention the disk he had been downloading. When Velois went back down the stairs, Mac took out the disk and put it back into his jacket pocket. He wanted time to go over the information he had found, examine it, organize it. He knew he would have to explain it at the debriefing the next day. Picking up the computer, he tucked it under arm. and placed it into the rear of the van outside.

The agents were snapping photos, sifting through clothing, dusting for prints, bagging up anything left by the intruders. Everything they found would go to the crime lab on their return to headquarters.

Opening the door to his second floor walk-up apartment always gave Mac a comfortable feeling. It was his home, his place away from the pressures of his job, and the huge, busy city he now had called home for nearly two years.

As was his habit, he always walked to the second bedroom where he kept his computer, and his next most important possession, a Tarmac, 10 speed bicycle. He always had to check to make sure his precious possessions were still there, that no one had broken in and stolen them. Where he grew up in rural Kansas, no one even locked their doors.

2:13 A.M. read the clock on Mac's kitchen stove when he turned on the burner under the tea kettle to make a cup of tea. He took the disk from his pocket, booted up his computer and placed it in the slot. He began to examine what he had been able to save. While sipping his tea, he scanned the information he had found on the disk. First thing he saw was an Email from a Swiss bank, another one with sorting numbers from an offshore bank in the Dutch Antilles. He studied those numbers for a moment. Plus there were two Emails in Arabic from much the same source as the one he had located before. He would need a translator to understand those.

At the end of the disk, he found another e-mail in English mentioning Las Vegas. He quickly burned a copy of the disk, and hid the first copy inside a James Patterson novel. He would take the original to headquarters for debriefing tomorrow, 9 a.m. sharp. He was excited to translate those emails that were Arabic and find out what they contained.

Once in his bedroom he cracked open the sliding glass door to the small deck. For a moment he enjoyed the cool, slightly foggy night, but then stripped off his clothes. He quickly showered, and felt coolness from the damp September night still clinging to summer. He lay down and pulled up a sheet to catch a few hours' sleep, but his mind questioned the mention of Las Vegas in the e-mails. Had the terrorists decided to attack America's Adult Playground? AKA,'Sin City'? Would what happened in Las Vegas, really stay in 'Vegas?. Or would it be known all over the world?

CHAPTER TWO

———— ♦♦♦♦♦♦ ————

C LAIRE TALBOT SLUMPED over her desk in the doom room she occupied. She was reviewing for an exam on large animal anatomy she had at 9 a.m. the next morning. She was a student at the Veterinary College in Boulder, Colorado.

She stood up and stretched going through an arm and shoulder exercise. She worked through these short exercises to avoid the stiffness that came from sitting for long periods. Suddenly her land line rang, and she whirled around to see who would be calling. Her small clock read 10:37 p.m. It was late for her brother or mother to be calling. "Room 364, Claire Talbot speaking."

"Claire, oh I'm so glad I caught you in your room. I called earlier, but I guess you were out." The words came out in a rush.

"Suzanne! My goodness how are you doing? Why are you calling, especially so late?"

"I know it's late, but I had to put Justin to bed before I had time to call. I just had to give you the *news*."

"What news? What could be happening in Rawley, Utah that would be considered newsworthy?"

"You forget to include St. George. It's about Neil Bradshaw. He had an accident and was killed."

"Dead!?" Claire sucked in a ragged breath, coughed and tried to clear the tremors from her throat. "How? When?' Claire had a momentary attack of grief, and she could not stop the tears forming in her eyes, and trickling down he cheeks. *Oh God, not Neil!* Yet, because of the last time she saw him, she was full of anger, and felt only the deep pain he had caused her. *No, she couldn't give in to grief, not now.* She coughed and took a ragged breath. "What kind of accident? Did he trip over his nine iron on the golf course?" Claire covered her pain with heavy sarcasm.

"No- - - - - - -." He drove his new Acura convertible into the corner of a brick building. *Massive Head Injury, Alcohol a factor.* "Sorry, just quoting the death certificate." Suzanne said.

"You'd know since you work in the St. George ME's office." Claire quipped. "How is his present wife taking all this? From what I remember she was wife number three."

"You mean Sally? She's grieving properly. Wearing a little black dress with a thigh high, full skirt, and of course sniffing though a little black veil into a white lacy handkerchief. I visited the mortuary this evening."

"When's the funeral?" Claire asked. "I supposed I could send Sally a 'Get-over-your-loss-card'.

"The funeral is the day after tomorrow. However, the main reason I called is that you need to be here."

"I'm in the middle of my third semester in Vet school. I can't leave now." Claire voice showed her irritation.

"I understand that. However, Ted Huffington, Neil's attorney called and told me that we both need to be at the reading of Neil's will and trust. And he was very serious."

"Suzanne, you're kidding, - - - - - - - -, are you not?"

"I speak the honest truth. If you leave tomorrow early you can make it by 12 Noon, Saturday to the funeral, here In St. George."

"Okay, let me think." Claire began to pace the narrow room. - - - - -. I have an exam tomorrow at 8 a.m. After that I could start driving. Then I could leave Rawley early Sunday morning, and make it back here in time for my Monday morning lab, and Monday noon, lecture." Claire mumbled.

"Great. I think it's important you come with me to the reading of the will." Suzanne sounded relieved.

"I'll stop by you place of business on the way home." Claire said

"Take it easy, I know how you like to push that Honda of yours."

"Going across umpteen miles of southern Colorado and then into Utah isn't 5 O'clock traffic, you know."

"Just take it easy." Suzanne ordered.

"What the weather like down there." Claire asked

"The usual weather for early October. Days are still hot and dry, but the evenings are cooler."

"I'll see you tomorrow, late. Thanks for call, even though I wasn't thrilled with the news."

"Oh, by the way, I'm not living in St. George anymore. I'm back in Rawley, at my mother's house." Suzanne sounded too offhand at this new situation.

"At your mother's? Why? Where's Andy?"

"I'll explain it all to you when you arrive." Suzanne let a long sigh escape. "See ya tomorrow. Bye."

Claire held on to phone for a long moment. *I thought I was finished with Neil Bradshaw.* Claire hadn't laid eyes on him for well over a year. A man she thought was the 'one'. She believed he cared for her, as she did for him. Damn it, she had *loved* him. He had been her boss, her mentor, her first and only lover.

She felt a jumble of emotions. Grief, anger tinged with sadness. Yet somehow, way down deep, a sense of relief. Right now she couldn't dwell on what might have been. She swiped at the tears on her face. She marched into the bathroom and splashed her face with water. Then stripped and took a shower. Standing, wrapped in a towel, she pulled out her suitcase from a shelf in the closet. Later she stood staring at her small wardrobe hanging in the closet. She's need lightweight clothes to wear in St. George.

The drive from Boulder Veterinary College to St. George was close to Six hundred miles, and across two states. Once she picked up I-70 she had another nine hours to drive. Her old Honda Accord could still eat up the miles, with the air conditioning blasting, and could keep her in relative comfort.

Once she had cell phone range, she called Suzanne still at the STME office and asked about the time of the reading of the Neil's will.

The old morgue was still found in the St. George Regional Hospital. Corpses came in from the hospital itself as well as, bodies were brought in from anywhere in the county. The waiting period for autopsy, examination, or even for the family viewing became longer and longer. And the bodies began to stack up, a new building for city-county services was under construction but not yet finished.

Claire went down to the basement level in the elevator. As the sliding doors opened she was assaulted by the cool, slightly dry air, and the faint, unmistakable odor of death. She knocked on the door of marbled glass and rattled the door knob. "Suzy, you in there?"

Through the frosted glass, she could see a fuzzy outline of her friend. She could make out her petite figure and white coat.

Opening the door marked Hospital Morgue, Suzanne pulled Claire in. "Hey you made it, and in good time, too." She pulled Claire into a bone crushing hug.

Claire smiled down at Suzanne. "It's good to see you, too. I stopped by to see what tomorrow's activities are going to be, what time exactly and where."

"Okay the funeral is at 12 noon, the graveside is at 2 p.m., and the reading of the will is at six in the evening." Suzanne handed Claire a printed schedule.

"I'm surprised she's not shipping the body back to Virginia." Claire said. "He was born and raised there."

"No, she bought drawers in the mausoleum, next to a spot she previously purchased, plus another one for her next husband or son, whoever needs it. I suppose I should correct my grammar and say the next man in her life."

"She's planning to bind Neil to her in death, as well as life. *How Sweet.*" Claire couldn't keep the sarcasm from her voice. Hating the painful emotion bubbling to the surface, Claire blinked and turned away from Suzanne. "Well, my mind is fuzzy and my eyes are burning,

I'd better get on the road to Rawley. Hopefully, some decent sleep will improve my black mood. So I'm back on the road. My land line is on vacation mode, so call me on my cell."

"I know you're bushed, but you look good. You've lost more weight, and I love this new Princess Di hair style. It shows off your 'white lock' to an advantage. I'll see you tomorrow. I'm glad you decided to come home, even it is just for the weekend."

"You don't look so bad yourself; Still sporting the blond curly hair and, those innocent blue eyes. If people only knew what lurks in that head of yours." Claire laughed. "See ya tomorrow."

Home was eight miles, slightly north and west of St. George. Claire drove into the dry and dusty hills of the town of Rawley. The house she sought was an old farm house sitting on ten acres of land. It was a white clapboard structure with a new black roof. Two years before she had purchased it from her parents. This is where she had grown up.

A few years earlier, her mother had begun to have attacks of arthritis. She seemed to do better in a milder climate. Her parents tried living in various beach cities in Southern California. Even though St. George was wickedly hot in the summer, the winters here could be chilly, sometimes downright cold. So they moved to a small town north of San Diego two years before. Her mother's health improved and Claire bought the family house. Claire hadn't been home for ten months, and she knew what she would find inside. The place would be hot, and everything would be covered with a layer of dust.

The house sat on the north side of the road, under the shelter of large old trees. Old trees with gnarled trunks, survivors of the desert heat, wind, cold and sometimes a blanket of snow, but gave welcome shade in the summer. She had loved this house for all of her thirty-one years.

She found her set of keys in her small backpack, and put the key in the lock, but it would barely turn. This door had always stuck, but after much shaking and jiggling she managed to push the door open. As she expected, she was assaulted with heat and the smell of dust. The first thing to do was turn on the evaporative cooler. She had called a neighbor and asked him to take off the cooler's cover early that morning.

After dragging in all her belongings, she picked up her cell phone and answered a new text. It was from Suzanne. Rather than text back she called her friend.

"Meet me for breakfast before the funeral. Say the Waffle House at 10 a.m. I know you don't have any food in the house." Suzanne said.

'Usually I'm not much for breakfast, but okay." Claire said as her stomach made a loud growling noise. "Right now I'm going to drop, but tomorrow I want the whole story of why you are living with your mother and not your husband."

"It's not a pretty story, but okay. Tomorrow, 10 a.m." Suzanne clicked off.

As Claire set the phone down she took a hard look at her kitchen. She was tired and hungry, but she wouldn't be able to eat until she cleaned it. After digging out some cleaning supplies, she set to work. After the kitchen was reasonably clean, she opened up a can of soup, found a partial loaf of bread in the freezer, and made a cup of tea.

Next she tackled the bathroom. It after midnight when finished she dusting, vacuuming, and changing her bed, but she was pleased with her efforts. Though exhausted, she took a quick shower. Finally she 'hit the wall' as she stood staring at the contents of her closet. She closed her eyes for just a moment and found herself slumped on the floor. Picking herself up, she slid between those clean sheets, but woke up three hours later to turn off the bedroom lamp.

The next morning after a cup of strong coffee, she knew she needed to search her closet for something suitable to wear for all of today's 'festivities'.

She finally found a royal blue, short sleeved knit dress, and the matching pumps. She also found an appropriate long strand of pearls and matching earrings. In the back of the closet she managed to drag out a white cotton shrug. This was in case the church or chapel would be super cool. After all she had acclimated to Colorado Mountain weather.

The restaurant was a landmark of sorts in St. George, and rather crowded. Claire spotted Suzanne three tables back in by a window.

"Great, you managed to get a good table. Have you ordered?" Is Andy watching Justin?" Claire asked.

"Andy's in Las Vegas." Suzanne said in a flat voice.

"What's Andy doing in Las Vegas?"

Suzanne frowned and played with her tableware. "He took a job down there about six months ago. Better money, better chance for advancement."

"Why aren't you in Las Vegas with him, you're still married to him aren't you?"

"We- - - - -sort of, broke up. I didn't want to live in Las Vegas. Living there would be a terrible influence on Justin to grow up there." Suzanne was talking too fast, her voice rising with emotion.

Claire could see she was upset. 'Oh Suzy, that's not the way things should be. You two were so much in love. Isn't there some chance- - - - -.?" Claire watched Suzanne begin to dab at her eyes and sniffle.

"We hassled over the situation endlessly. Now he's in police training down there He's going to be a cop in Nevada's 'sin town'. It's too dangerous! Besides I have a good job here. I'd have to find another position, and day care for Justin. Housing is so expensive down there."

"So where's Andy living? You said you moved back with your mother."

'The LVPD found Andy an apartment. They take care of their own." Suzanne shook her head.

Claire gave a snort of disgust. "And how much influence was your mother in all this?"

"Well, you know Mom, she likes her children and grandchildren close by."

"Did you remind her that Las Vegas is only two hours away?"

"Yes." A long silence - -Then Suzanne glanced up. "Oh, here comes our breakfast." Suzanne was intent watching the server set plates of food on the table.

"What did you order for me?' Claire asked frowning.

'Waffles, you'll see." Suzanne flashed a wide smile. "You'll love this flavor."

CHAPTER THREE

———— •••••••• ————

T HE FUNERAL WAS held at a new funeral business: Crawford Mortuary. In the past years, in the town of St. George, the major religion was the LDS Church. The funerals were usually held in the ward chapels. But now the city had become a major destination for those retiring, along with a college age population attending Dixie State College. The growth in the area was booming, which meant the city had to provide services for an older population, most of which were affluent. And for the college group there was a shortage of student housing. Most of the dorms available were old and insufficient. All of this growth made the population of the town more diverse.

As Claire and Suzanne entered the chapel, Claire was surprised at the large number of people in attendance. Neil had rented an old building and set up his veterinary practice nearly nine years earlier. Most of his practice was treating cats and dogs, but Neil would take a look at a rabbit or a bird now and then. Claire recognized many of owners of these animals in the chapel.

Claire had gone to work for Neil close to nine years before. She had attended Dixie College for two years. Even though now it had grown to a four year college, she ran out of money, and needed to seek employment. On her father's farm she always been comfortable with animals of all kinds. Her major at the college had been biology. And she took courses of both human and animal anatomy.

When she called the *Bradshaw Small Animal Clinic* and asked for an interview, Neil hired her on the spot. He was impressed with her work, and they had grown to be close friends and later on began to date.

When Claire's parents decided to move to Southern California, Claire had saved enough money to put a hefty down payment on the house, and bought it from her parents. At about the same Claire was considering a marriage proposal from Neil. Although she knew he was several years older than she was and had been married before.

One evening Neil took Claire and her parents out to dinner. Neil drank too much, and Claire's father, who does not drink alcohol became disgusted with this man who spoke of marriage to his daughter. When the Talbot family arrived home, Claire's father told his daughter she would be unhappy if she married Neil.

Within a few weeks Neil's attitude toward Claire did a one-eighty change, along with a change in his behavior. He began coming into work with a hangover. He was even drinking on the golf course. One day Claire caught him giving a dog too much anesthetic during a surgery, and Claire had to take over and finish.

Several months earlier, he had hired Suzanne, and began being late to or absent from the clinic more and more. This left the two girls to care for the animals. With Claire and Suzanne to run the clinic, Neil took more time on the golf course and more time to 'unwind'.

The last 'straw' had been Sally. Pert, little, bottle blond Sally, the computer expert. She knew nothing about the diseases of animals and what it took to care for them. Yet, Sally was very good at the computer. She could order supplies and animal food more efficiently and cheaper than Claire had been doing as office manager.

Sally refused to help clean up the animal cages or scrub down the clinic, or even lift a dust cloth to the artificial plants in the waiting room. Before Sally, everyone who worked at the clinic helped to clean up, straighten, and scrub floors at the end of the day.

Within two months Sally had hired four girls who would do much the same work as Claire had been doing for over seven years, and Suzanne for several months. She hired these girls at entry level wages, and no health insurance. Suzanne quit is disgust, quickly found a job at the city morgue. Sally cut Claire's hours to only the days Neil did surgery. She knew Claire was the best tech to do that work. Sometimes she had to save an animal when Neil screwed up.

Claire hung on a month longer, while she applied to veterinary schools across the country. Strangely, Neil wrote a glowing letter of recommendation for Claire to the school in Colorado, where he had received his training. Finally, she was accepted at the Colorado Veterinary School. She had begun her class work there three semesters before. She found the class work went hand in hand with all the training she had received from Neil.

The graveside service took place in the lawn behind the new Mortuary. The day was warm, around 80 degrees, though the outside service was short, it was too long for Claire. The October desert sun beat down on Claire wearing the dark blue dress. She took off the shrug, but then put it back on. She was unaccustomed to wearing anything but flat shoes, and hated standing on the damp grass in dress shoes.

The widow, Sally wore the thigh high black dress along with four inch heels. She finally was brought a chair, and a line of chairs were added. Claire had compassion for Nathan, Sally's eight year old son from a previous marriage. The poor kid was forced to wear a suit and finally the coat came off. Emma, Neil's first wife and her ten year old daughter dropped into some chairs behind Sally. Emma seemed bored and sleepy.

After the final prayer, Claire and Suzanne hurried from the grounds to Suzanne's waiting car

"Boy, am I glad that's over with. I need to go home and peel off this dress and shoes and jump in the shower." Suzanne said.

"Yeah, it's pretty warm, but you elected to wear those three inch heels, and a black print dress."

A shower sounded like an excellent idea. "Hey, I'm not climbing back into this dress for any reason. I'll find something cool and subdued to wear this evening. Definitely some slacks." Claire said. "I'll pick you up, what 5:30 p. m? We should make it to the law office in plenty of time. Actually the main reason for attending this will reading is because of all the high drama." Claire widened her eyes and laughed.

"Ah, Mamselle, Tonight, all will be revealed." Suzanne laughed gleefully, after her poor imitation of the master detective, Poiret.

The law offices of Brinker, Brinker, and Huffman were located in a new strip mall north of St. George in the town called Washington. The offices wrapped around the corner of the sprawling building, with a fair amount of parking on the east side and offered two entrances. One on the front of the building, and the second entrance to the north where there was more parking.

As Claire and Suzanne walked in it was two minutes past 6 p.m. that Saturday evening, and they were the first people to arrive. A young secretary stood behind a long table laid out with coffee, sodas, and plates of snack food. She looked up, holding a clip board and smiled brightly. "Could I please have your names?"

Claire and Suzanne watched her make notations on the clipboard. "Thank you for coming. Please help yourself to some refreshments."

There were paper cups, small plates, forks, spoons and napkins. Claire picked up a cup full of ice, a can diet coke, and a few vegetables and small slices of fruit on a paper plate. Suzanne did much the same.

The secretary turned from taking the names of some other people and said. "Please go into the conference room."

Suzanne indicated two chairs at the opposite end of a pile of paper work laid out at the other end of the long table. Claire and Suzanne watched David Huffman and Sally stroll in and sat down near the paper work end of the table.

Sally glanced up and stared at Suzanne and Claire but made no acknowledgement.

"Well I'm glad I didn't come over here in a dress. I went for comfortable, and it seems Sally did too, I wonder if she glanced into the mirror, and checked her rear end in those white slacks." Suzanne said.

"Those slacks *are* a bit too tight." Clare agreed.

"A *bit?* Is that the new term for a size too small." Suzanne raised her eyebrows. "I suppose I should be kind, after all she is the widow."

Other people began to fill the conference room. Soon Dave Huffman stood and glanced around the room. "Ladies and gentlemen, Please." He said. Calling the group to attention, he cleared his throat, and introduced each person around the table. Lastly he introduced Neil's banker, Sid Franklin.

"We're gathered here tonight to read the last will and testament of one deceased, Neil Aaron Bradshaw." David picked the top sheet from a stack papers. *"Being of sound mind----------------, he droned on.* He described the day of Neil's death. Then he explained the legality of a revocable trust, the tangible goods that had been placed in the trust; Stock, precious metals, real-estate, and some other materials that could be moved in and out of the trust.

David picked up the next sheet of paper. "First, Neil has bequeathed savings bonds, to go to the local animal shelter. Net worth $2,000 dollars. Second, he gave his house, and furnishings, the two automobiles to Sally Ellis Bradshaw. On third sheet of paper Neil bequeathed, his brokerage account to Suzanne Freeman, for her son Justin's college education.

Suzanne's reaction was of genuine surprise. Her hand touched her chest. "I- - - - - - I'm amazed that Neil would do that for my son, and I'm very grateful."

"I bequeath my half ownership in the new golf course in Hurricane to my daughter Emma. Tom Naylor owns the other half. He will help Emma and her mother to understand Emma's role in this venture."

"Oh, please see me after the meeting." He glanced up. "And I need to speak to you, Suzanne, There are stipulations to this account: how you must deal with this brokerage account."

David directed his attention to the next paper in the stack. The next words David spoke had everyone in the room riveted. *"I bequeath my veterinary business, all buildings, grounds, vehicles and contents of such building to Claire Talbot.*

Claire's mouth flew open and the audible sound heard was. "What?"

Sally screamed. "NO! He couldn't have done that. Couldn't, would never do that. There must be some mistake." She stood red faced and shaking.

Suzanne swiveled her body toward David and flashed a benign smile. "Could you please read that again, David?"

"Of course." David directed a tiny smile to Suzanne, picked the next paper in the stack and stood. "I'm now quoting from the will directly. *Claire Talbot was instrumental in building my business and reputation from its inception. She worked long hard hours, became an apt pupil in animal care for seven long years. If anyone deserves to continue to operate Southern Dixie Animal Hospital, it is Claire. If she chooses to continue to operate the clinic, or sell it or even rent it, it is her decision. The proceeds of any sale will go to her.*

Sally jumped to her feet and leaned over David. "He can't do that? Give the clinic to that uppity bitch." She turned to stare venom across the room at Claire.

David sat calmly at the table and gazed coldly up at Sally. "He could and he did. It's all perfectly legal. He never put it your trust. The specific directions as to who inherits his business were changed recently in a codicil." He stood and smiled in Claire's direction. He brushed past Sally and strolled down to where Suzanne and Claire were sitting.

Claire felt body and mind go into mild shock. "Ms. Talbot. Please see Ms. Turner in the foyer and make an appointment for a convenient time on Monday morning. Will that work for you?"

Claire could only give him a brief nod. Her throat felt bone dry. She took a hurried sip from her diet coke.

Suzanne could not wipe a wide smile from her face. "Good work David. I'll have Claire here Monday morning." She turned to Claire and put a hand under Claire's elbow. "Come Claire it's time to leave."

Claire allowed Suzanne to lead her to the secretary in the foyer. "Ms. Turner, is there an opening for Claire and me? Say 10 a.m. Monday morning?"

The young girl checked her paperwork. "Yes, ma'am, 10 a.m. is just fine."

"Thank you." Suzanne directed Claire to the front door. "Claire, give me your car keys. You're in no shape to drive."

Claire fumbled in her purse and handed the keys to her friend. Once they reached the car, Suzanne turned to Claire. "Are you interested in any food?"

"Food? What I need is a drink."

"Okay, I'll drive over to the Hilton. That hotel has a nice quiet bar."

"But you don't drink." Claire murmured.

"Ah, but I've known you do so on occasion." Suzanne began the drive across town to the hotel.

CHAPTER FOUR

———— ✦✦✦✦✦✦ ————

C LAIRE AND SUZANNE walked into the offices of Brinker, Brinker and Huffman at precisely 10 a.m. Monday morning. All weekend Claire had walked around her house trying to do some cleaning and clearing out, but she found herself standing with broom in hand staring out her kitchen window, or leaning on her front porch after she had turned on the sprinkler, and watching the spray flow back and forth for long minutes.

Her mind was in a fog, and found that whatever she thought she should do, she couldn't remember. Should she forget the whole clinic thing and go back to college? But she did nothing to plan a return to Boulder. She didn't have her veterinary license. She would need a licensed vet to come and work at the clinic. She could go back and run the clinic as she had for several years. Or sell it and return to her unfinished education. She finally decided that sitting down with David on Monday was her best option.

"It's nice to see both of you this lovely sunny morning." David came around his desk and offered each a chair to sit down. "May I have something brought in, coffee, a soda, ice water."

"No, I'm fine. Claire said.

"I'm good." Suzanne answered, and smiled.

"Okay." David sat down in his large leather swivel chair behind his gleaming cherry wood desk. "Claire, have you had any thoughts or plans as to the future of your clinic?"

"My clinic?" Oh you're correct. It *is my clinic*. I've thought of nothing else all day yesterday. My original plan was to drive back to Boulder early Sunday morning, but of course it's Monday and I'm sitting here in your office."

"I believe I can help you with your decision. Let's start at the beginning." He opened a file. "The Southern Dixie Animal Clinic has a mortgage on it. It is a ten year mortgage and as of last week Neil sent the September payment on it. Secondly there are fifteen more payments to be made until mortgage company is satisfied."

"You mean paid off." Suzanne said. "And when did he change the name of his clinic?"

"Exactly. Also the three girls who were employed there are willing to return to work, when you reopen the clinic. So you'll have a staff of sorts ready to resume their jobs there. Thirdly, Neil had a vet doing an internship there last year. I took the liberty to call her last night. She lives in Mesquite, Nevada. Her name is Olga Vauneu. She is naturalized citizen originally from Russia. Her English is excellent, and right now she is only working three days a week in Mesquite. Oh, and as far as the name change, I think Sally did that."

"How did Neil and this Russian lady get along?" Claire narrowed her eyes. *Sometimes, Neil could be such a screw-up.*

"Here is a folder with Neil's notes about working with Ms. Vauneu. Along with her name, address, phone numbers and a copy of her license to practice veterinary medicine. Here are the clinic's bank statements. You will find the clinic's billing on the computer." Neil took a small envelope from the file. "Here are the keys to the clinic and the van that is parked out back."

"What about Sally?" Suzanne asked and raised an eyebrow.

"Sally, as you both noticed Saturday evening, is not happy with the way, and to whom Neil left his assets. However, I talked with her, and explained to her that this is what Neil wanted. He wanted you to have the clinic, Claire." David's eyes met Claire's.

Claire took a deep breath and shook her head. "But why now? When he moved Sally into the mix twenty months ago, I was summarily booted out of there." She glanced over at Suzanne.

David cleared his throat. "The marriage was not, how may I describe it, as satisfying to Neil as he thought it would be. He knew Sally could not run the clinic the way he would have wanted it run. He had regrets about your relationship with him. He felt he let you down. But you were the *one* individual to work the clinic, and love and care for the animals."

David stood and slid the keys across the table. "Here are the keys. Go look it over and decide what you want to do."

Suzanne scooped up the keys. Then she sat down again. "Before we leave, I'd like to know about this brokerage account left to Justin."

"Okay. Mainly it's restricted. You must leave it alone, and let the contents grow financially and make the kind of money Neil envisioned when he bought the stock. I'll tell you this much. By the time Justin is ready for college, it will be worth four times what it is today."

"Okay, what is the major stock in the account?" Suzanne asked.

"Google, 50 shares." David smiled. "Oh and it does pay dividends."

"Google?!" A bright smile crossed her face. "Oh, I think I can sit on this for a while."

Claire smiled but shook her head slightly. "Please don't tell your mother, Suzie."

Suzanne frowned but gave a little nod. "Right, that would not be a good move. Come on Claire, let's go over to the clinic and take a look. We've got an hour before I have to pick up Justin from kindergarten."

"Thank you David for being such a good friend to Neil. Apparently, he really needed you." Claire swiped at the tears filling her eyes, and fumbled for a tissue in her purse. He nodded and handed her the clinic folder.

"Call if you need any help." He walked his two clients to the door.

As Suzanne drove back into the business section of St. George, she turned to Claire. "See, I told you, you'd want to go back to the animal clinic and take a look around. Besides, I haven't been in the place since

I quit. See, as I explained, it would be better if we drove two cars into St. George from Rawley."

"Are there other things you told me to '*see*' that I need to remember" Claire said.

"Humm. My advice is usually good." Suzanne straightened the rear view mirror. A few streets later, she turned into the driveway which led to the rear of the animal clinic.

One they were in the building Claire felt a strong sense that this place *was* destined to be hers. "It's clean and looks pretty good." As she walked around opening drawers and checking some of the animal cages, she smiled and turned to Suzanne. "You were right this time. I do want to take charge of this place. I may as well call the vet in Mesquite from here so that she will have this phone number. Make this my business phone."

"Good, I can put in a few hours in the mornings here while Justin is in school. I know you'll need to drive back to Colorado and clean out your dorm room and speak to the administration about your earned credits. While you're gone I can come by every day and check on things. I'm sure Sally would love to sabotage the place, if she could."

"Thanks a bunch Suzy." Claire walked over to her friend and gave her a hug. It looks like I'll need you to be my friend and a nag. We've somehow must get you and Andy back together, and your marriage back on track."

The Southern California FBI field office had run out of leads. Only two individual's fingerprints came up on Interpol and one of those was found on IFIS. The first man they were able to identify was Ari Hakim Barouq. He had been in the U.S. since the terrorist attack in Florida. One stray fingerprint of his had been found in the suspected killer's apartment. He was originally from Yemen and been with some of the original leaders of ISIS' payroll.

The second set fingerprints were identified and on Interpol were from Zuhdi Hassim. He was suspected in the investigation of the Subway bombing in England. How both of these men plus at least four others got in, and have been in the United States for a fair amount of time? This was the first time they had been in Southern California. The Bureau had its suspicions, but no clear evidence.

Mac had traced every Email, but one. Only a single lead on that one, mentioned the destruction of some kind in Las Vegas.

Tom Velois decided to give the Las Vegas director a call. Since 'Vegas had no leads, he convinced the director in Las Vegas to begin checking with the LVPD.

The local police department had now received a threat mentioning 'taking down the corrupt world' of their fair city. Once the local field office received the email from the police department, the director called Strickland and asked for help. "Anything you can tell mw would be helpful, V.I."

"Have your people come up with anything, threats, strange activities in places outside of the city?"

"We've assigned two of my best agents to work on your inquiry. They have been checking with all the divisions of local police. The police have received two emails. Both were a mix of English and Arabic." Director Strickland said.

"Let me know if you need any help. I have a fine field agent, Dexter Macandlass, and his partner Theo Kastanis. Macandlass is amazing, He can turn a computer over, stand it on its head and make it sing Dixie."

"Great. I'll contact you if anything else comes up." V.I Strickland said.

CHAPTER FIVE

————— ◆◆◆◆◆◆ —————

S IX DAYS LATER Theo and Mac drove to Las Vegas. They were told to stay at a specific motel and were directed to the local FBI office when they arrived.

The next morning they returned to the field office and met with special Agent Dan Forester and his partner Marla Bunker. They went for a midmorning briefing at the motel coffee shop.

When Mac met Dan Forester, he noticed that the man was close to his height, but heavier. The extra weight seemed to be in his wider shoulders, and muscular arms. He looked trim and strong.

After introductions, Dan began to brief them on the progress made in their investigation. "When the police detail checked this particular area, they found things pretty quiet. One of the officers noticed a big dog, probably a yellow lab mix, wandering around some old abandoned warehouses west of the airport. At times those warehouses are used when some heavy freight needs to be stored for a few days. The next time the patrol checked the area, the dog could not be found. We believe someone found him and pulled him inside."

Marla laughed. "Another strange thing about one of warehouses occurred. Someone had washed the windows high on the eastside. It was a partial cleaning of a second story level. Anyway, the windows had been cleaned."

"Facing east,- - - Mecca." Mac mused. "Muslims would want clean windows to face Mecca while they pray. It would take a woman to notice that."

"So, it's not just housecleaning. then?" Agent Forester's face quirked into a grin. "I didn't know house cleaning was high on their list, unless some woman does it."

"A woman or the junior member of the group. They get the grunt work." Mac said with a sly grin.

"At any rate the local police will keep up their surveillance. If it looks like something illegal is going on, we'll have grounds for a raid." Dan said.

The next day MacCandlass and Forester were 'brought up to date'of some interesting news. "A delivery truck came through the area, and hit a big dog. The driver said it was a yellow lab mix. It managed to hide or was pulled into a particular warehouse. It could be the one with clean windows."

"Then we know people are in there, and possibly with an injured dog. "Mac said.

It was well past midnight when Mac, Dan, Theo, and another agent named Wielding plus four of Las Vegas 'finest' quietly drove up to the side entrance door of the warehouse. All was dark and all was quiet. Theo banged on the door and announced "FBI, Las Vegas police. Open up!"

They went in with powerful flashlights searching every corner of the building. The light picked up a garage door at the far right end of the back wall. The door rolled up and behind it, an old blue Mercedes roared to life. At that second Mac shot up the stairs and spotted a glowing screen of a computer. He ran to it and picked it up.

A bullet grazed his shoulder and a voice said. "Ah, Mr. computer geek, I got you."

As the bullet whizzed by his head, Mac ducked and it grazed his shoulder. The butt of a revolver slammed into the back of his head. Pain shot through Mac's head and shoulder, then dizziness and the floor came up fast and last, blackness.

Below, flashes of gunfire were aimed at the incoming FBI and police. When Forester realized they had been ambushed, he yelled. "Get out!" Suddenly his arm burned and fell useless. Yet he made it out, and to his FBI car.

Following him were three police officers, Wielding, but no Theo and no Mac.

"Just what happened in there?" Detective Brown croaked, his voice hoarse with fear.

An unconscious Mac was dragged down the stairs by his feet, and his captor yelled for the youngest of group to help the leader toss Mac into the trunk of the waiting Mercedes. Mac shared the trunk with an injured yellow dog.

Four men jumped into the car and Zuhdi, the driver yelled. "Where's Hannique?"

"Dead. Do we leave his body for the enemy?" Aukmed asked.

"He is in his glory, now." Zuhdi answered.

"But the Americans, they will find out who he is."

"Dead, he cannot help them. Dead, he cannot hurt us." We go to the safe house." Zuhdi gunned the older car around to another road and left the warehouses and headed north to the freeway.

Dan Forester though wounded, called for backup from the FBI, and Detective Brown called the Las Vegas and yelled for 'back up'. for the investigators. Once the teams arrived they decided to wait until daylight. They posted fresh men to guard the area until the investigators returned.

Officer Brown insisted Dan Forester be driven to the nearest hospital to check on his arm and shoulder. Finally Brown drove him to Las Vegas South, Medical Center.

Once Forester was examined, the bullet wound was deemed not serious, but could become infected without treatment. The emergency room doctor insisted he stay at least 12 hours, gave him a sedative and found a bed for him to rest.

The terrorists' safe house was located 15 miles north and west of Las Vegas. From the freeway, Zuhdi turned west on a well - traveled but unpaved road. Once across a flat area of the desert, the road curved up into the mountains and the desert gave way scrub bushes, larger plant life, then to small trees. They passed a dry river bottom, and finally Zuhdi drove the car up and around a curve to an old farm house nestled in a stand old half- dead trees. The trickiest part of the drive was a curve in the road that narrowed and angled before reaching a fairly flat place near the house. Behind the old house stood an ancient shed, boulders and more trees, but finally a space to park a car.

The Mercedes, badly in need of shocks and struts, bounced and lurched its way up to the house. Zuhdi parked behind the old house. It was an uneven spot where the ground tilted down so that part of the automobile sat on a curve. Because of the uneven ground, the driver's side door, when opened scraped the hard packed dirt.

The four terrorists pushed at the front door. The hinged lock on the door was broken and hanging by one screw. The only light fixture in the front room was an old western style wagon wheel with only two bulbs of five lighting the room when they flipped the switch. There were four used folding chairs bunched around a badly scratched table under the light fixture. The only other piece of furniture was a filthy, mud colored, sagging sofa and had been pushed into one corner A spring had popped through the worn cloth covering on the sofa.

"Get the FBI geek." Zuhdi ordered, he had become the self- appointed leader of the group. The youngest, Jahreal, and barely eighteen years, and his brother Ari Hakim, stomped down the three stairs off the sagging front porch shuffled around back and opened the trunk of the car. Mac and the dog lay inside, both unconscious.

"He's heavier than he looks." Ali said as he and Jehreal struggled with the unconscious Mac. They carried him into what the men used as a bedroom with cots lined up across the small room.

"Is he awake yet.?" Zuhdi asked.

"No he seems to be unconscious." Ali said.

"Ah, he plays at sleep." Zuhdi growled. He grabbed a half smoked cigarette from a cracked ashtray in the middle of the table and lit with a lighter from his pocket. With cigarette dangling from his lips he smacked Mac hard across his mouth. Nothing happened, no reaction. Zuhdi smacked him in the jaw. Still no reaction. Zuhdi tore the sleeve of Mac's shirt grabbed his arm and burned the inside of Macs arm. They heard only a small moan.

Zuhdi swung around and grabbed Ali by his shirt. "What did you do to him? You were to subdue him. Not render him useless."

Ali Hakim dropped his head and shrugged, then lifted his hands, palms outward in a gesture of ignorance. "Maybe I hit him a little too hard?"

"Get him awake! We need to know what he has discovered on our computers." Zuhdi left the room.

"Perhaps he had a suicide pill, or tooth?" Jahreal said.

"No, not Americans, they don't believe in suicide." Zuhdi paced from the room and then came back.

"Could I examine him? Perhaps I can discover how he is injured." Jaheal asked swallowing his timidity.

Zuhdi threw up his hands. "Do it."

Jahreal knelt next to the cot where Mac had been laid. He began touching his hands arms and legs. Next he picked up his head, and felt his head and neck. Gently he moved his hand across the American's upper back. "He has quite a bump here, and lump here." Jahreal gestured to the side and back of Mac's head. "Perhaps he has a concussion. Also there in a bad cut behind his ear. It no longer bleeds, but,-- - -.

"And how would you know that, my young *doctor*?" Zuhdi sneered as he paced back and forth in the small bedroom.

"I, ah- - -" Jahreal opened his had hands on his thighs, and dropped his head.

"He talks of being an animal doctor. He reads many books." Ali spoke up. "Perhaps I hit the American too hard, or his head hit the stairs as I dragged him to the car."

Zuhdi ground his teeth in frustration. "What good is he to us? If he is unconscious, perhaps near death? None I tell you. Shoot him. Bury him next to your precious dog."

"No!" Aukmed ran into the room. "Bullets can be traced. Have you not seen the CSI program Here in Las Vegas they will find the body, dig out the bullets, and- - - - - - -."

"Then, what do you suggest?' Zuhdi stopped and folded his arms across his chest.

"The drugs Jahreal stole from the dog and cat hospital. You still have more left, do you not?" Ali asked his brother.

"Yes." Jahreal swallowed hard and gave a nod. *I had no time to inject the dog before the police raid.*

"Good, give him the injection and we'll bury them together."

Jahreal went back to the old sink in the little kitchen and worked on preparing two injections. The drug he planned to stop the dog's heart with one and use the Ketamine with the other. He did not want the dog to suffer so he put most of the heart drug for the dog. What was left he would shoot into the American. He did not want either of his *patients* to suffer. He went out, lifted to lid on the trunk and injected the dog with the drug. Next he went in and picked up the other syringe and used it on the American.

Ali Hakim went outside, and with an old shovel he had found, began searching for a place to bury the dog. He came back in, wiping sweat from his face with his shirt sleeve. "The soil is very shallow, Just under it, one finds tree roots. We cannot bury the man here."

"Ah, I *know*. Take him to Utah." Zuhdi said and laughed. "The sheriffs there are slow witted, stupid cowboys. They won't know what to do with a body in a ditch."

"How far is Utah?" Jahreal asked.

"From the map I studied, I believe about a 100 miles." Aukmed said.

"Good, you then can drive the American to Utah, and Jahreal can go with you and keep you awake. Take off the American's shirt and pants, shoes, wrist watch, and wallet. We could use them around here." Zuhdi ordered. "And you Ali Hakim, can bury the dog. I'm going to bed."

CHAPTER SIX

———— ✦✦✦✦✦ ————

T HE DRIVE DOWN the mountain was more eventful, than to reach the I-15 freeway heading north. Most of the drive to Utah was just freeway. The last thirty-eight miles through the Virgin River Gorge, though a challenge, tested Aukmed's driving skills and the car's front end.

In the east the sky began to turn from black to gray. "When we cross into Utah, look for a ditch or stream where we can drop the American. Then we will find a convenience store and breakfast."

"What is the St. George, Aukmed?" Jahreal asked.

"I believe it is a temple, built by the early Mormons. It is an honor to their prophet who believed in polygamy and sent his followers here to live. A few of them still have more than one wife."

"Some Muslims have more than one wife." Jahreal said.

"Possibly, there are still some enlightened Americans living here." Aukmed laughed

Back at the warehouse in Las Vegas, the CSI team from the LVPD had begun their work. The FBI knew of the skills and fine laboratory the City of Las Vegas had. The two bodies, one of the policeman and the other a terrorist were driven away to the lab. The team continued to seek fingerprints, anything the four suspects may have left that would help in identifying them.

The major question was the disappearance, possibly kidnapping of Theo Kastanis and Dexter Macandlass. Blood stains were found on the stairway leading up to the office where a computer was found. They also found a piece of fabric from Mac's shirt and a spent shell casing. Now the CSI team would take all the evidence they found and return to the lab.

Dan Forester managed to wake mid-morning and check himself out of the hospital. He took a taxi straight to FBI headquarters, but the only people there on a Saturday was Marla and his boss Strickland. "What's going on with the investigation?" Dan asked

Marla brought him a mug of coffee. "Sit down Dan. It's all in the hands of the CSI. They're still working though the warehouse. There's nothing for us to do here. Kastanis is missing and so is MacCandlass. We know Mac went up to grab the computer and the CSI found blood on the stairs. The theory is that both Kastanis and Mac were kidnapped and one of them was shot. Go home, take it easy. If we get any leads we'll call you."

"But is there's anything *we* can do?" Dan bit back the pain in his shoulder.

"Not now. Go home. Take it easy. Watch a football game or something."

"Is my car still down in the parking garage?"

"If you left it there last night, then it probably is." Marla said.

Dan painfully opened his desk drawer, and with his left hand he fumbled and found his key ring On it were car keys and the key to his apartment. "Okay, make sure you call me if anything comes up." Dan stalked out of the office and slammed the elevator button going down.

It was Saturday night and Claire was again doing clean-up work. Now that the Southern Dixie Animal Clinic had been open nearly a week, Claire needed a vet, and hired Olga Vanneu. Living in Mesquite. She had come in for the day to become acquainted with the clinic. The woman had left only an hour ago, and Claire had more cleaning to do.

As she stared at her mop bucket, Claire decided that it was a good thing that the clinic was not too large. There were two examining rooms, a front office, a small storage area, and small airless cubical that had become the manager's office It had barely enough room for a desk and filing cabinet. The building had been built with a partial basement. Claire used it to store large bags of animal food. Down those twelve stairs resided an old sofa Neil had brought in from his first apartment. There was also a small bathroom with a shower. The only windows down there were high, small windows on the west wall. Claire finally finished up and was hungry and exhausted She walked into her office, gathered up her belongings, and began shutting down the lights. Her car was parked out behind the clinic, and as she turned out the inside lights, the office phone rang. *I'm going to ignore that. Whoever it is can leave a message.*

As Claire climbed into her car and her cell phone rang. She sighed and it pulled out of her purse. "Hello?"

"Claire I'm glad I managed to find you. I need you soon, actually right now."

"Suzanne what are you talking about? Are you at work?" Claire asked.

"Yes. Please come over to the hospital, right now and bring the clinic wagon."

"Bring the wagon?!" What are you talking about?" Claire asked, getting exasperated. She stood in the parking lot for a moment and stared at both vehicles. But then she climbed into the clinic wagon, started the engine and began to drive in the direction of the hospital. She knew Suzanne well enough that something definitely was up.

As Claire drove, Suzanne went on with her plea. "I need you come over and look at one of my 'clients'." Suzanne said excitement in her voice.

"A corpse? You want me to look at a stiff?"

"Yes, because I don't think he's dead."

When Claire reached the parking lot of the hospital, she called Suzanne. "Where do you want me to park?"

"Park as close to the loading dock as you can. You can climb up the side stairs, and no one will ask you what you're doing out there. Take employee's elevator down to the morgue."

Claire sighed, stepped out of the van, and made her way to the lower level and the morgue. Suzanne's, 'area of the dead' as she called it. Claire knocked softly on the frosted glass door.

Suzanne pulled the door open and immediately grabbed Claire's arm and propelled her into the morgue. She led Claire over to a sheet covered body which seemed very still.

"If it isn't Bradley Cooper I'm not interested." Claire stood by the gurney with arms folded.

"Very funny, Claire. This guy could be as tall as the actor."

"Okay what makes you think this individual is still vital? Why don't you call upstairs and ask an MD to come down and check him over."

"Because he begged me not to, said," *No hospital.* "He sat up, pushed the sheet down and begged me. Then he sort of collapsed, and since ten he's been pretty quiet."

"The corpse said. 'No hospital'?" Suzanne, what's the catch? When did you get him in here?"

"The highway patrol troopers brought him in late this afternoon. 'Said they found him in a culvert half wrapped in a garage bag. The stream bed just inside the Utah border, northbound near the freeway. Some kids playing in the ditch found him. His hands were tied behind his back. So I began a file and cleaned him up and did the usual measuring and weighing."

"As I worked on him I noticed he was very cold, but not in rigger. Some areas of his body were colder than others. Like behind his ears. There is a laceration on his left shoulder." Suzanne pulled down the sheet and showed Claire the long cut.

"This is a strange laceration." Claire said. "I wonder if he's a victim of a hit? Perhaps that's why he doesn't want to be in a hospital. You say he was on the northbound side of the freeway? He may have been dumped here, because he's in trouble with the mob in Las Vegas?" Suddenly Claire's fatigue disappeared, and curiosity replaced it.

"Did you bring the animal van over here?" Suzanne asked. "Hey if he's a victim of a hit, maybe he's afraid they'll come here and finish the job."

Claire frowned. "Yes, the van is parked close to the loading dock. You're thinking of smuggling him out of here aren't you? Where are we going to take him?" She stared a Suzy. "My place? *Oh no!* But, first, let's see if he's still alive."

Claire picked up his right hand. She felt for a pulse, but found nothing. Pick up his left hand and noticed a burn nearly at his elbow. "Hey look a cigarette burn. They must have tortured him. "Suzy, do you have a stethoscope?"

"Yes, here." She handed the instrument to Claire.

Claire listened to the man's throat, right side for a pulse. Claire could hear and then feel the thud of a beat on the guy's throat. Then nothing, a long moment, then another. Claire began timing the beats. "Amazing! His pulse is just a little over 40 beats per minute." She went on to feel his long arms, chest, neck and lastly his arm pit. "He's alive." She examined his torso, lean but muscular, long legs, wide shoulders, basically a lean, strong individual. "With a pulse rate of forty, he must either swim, or ride a bicycle for exercise. Did you weigh and measure him?"

"Yeah." Suzanne picked up a clipboard. "John Doe weighed in at 189 lbs. and 75 inches tall. He's kind of a hunk, isn't he?" Suzanne grinned.

Claire lifted the guy's head and felt his head and neck. "He has lump behind his ear, and a nasty bump to the rear of his head. His face is bruised, and jaw, red and swollen. With his fair skin, it's even more noticeable, along with the copper-red hair. His arms and legs have a good tan. I'll vote for the bicycle, and also he might have a *mean* concussion, or worse." Claire dropped into a visitor's chair. "My blood sugar has tanked."

"I'll fix that." Suzanne went to a small refrigerator and pulled out a carton of milk. Next she reached into a drawer and tossed a protein bar at Claire.

"Oh, thanks Suzy." Claire took a long swallow of the milk and a bite from the bar.

"A girl has to take care of herself and be prepared." Suzy laughed.

"Okay, now I can see why you think we should get him out of here. Where do you propose to take him? We also need to warm him up. It would be a crime for him to die from hypothermia after all he's been through." As Claire stared down at the John Doe, she spoke softly. She turned to Suzanne. "Where do you propose to take him?"

"The clinic. We can put him in the basement."

"And how do you propose to get him out of here and down the clinic's basement stairs?" Claire put her hands on her hips and glared at Suzy.

"There's a new gurney, and it goes up and down stairs. A young guy, an EMT from Bountiful invented it. He started up a company and the hospital bought four of them, and the City of St. George has ordered more. I have one down here." Suzanne went into her office and brought out the folded gurney "It works like a charm."

"Okay, miss smarty pants, how are we going to get him past security?" Claire asked.

"Out through the service entrance. There's a motorized dock that goes up or down. You drive the clinic van over there. We'll load him from the dock. *Piece of cake.*"

"When's the shift change?" Claire asked.

"Eleven p.m."

"Okay, Its 10:40 p.m. right now." Claire studied her wrist watch.

In the next few minutes the girls loaded the JD onto the new gurney, carefully wrapping him a large sheet, a hospital blanket and made sure the sheet was draped loosely around their *patient's* head. They put him in the service elevator and hit the button up for one floor.

"Now, go get the van and park as close to the dock as you can." Suzanne ordered.

Claire stood outside next to the van and waited for Suzanne and the 'close to death' JD. She parked the van so the animal hospital logo did not show. *We can't do this. We're breaking all kinds of laws state and federal.*

CHAPTER SEVEN

———— ✦✦✦✦✦ ————

"E VENING, SKEETER. HOW'S it going?" Suzy spoke to the orderly on duty at the loading dock.

"Fine Suzanne. What you got there, a stiff?"

"Yeah, the mortuary called. The family can't afford to have a big funeral. So they want the guy cremated ASAP. It's a rush job. They're getting ready for the body now."

Claire within hearing distance of Suzanne's excuse, and sighed. But decided she's better play along. She reached in the rear of the van and found a ball cap of Neil's and a big sweater. She dropped her voice into a lower register. "Over here ma'am." She called out.

"Oh good there's the van now.' Suzanne said brightly. "Skeeter, can you lower the dock, please?"

The orderly went to the rear of the dock and touched some buttons, and manipulated the controls.

Suzanne and the loaded gurney slowly came down. Claire got into the van and backed it as close to the edge of the dock as possible. Claire was amazed how easily it was to adjust the gurney to height of the rear of the van.

Suzanne and Claire eased the JD into the rear of the van, and Suzanne folded up the gurney. She pushed it along the side of the van, and Claire locked the rear doors. Then she climbed infront with Suzanne and they drove away.

With some struggle, the two girls managed to lower the JD on the new gurney down the stairs into the basement of the clinic. They pulled out the sofa bed and opened it. Claire had swept and cleaned the room and vacuumed the sofa bed two days before. "We need some sort of bedding. I'll go upstairs and I'll see what's available." Claire said. She came back with a pillow, and one sheet and a stack of animal blankets.

"Okay, I'll make the bed and you go get an IV and a stand." Suzanne ordered.

A few minutes later Claire returned with the IV system, an old tee shirt and some men's socks. "He's still so cold, I think this will help warm him up."

"Wasn't there a space heater in the bathroom?" Suzanne asked. "I'll go see." She came back with the small space heater.

"Where are we going to plug it in?" Claire asked. She searched the walls for an electrical outlet. "The only one is in the bathroom. It shows you how old this building is."

"Come on, let's get him in the sofa bed." Suzanne ordered. They lowered the gurney and slid the JD onto the bed. "I used one the blankets for a cover on the sofa, next the sheet and- - - - - -.

"Here, I'll put the waterproof pad on the sheet." Claire said. "What goes in must come out." She spoke as she threaded the IV needle into the man's right arm. "We don't know how long he lay in that ditch. I'm afraid he's a candidate for pneumonia."

Suzanne finished wrapping the JD up. "Come on, I need to go pick up my car and get home to my son. It's well after midnight."

Claire dropped off Suzanne at the hospital and drove back to the clinic to check on this poor guy, now a guest of the clinic. She feared he would die on them, and then they'd really be in 'hot water'. She went down stairs and touched him. *Damn, he was still too cold.* She tucked the blankets around him, and grabbed another bag of IV fluid.

Claire had been up since just after 6 a.m. that morning. She barely made it home without falling asleep. All she could think of was a hot shower. She drank some milk and made a quick peanut butter sandwich. Once she lay down she fell asleep instantly.

Sunday morning, a little after 10 a.m. Strickland called Dan. He had just begun to watch. *NFL Today.*

"Dan, we have some new information concerning the disappearance of Agent Kastanis. Please come into the office for a few minutes."

"Sure. I'll be there in 15 minutes." Dan moved a quickly as his wounded would let him. But walked into the FBI office and there met his boss V.I Strickland, and the director of the Southern California Office: Tom Velois. And another man Dan had never met.

"Sit down Dan. This is the director, Thomas Velois and Chief of CSI, and from the Las Vegas Police Department, Samuel Kerr." They all sat down around the small table in the break room.

"We found Theo Kastanis two buildings west of the warehouse, area of the crime scene. He had been shot twice. As the medical team loaded him into the ambulance, he kept murmuring: *They said they wouldn't shoot me. They said they wouldn't shoot me.* "His prognosis is not good. He *possibly* may not make it. We also found bits of glass from the tail light of the terrorists' car. From that we were able to find, we discovered the year it was manufactured."

Velois spoke up. "At the first raid in California, Mac shot at their car, and the tail light exploded. Sadly, they found no evidence as to where they took MacCandlass."

"We found the identity of the dead Muslim: Hannique Maroque probably from Iran. We found him on Interpol. There also was a picture in his file. It was taken last Christmas time in Montreal. He most likely has been in Canada and now the U.S. for some time. One item of interest: In his pockets he had small cards, a fist full of them, printed in *English*. The cards read: *Sons of Allah, Authors of Your Demise.*

"There's more. But it is a Sunday, and not much can be done until tomorrow. Come in ready to work tomorrow morning." Strickland said and stood up. "Go back to that football game, Dan Forester. And while you're doing it, rest that arm."

Claire woke up with a start. She glanced at her bedside clock. It read a few minutes past 9 a.m. There was light coming in from the half- closed shutters on her bedroom windows. *The John Doe. I need to check on him.* She jumped out of bed and ran around the room looking for some clothes to put on. Finally she found a pair of jeans and tee shirt, and slipped into a pair of tennis shoes. Next, she scurried into her bathroom. *Should put some make-up on? No time. Besides he won't care if I'm barefaced or not.*

Where are my purse and keys? She galloped down the stairs to the kitchen and found purse and keys on the table. She grabbed an extension cord from her pantry door. As she locked her kitchen door, she again found it stuck when locking it. *Someday I'm going have to call a locksmith.*

Fifteen minutes later, she hustled into clinic through the rear door. For a moment she stopped to listen for any sounds coming from the basement. The only sound she heard was sound of the air conditioning unit. She eased down the stairs with the extension cord and went to her patient.

He lay so still, almost in the same position as the evening before. But as she bent close to him she could hear his slow regular, breathing. Next she took his temperature. It read 95.9 F Good. His body temperature had risen from the night before. Bur he was still too cold. Perhaps a warm bath would help, and she connected up the space heater. With the extension cord, the space heater could be close to the sofa bed. She went upstairs for a large basin, towels and some soap. She methodically began to bathe him.

As Claire worked she could not but admire his strong, lean body. She found a slight wound at the top of his left shoulder. It was like a bloody scrape tearing the flesh. Could this be a bullet wound? She'd better treat that. Her theory that he was a victim, or some *wise guy,* from Las Vegas went up a notch.

Once she finished the bath, she went back upstairs and brought down meds and bandages to treat the wound. She wished the clinic had a blood analysis machine. She doubted a concussion would keep him unresponsive this long. Something or some drug was keeping him in a coma. She thought about drugs used on dogs to keep them sedated. She would need to check the animal drug reference book upstairs.

After tucking him in, she decided to hang around the clinic for a while. She walked upstairs to make some coffee. She'd use this time to work on the clinic bookkeeping.

Three hours later Claire went downstairs to check on her JD. She took his temperature, and it had come up two tenths of a degree. Claire breathed a sigh of relief. For some reason this patient of hers had become important to her. She wanted him to awaken, and hoped he would have no permanent impairments.

Claire worked on the clinic's accounts for another two hours, but hunger forced her to go out briefly for a breakfast sandwich from Burger King. By early afternoon, she had finished getting the clinic ready for tomorrow and the new vet beginning her first day at work. Claire went downstairs and found the basement quite warm. She disconnected the space heater and took put it away. Last before leaving, she checked her patient and took his temperature. It went up 4/10s of a degree. *This is even better.*

Driving home she thought about the various drugs and their effects on dogs and people. The fact that JD had grabbed Suzanne's arm and spoke briefly, Claire decided that he may had been given Ketamine. She knew that people used as a recreational drug, which meant that it was easily obtained. That thought opened up other possibilities as to how he had been given the drug.

When Dan reached the FBI offices early Monday morning, Strickland came into his cubicle soon after. "We've another meeting with CSI and Home Land Security. Would you go down to the bakery on the main floor and pick up an order I placed about an hour ago. Thanks. Marla brought in her big coffee pot. We should be ready when everyone arrives."

When Dan returned, some of the others had already arrived. Marla had the side table set up with a 30 cup coffee pot. Also there were large, paper coffee cups, sugar, cream and large trays for the bagels and donuts. She took the bakery items and spread them artfully on the trays.

V.I. Strickland invited everyone in to sit in the largest room in their offices, and partake of the morning treats.

Soon he called the meeting to order. "First we'd like to hear from director Kerr and his assistant, Sandra Bellos of the Vegas CSI."

Kerr opened his large folder. "After examining the warehouse in question and the surrounding area, we first found glass from the rear of the Mercedes the perps drove. We believe it came from a light blue 1996 C400 series, Mercedes, a four door sedan. It was originally purchased by an older man in Las Dinas, California and stolen from a supermarket parking lot last March. The original owner had left the windows down.

We found out what the perps liked to eat: American fast food, and junk food from convenience stores. We also found a small bag of dog food and dog droppings. We located a box of nine-mil shells, some cleaning supplies and a large drum of water. We're having the water analyzed. The water may lead us to their 'safe house'. As far as the whereabouts of MacCandlass, all we have is a piece of his shirt, and a spend shell casing found in the second level of the building. We believe he was mortally wounded, or else close to death. Also there were blood stains on the stairs leading down to the main level. We've analyzed the blood and it matches MacCandlass' blood type.

Kastanis is very critical, from two gunshot wounds, and his diabetes is serious. He may not survive." Kerr shuffled his papers.

"Thank you Mr. Kerr" Strickland said and stood. "Our other loss was Officer Roberto Valdez. His funeral is scheduled for Wednesday. There will be a motorcycle escort and full honors." We are saddened by the losses we've all suffered. However the search goes on to find and eradicate this city, and this nation of these terrorists." Thank you for helping us to locate our enemies, domestic or international." Strickland sat back in his chair.

CHAPTER EIGHT

———— ✦✦✦✦✦✦ ————

MAC WAS DREAMING of dogs. Angry, barking dogs. Growling dogs with their teeth bared, mouths dripping with saliva, and they were after him. He ran as fast and far away as he could, but they still chased him. Just as the largest dog, a big black Doberman, sank his teeth in Mac's leg, he opened his eyes. He lay there in a sweat, his heart pounding hard for what seemed long minutes, but as he calmed his eyes drifted closed. Sometime later he opened them again, and trained them on the ceiling. A strange ceiling, not very high, and a type he'd not seen before. The light was dim in this place, but the ceiling was made up of tiles, and they seemed to sparkle.

He moved his right arm, and found it was taped, to what? An IV? He lifted his arm and could see it was attached and could touch the IV line. As he turned his head and it ached, and his vision blurred. He lay still until his head hurt less. Was this a hospital? It was unlike any hospital he had ever been in.

He lifted his shoulder and twisted his head to the left, and again it ached. Lying back down and breathing in and out helped to calm his fast heart rate, and ease the pounding in his head. He closed his eyes, drifted off and dozed for a while.

Again a barking dog roused him. But this time the dog seemed smaller, and yapped as if it were in pain. The sound came from somewhere upstairs. He slowly came up on both elbows and several feet in front of him he could see a set of stairs leading up. If this was a hospital, they had put him in the basement.

He lifted the sheet and several blankets and gazed down at his body. He was wearing a tee shirt, a pair of baggy boxers, *I never wear boxers,* and some heavy socks. There was a tube taped to his left inner thigh. With his hand he followed the tube and it was in *Him.* A urine catheter. He must have been in an accident or injured somehow. THINK. The only thing he was aware of was his pounding head and a stinging pain in his left shoulder. The best thing for him to do would be to lie back and relax. Maybe some memory or scene would come to mind.

Later, he woke because the sun had moved to shine through the small windows high up on the wall. It must be afternoon, and this wall next where he was lying had to be located on the west side of this building.

There must be a door at the top of the stairs, and now it was open. He could hear voices, feminine voices. Sometimes two sometimes more. One of them came from an older woman and one from a younger female. Her voice had a husky quality, and when she laughed, her laugh that had a musical quality. She laughed often, and he liked her infectious laugh. The voice of the older woman, suggested that she did or had smoked. She cleared her throat often and coughed now and then.

Since he was trapped in this basement, he decided to listen to the conversations for clues to where he was. He couldn't seem to focus very long and again grew sleepy. When he next opened his eyes he noticed that the sun had dropped below the high west windows, and room was growing dark.

He heard a door slam. A few minutes later he heard footsteps on the stairs coming down. He pushed up on his elbows, but his vision blurred and his head pounded

A woman walked to his bedside. "How are you doing JD?" She spoke in a soft voice. The voice he had been listening to all day. She touched his shoulder. "Are you any warmer?"

He reached up and grabbed her wrist.

"Oh!" Startled. "You're awake." Her eyes widened and she pulled back, but returned closer. 'I'm glad you're awake, but please let go of my wrist." A shaky smile came with her words.

"What is this place?" He croaked out. His throat felt as if he had been running for miles or biking uphill for hours. So dry he couldn't swallow.

"Hold on. I'll get you some water.' She turned and dashed upstairs and quickly returned with a mug of water, and paper cup.

She poured some water into the paper cup. Picked up the pillow next to him and shoved it under his head. "Slowly, don't gulp." She watched him swallow, and poured more water from the mug resting on the floor and filled the little cup again.

He drained the cup. "Now, where am I? What is this place?"

"This is a veterinary clinic, and the patients are usually cat and dogs." She tried for a smile.

"Why am I here? It's getting dark down here." He asked.

"Let's take care of the light, first." She went to the wall at the bottom of the stairs and flipped a switch. Two recessed flood lights came on in the ceiling. "As to why you are here, it's a long story. Let's take care of your primary needs, first. Your body temperature was so low, and you were dehydrated. And you have a nasty bump on your head. We were afraid you might die." She talked fast and looked down on him as any caregiver would.

He could see short, wavy brown hair with a nearly white streak in front. Even from his angle, flat on his back, he could estimate that she was tall, trim but not skinny.

Now that he had drunk water, his stomach growled, and he put his hand on it.

She made that lovely laughing sound. "You must be hungry."

"Yes, I could eat something. Where are my clothes?"

"Sorry, you came in with no clothes. The clothes you are wearing are some Neil left here." She said. Dark sadness filled her eyes for a brief moment, but she blinked and shook her head. "It's still quite warm outside. I think you'll be okay to ride home. Once there, I'll find you something more suitable to wear."

"How did I get here, and from where?" He asked.

"My friend Suzanne and I brought you over here. It was the best alternative." As she spoke she deftly removed the IV from his arm. "I'm going to look for some shorts. Be right back."

He watched her bound up the stairs, but come right back with a pair of shorts that you'd only see on a guy over 40 wearing on some golf course. "Ah, before the shorts, lady, would you take this tube out of me?"

Her face and neck took on color. "Oops, I forgot the catheter." She went through a door opposite that stairway and quickly returned with a washcloth and towel. She walked around to left side and tucked the covers around all but his left leg and groin area. She gently pulled the tape away and freed him from the tube. She handed him the small towel.

He realized she knew what she was doing. She seemed very professional, and handed him the shorts. He dragged the ugly larger sized shorts around him.

"Now we need to get you up. Swing your legs out and down." She pulled him up to a sitting position. "Okay, this sofa bed is low, and you're quite tall. She put her hands high on his sides. "Now put your hands on my shoulders."

He barely stood up, but had to sit down again. "Whoa, I'm a little dizzy."

"Sit there a moment. It's your blood pressure. It has to rise up with the rest of your body. I've had dogs stand up after surgery, and just fall over. Usually, though, dogs are smarter than that, but cats don't stand until they know they can."

He could tell that she was uneasy with him. Yet she had treated him as any medical professional would. His head cleared and he managed to slide his feet to the floor. He stood and felt queasy, and had a head rush, but she held onto his arms to steady him.

"There's a bathroom over there." She pointed to the door opposite the stairway. She picked up the ugly golf shorts, and handed them to him. "I'll wait to help you up the stairs She supported him as he walked across the room. When he came out of the bathroom she was sitting on the stairs.

"Now we're going upstairs. Put your hand on the railing. "You go up, first."

He moved up the first stair and then another "I can make it up the stairs okay, I think."

She followed closely behind him. Once he reached the top stair, the bright overhead lights of the clinic blinded him. She grabbed his arm and moved him to a chair.

"Stay there. I go out and unlock my car." She picked up a sack and her purse and walked out through a heavy metal door painted white. It led out outside in a western direction, he decided. She returned and helped him, by putting her hand under his elbow. "There are two steps down to the ground."

He did better on these steps, and they walked to an older Honda sedan. Once he was in the car, she belted him in and drove out of the parking area to a rather busy street and turned west.

"If you look in the glove box there may be a pair of sunglasses."

He found them. She drove west into bright sunlight, but soon the sun dropped below the horizon and he could see the road. Now they left the city, and the businesses turned into subdivisions, and then to older houses on larger lots with larger trees and some with green lawns.

About twenty minutes into the drive, the landscape changed to areas of larger lots, some farm land and big old trees. A few minutes later she slowed and turned right, onto a gravel drive on the west side of an older white house with a wraparound porch, and a black roof. On the west side of the house was an old barn, but she stopped close to what looked like a side door of the house. She shut down the engine and walked around to what seemed to be a kitchen door. Even with a set of keys, she struggled with the lock, but finally the door swung open.

"Come on, I'll help you inside." She helped him into a pleasant kitchen and led him to an oval shaped bench built into a bay window facing north. He could see farm land across the way, and it seemed natural and familiar. The bench was covered with imitation leather in black and white. In fact the whole kitchen was black, white with silver- gray appliances, and a black and silver stove. He liked the color scheme. It was a comfortable contrast to the age of the house.

There was a doorway to a short hallway from the kitchen. She went into a door and he could hear water running. She returned and went to the refrigerator and grabbed a carton of low fat milk. She poured him a glass. "You need the liquid and the protein. Drink this while I find us some dinner."

Soon she set a steaming bowl of chicken noodle soup in front of him. As he smelled it his mouth watered, and the first spoonful burned his tongue.

While she fried bacon, she cut up a loaf of French bread length wise and covered one half of it with slices of tomato, cheese and bacon. Into the oven it went under the broiler. Taking it from the oven she cut it into four slices.

As he ate he realized how hungry he was. His stomach felt like a bottomless pit. The food disappeared so fast he couldn't remember how tasty he knew it was.

Once every crumb was gone, he sat back and now he felt heavy, sleepy from his full stomach.

"Could you eat another sandwich, or would you like to wait a little later for some cookies and ice cream." She asked.

"I could still eat more, but I don't want to toss it all up, so I'll stop now." He sighed.

"Most likely, it's been three days since you've eaten anything - - - -.

"Three days?" How long was I- - - - - I mean since you brought me to your clinic?"

"Since Saturday night. Now it's Monday evening. You could have lain in the ditch for a whole day before they brought you in to Suzanne."

CHAPTER NINE

————— ✦✦✦✦✦✦ —————

"W HAT DITCH?" HIS eyes widened.

"You don't remember." She gazed at him, sympathy in her eyes. "Of course you don't. You were probably unconscious when they dumped you." She informed him.

"Who dumped me?" He sat back and frowned.

"Do you remember anything?" She waited a beat. "Okay let's back up. Think, while I tell you why Suzanne and I sneaked you into the clinic." She went on to tell him about Suzanne's phone call, and why she believed he was still alive. "That's why you woke up in the animal clinic's basement.

Now, can you remember any group or individual who would want you dead? And then would dump you in a ditch just inside the Utah/Arizona border. Particularly since Las Vegas is only two hour's drive from here."

He felt only astonishment. "Someone or more than one individual dumped me in a ditch in the desert?"

"Yes, the UHP, you know highway patrol, brought you in, but luckily for Suzanne and me, he didn't have time to do the paper work on you. He had to go unsnarl a three car accident. Suzy has worked in the morgue for over two years, and to her, you just didn't have the usual the corpse criteria. The morgue is in the St. George Regional Hospital, and it's usually quite busy." The words flew out of Claire's mouth.

"Why didn't you or your friend, is it Suzanne, call up stairs and ask an MD down to look me over?"

"Because you begged her not to. You reached up in you semi-dead situation, grabbed her arm and said "No hospital."

"Okay, now you back up.' he said. You've never told me where I am exactly. What city. I figured out, driving to this house, that this is the southwest, a desert city." As he studied her, he noticed her golden, brown eyes, and a fringe of dark brown lashes. He may have been in dire straits, but he enjoyed talking with this attractive girl.

"Oh, that's right. I assumed that you knew where you were. Okay, this is a little town called Rawley, on the outskirts of St. George, Utah. We are located in the far south-west corner of the state of Utah. Since Las Vegas is only a two hour drive from St. George, we assumed that you were somehow involved with the mob in 'Vegas. That you had crossed them in some way. Or you're a *wise guy*, and they figured you out."

"Wise guy! Like an undercover cop, or with the FBI?" He sat back and smiled. He liked the idea of being a 'good guy'.

"And the reason you had no clothes, is that they didn't want you identified. So if you remember your name, we can work from there and get on the computer and find out who you work for. Unless, you only used an alias with them. With your red hair and green eyes, you don't look like a terrorist."

"I'm- - - - -I'm -----------------?" He stopped and stared at her. He dropped his gaze and studied his empty plate. Panic clutched him, and it became hard to breathe. He took a choking breath. "I can't remember. I can't remember my name, what my name is."

She continued to stare at him for a long moment. Again, he noticed sympathy in those brown eyes. "You don't recall your name? She shook her head. Do you remember where you lived or have lived?"

He shook his head. "No." He felt the blood leave his head, and his arms felt useless. He wondered if he might just die right here in Claire's classy kitchen.

"Hmmm? Well, you have a rather nasty bump on the side of your head, and most likely a concussion. Which could cause brain swelling in some cases. Short term memory loss is fairly common. Especially all the trauma you've suffered, plus what happened before you were dumped. I believe you were tortured."

"So that's why I can't remember anything? Your theory anyway." He frowned.

"My theory is that you were drugged, with what I don't know. I feel that drugs are a major factor in your memory loss. When you were found your wrists and ankles showed that you had been tied up. You have a burn on the inside of your left arm. You have a bruise on your face, left cheek. Your jaw is swollen, and you have an abrasion on your right shoulder, which looks very much like a graze from a bullet." She looked down at her plate and sighed.

"We've been sitting here speculating for some time. Come upstairs and I'll take you to a room where you can rest. It is or was my brother's room. But he's in medical school back east. I called him earlier, and asked him if you could use some of his clothes. He said that was okay. He's nearly as tall as you are, but maybe thinner."

"What did you tell him about me?"

She shrugged, and her face curved into a little smile. "I told him that you were a friend of mine from school, and you had flown over here and the airline had lost your luggage."

"How old is your brother?" Mac asked. "And why does he still have his belongings in your house?"

"Because he used to live here and he's younger than me, twenty-six. I'll tell you what. When you remember something about your prior existence, and share it with me. I'll tell you something about my past, okay?" She flashed a grin.

"So come upstairs, and you can rest. In a while, I'll bring you some cookies and ice cream if you like." She guided him to the front of the house where a stairway led up to the second floor.

Once upstairs, he could see a wide hallway and a door on the right side, and another door more to the front of the house. It was an interesting one and a half story structure.

She opened a door on what he decided was on the west side of the house. The room was of average size, but decorated in a spare, masculine style. The west side of the ceiling slanted. And there was a window close to another door on the west side of the room. She pushed that door open, and revealed a long narrow bathroom with a frosted window looking out the west side. There was the usual shower, vanity, and toilet. In the bedroom, the north wall had three square windows high up on the wall. In the middle of the room was ceiling fan. And beneath it stood a queen sized bed. On the east wall was a closet with sliding doors. There was a small desk and chair close to the window on the west.

Though it was dark, he could see Claire's car below. "Mind if I look in the closet?" He asked, and slid one of the doors open and there were a few clothes on a hanging rod. Jeans, shorts and a few shirts, and on both sides of the closet were built-in shelves. There he noticed a stack of tee shirts, and some flip-flops.

She pulled down the dark blue and gray quilt. "There are sheets and a blanket on the bed. It's still quite warm, but the air conditioning doesn't run too much at night anymore." She walked into the bathroom and brought back a bottle of Ibuprofen. "Because of your weight and size, you can have three of these pills for any pain you have. Do you want some now?" She asked.

"Yes. I could use something for my aching head." She dropped three pills in his hand and went to the bathroom and brought a paper cup filled with water. "Thanks you." He said.

"I'll let you settle in, then." She hesitated at the door as if she wanted to do say something, but left it slightly open and walked down stairs.

He found a new tooth brush in the bathroom and a small tube of toothpaste. Moving that brush around in his mouth made him dizzy and increased his head ache. He flopped on the bed, closed his eyes, and soon fell asleep. Sometime later she must have covered him with the quilt. Even in this impossible situation he found himself, he felt a measure of comfort. And he slept until morning.

Late that same evening in Las Vegas, Dan Forester woke from a strange dream. *In it he followed the old blue Mercedes to a strange old house in the country, but lost it in a cloud of dust.* He sat on the edge of the bed. As mind cleared he realized that the terrorists must have a safe house somewhere close. It could be in an apartment, or old house? Tomorrow he should grab his new partner and go searching older neighborhoods for that car. Plus there had to be one or more individuals financing the terrorists here in the U.S.? Somehow these terrorists must receive instructions. Perhaps as simple as a cell phone call from the money source. There could other 'cells' in the U.S. like this one. He felt there had to be is an individual who sends them money, But where does the finance man live?

When Mac awoke Claire had already left for the clinic. She had made a pot¡of coffee and left some for him. She also left a clever note on the refrigerator It read: *Search me because there's all kinds of food in here. Just open my door. Make yourself a nutritious breakfast.* True to the note, Mac found eggs, bacon, bread, oranges and juice. Along with and a package of Rhodes cinnamon rolls. Maybe he would decide to bake them. After some breakfast he cleaned up carefully and left the rolls out to thaw and bake later. Since he was here alone, he decided to explore the house.

The front of the dwelling was typical for the style of the house, a bungalow. The living room had a wood burning fireplace on the east wall that had been updated with natural brick trim. There was a brown and beige tweed sofa, matching love seat and an easy chair in crème tweed. In the dining room, he found an older, but well cared for dining room set of cherry wood with six matching chairs and a china cabinet.

Through an archway from the living room were the stairs that led up to the story-and a half second floor and the bedrooms. Tucked behind the stairs he found a half bath, and next to that, a room that was originally a third bedroom, which now was a den-TV room. In one corner was a computer set up, but no computer. He needed a computer, and he didn't know why. It was as if he were a concert pianist and had no piano to play.

There was a comfortable sofa which made into a bed, and there was a sliding door closet. On a corner shelf he found a stack of yellow legal pads and a box of pencils and some pens in a jar. He took one of the pens and a pad. If he had a flash of memory, he would try to write it on paper.

The sun slanting through the window of the kitchen door attracted his attention. As he opened the door it stuck, and he had to give it a hard twist to swing it open. The warm October breeze felt wonderful, and he stood outside and soaked up the sunshine. A few minutes later he glanced over at the barn. That would be the next place to explore. Near the front of the barn was room for a car. He suspected Claire parked her car here when the weather turned stormy. On a hanger high on the other side of the barn was a bicycle. As he studied the bike, it seemed to give him a feeling of joy. Some where he had a bicycle, The bike he owned was a better, more expensive model, but this one would be great, if he could ride it. As he examined it he realized the front tire had a rip in it. If he could get a new tire, he could change it out, and fix whatever needed to be done to make the bike road worthy.

Finally he remembered that he came out here to find tools to fix the kitchen door. He found a box of tools and an old saw horse against the back wall. He would need it when he took the door off its hinges.

As he worked on the door, he systematically examined his predicament. He couldn't remember his name, had no money, identification, no clothes. He stopped and gazed down at a pair of Claire's brother's shorts and the tee shirt that was a size too tight. He didn't remember what he had done to earn a living. He was totally dependent on Claire Talbot.

Was he really a low level mobster or 'wise guy'? Or perhaps a hit man who killed the wrong individual, or didn't do his job correctly. What about being an undercover cop? That felt ethically and emotionally better to him. He continued to work on the door, but the headache sneaked up on him. He was forced to go back inside and find the ibuprofen. While inside he put the rolls in the oven, because he realized he was hungry.

After a few minutes he felt better and set the timer on the stove and went back outside to work on the door. As he worked he thought about Claire. Why had she rescued him? Probably one of the reasons was to help her friend Suzanne. He was looking forward to meeting that girl. But right now Claire was stuck with him. Yet, so far she had done nothing but show kindness toward him. He owed her 'big time' huge amounts. How could he return the favor, the kindness? Once he felt better he would leave, but right now he didn't want to walk away from Claire.

Another thought crossed his mind. He could have a wife somewhere. Is that why he wanted to stay here with Claire, because he was used to living with a woman he loved? He studied his left hand fourth finger. It didn't seem to show any indication that he had worn a wedding ring.

The buzzer on the stove rang and he went back into the house, and took out the cinnamon rolls. He was nearly finished with the repairs on the door, so he put it back on its hinges. He tried the door a few times and it no longer stuck. He went back in and washed his hands, and suddenly was so exhausted he could barely stand in the bathroom. After taking a few deep breaths he climbed the stairs to the room where he had slept. He flopped on the bed, and fell asleep.

He dreamed of a large dark place with a high ceiling and dirty windows. He felt fear, and yet he knew he should do- - - - - something? But what? Later in another dream, he could see a woman's face. She had golden-brown eyes and a white streak in her hair. He liked listening to her laugh.

The sound of a car moving on the gravel under the window woke him. He eased off the bed and looked down. Yes, it was Claire and she had a brown sack along with her purse, He heard the door open.

CHAPTER TEN

————— ✦✦✦✦✦✦ —————

"JD, WHERE ARE you?"

"I'm up here. What did you call me?"

"JD, an abbreviation for John Doe. Hey, did you fix the kitchen door?" Her voice sounded pleased.

"Yes, I noticed that it stuck." He ambled down stairs and walked into the kitchen. "So I looked in the barn and found some tools. It didn't take me very long. What do you think?"

"Do you know that door has stuck, well, forever?" She laughed. "Thank you."

"Since I am your houseguest, I decided that I could be of some service to you. So you wouldn't throw me out, just yet." He tried for a smile.

She studied him for a long beat and shook her head. "I'm, not going to throw you out. I plan to feed you until you're feeling better, and help you remember- - - - - -things." She dug though the sack she had set on the counter. "I brought some ingredients for dinner."

He walked over to the counter. "I smell fish. What kind?"

"Salmon. I have a pretty good recipe, so I decided to bake the fish." She took a package from the sack.

"I remember liking salmon. Did you guess?" He dropped onto the padded bench near the oval shaped table.

"I didn't know, but salmon is good food for anybody, and you need good food to recover from your, ah,- - - - -- - - ordeal."

After dinner he helped her clean up, and he noticed a calendar hanging on the wall close to the doorway. "What's the date today?" He asked.

"You've lost your sense of days passing? Of course you would. Okay." She took the calendar down and spread it on the table. "Do you remember that's its October?" Her eyes met his.

"Yes, but it's because of the weather and the shorter amount daylight. I noticed that when I was in the clinic basement. That's especially important when you're harvesting- - - - -?"

"You lived on a farm?" She asked her eyes wide. "This is a good thing, - - - you remembered."

He closed his eyes for a moment. "Yes, I seem to remember driving farm machinery." He frowned and shook his head. "But where and when, I don't remember. Today, I glanced out the kitchen window, and noticed the crops in the field out there had been harvested. It that your property?"

"Yes, this house includes ten acres of farm land. I rented it out to the guy who lives through the field to the north. Okay, she sighed. Let's go on checking the calendar. Today is the 25th of the month. Next Wednesday is 31st. Halloween. That's why I bought the fish, I went to Costco for a bag of candy, and they were featuring salmon. Does knowing the date help you?"

"Maybe having this information will help me remember. I'll think about living on a farm. Right now I need some way to relax. 'Sort of clear my mind. How about some TV?"

It was a Tuesday and they watched NCIS, and then switched channels to watch part of a college football game. By 9 p.m. Claire was yawning.

"I'm not used to staying up very late, because I have to get to the clinic by 8 a.m. or earlier." Claire said. "If you want to watch more TV, you go ahead. "But I need to hit the sack" So I'll say goodnight."

"I want to watch a little longer. Is there news cast at nine?" He asked.

"Yes, but you need your rest, too." she said, gave him a little wave and went upstairs.

He switched to the Fox News channel, but the news seemed to be mainly about happenings in and around the State of Utah. After a few minutes, his eyes grew heavy. They burned and his head ached, so he eased upstairs. He took a shower, and opened the windows above the bed. There was a cool dry breeze, and it felt good. Just before he reached a state sleep, he decided living in a dry climate was pleasant. An individual would not have to deal with much humidity here. He knew where he had lived before it was humid.

Friday evening, just as Claire was about to close the clinic up for the night, the phone rang. *Maybe its JD, I'd better answer it.* "The animal clinic is closed for the night, and- - - - -." Her phone began.

"Hi it's Suzy. I have to work the day shift tomorrow and so I have the evening free. How's our JD doing?"

"He's doing pretty well. You want to come over for a visit?" Claire laughed.

"Well, yes. I found some old clothes of Andy's lying around. I thought I'd bring them over."

"Don't you think Andy will want them when you see him again?" Claire asked, her words came out sharp.

"Not really. I don't want to get into that situation with anyone right now, okay? I'm bringing dessert. What did you plan for dinner?" Suzanne asked.

"I thawed out some ground beef. I thought about making spaghetti, and salad." Claire answered.

"Sound's good, I'll be there in forty-five minutes."

When Claire arrived home she found JD in the den with the TV on, but asleep on the sofa. She left him asleep, and began dinner.

A few minutes later he came in and stood in the doorway with his hand on the top of the arch as if he needed to support himself. "What's for dinner?" He asked.

"Spaghetti, meat sauce and salad." As she spoke she began to cook the pasta. She turned to study him. "You don't look good. You have dark circles under your eyes."

Just then there was a knock at the kitchen door. Clare turned to let Suzanne in. "Evening Claire. Oh, hi JD." She carried in a tray covered with foil and set it on the kitchen counter.

He walked toward her and, just as he reached for her hand had a coughing spell. "'Sorry." He pulled a napkin from the holder on the table and wiped his face.

Claire whirled around, and pulled him over to the built-in bench by the table. "You don't look good. How do you feel?"

Suzanne went to the stove and turned the heat down on the bubbling pasta. She joined Claire near the table, and gazed down at the JD. "How do you feel? Oh, by the way, I'm Suzanne, and you don't look good." She turned to Claire. "You think the pneumonia you mentioned, is now a factor?"

"I don't think-------, pneumonia?" He said in a scratchy voice. "I felt okay until I woke up just a few minutes ago." He stopped and swallowed. "I do have a raw throat."

"Suzy, watch the pasta. I'm going upstairs for my first aid kit." Claire disappeared up the stairs.

Suzanne put on the tea kettle, and began searching the pantry for tea bags.

Between the two girls, they finished cooking dinner, and set a mug of tea by JD's place.

"Don't drink the tea just yet. It will change the temperature in your mouth." Claire said and waved a thermometer at him. "Open wide." She said, and waited for him to comply.

He scowled, but obeyed.

She counted out to 100, and then took the thermometer from his mouth. She leaned into the light over the kitchen table and studied the small glass stick. "101.3 F "She shook her head. "I'm afraid you have an infection."

Suzanne and Claire conferred together by the stove. "You said he was a candidate for pneumonia, and I think you are correct. Now where do we get some antibiotics?" Suzanne asked.

"Hey you two *caregivers*, I need to be consulted." JD said. He stopped for a long moment and stared down at the table. "Okay, I understand that you two can't take me to an insta-care place, but are you sure I need- - - - - -," A violent cough interrupted his words.

"Do you think you can eat some dinner?" Claire said. "Keeping your body nourished is doubly important now." Claire touched JD's hand. "Oh, your hand is very warm, however I think you should eat something." She turned and put a very moderate about of food on a plate and set in front of him.

"Don't you keep a supply of antibiotics at the clinic?" Suzanne asked.

"Yes, Dogs and cats can develop illnesses that require meds. Hey, you stay with JD here and I'll go back to the clinic and grab some penicillin." Claire was already on her feet and grabbed her purse.

Suzanne nodded. "Yeah, the sooner, you get JD to take some meds, the better." She turned to JD. "You aren't allergic to penicillin are you?"

He widened his eyes and shook his head. "I- - - - - don't know."

"His memory isn't too good right now." Claire said. "I'm leaving, be back soon." She banged out the door and the sound of her cars' engine could be heard.

"Well, I'm going to eat dinner now." Suzanne said. She sat down across from JD and began to eat.

JD scooped up a forkful and managed to eat a few bites. He sipped his tea. "I guess I'm not too hungry." He bit into the garlic bread. "This, I can taste. While we're waiting for Claire to return; Tell me about yourself. Claire said you've been working at the city morgue for four years?"

She smiled. "The way you phrased your question gave me the feeling that you are, or were in some law enforcement position. Or you have interrogated people before." She tilted her head and smiled.

"Okay. I'm Suzanne Freeman. I have a six year old son and live with my mother. Right now I am separated from my husband. He was a police officer here in St. George, but went to Las Vegas and was hired, at better pay. Right now I am an MTE, or medical examiner in training, and I like the work."

"Okay Suzanne Freeman, why are you not living in Las Vegas with your husband? Is it too difficult to find a morgue job in that town?"

"Las Vegas is *sin city!* It's a terrible environment for children. Besides, my mother tends Justin while I work. I'd have to put him in daycare or hire a sitter." She scowled at JD, shoved a mouthful of meat and pasta into her mouth.

"I would think in a city as large as Las Vegas, there would be various neighborhoods where normal families live and children go to school as in any other large American city. Have you really investigated that aspect of living with your husband?" JD had a coughing spell that stopped his words.

"How do you know about Las Vegas and not who you are?" Suzanne put her hands on both sides of the table.

"That *is* a good question. I seem to have general information in my mind, but not specific facts about myself. I found a pack of yellow paper, and I am writing down certain facts I can remember. Such as I know I've lived on a farm, and have some skills to repair- - - - -things." He stopped, coughed and took a large swallow to the tea.

"Because of my job, I am familiar with your—ah body. You suffered some torture. It's common for someone mistreated the way you were to develop an infection. Pneumonia is not exactly like catching a cold. Most of the time an individual has to have some trauma to his or her body. It's because the germs are all around us. Older people should get a shot to build immunity to the disease, but for the average youngish adult, it is not a problem." Suzanne said.

"Have you had an immune shot for the disease?" He continued to sip his tea, but then then he tried to clear his throat, which brought on coughing spell. "Yeah, my throat is sore."

"Yes, a few years ago. But it's because of what I do for a living." Suzanne replied.

He nodded. "Yes I can see that you are constantly dealing and handling the dead, you would need some protection." He took a bite of his food, and twisted the fork to pick up the pasta, but set it down again. "I guess I'm not very hungry." Instead, he sipped his tea.

Suzanne took their plates and rinsed them. Then uncovered the plate she brought and revealed several frosted pumpkin shaped cookies. "Justin helped me make these cookies. Try one, you might like them."

Claire returned with two bottles of penicillin One five hundred milligrams per pill, and the other a smaller dosage. She shook out one from the bottle and set it by JD. "Do you think you can swallow this pill?"

JD studied the long capsule. "I'll try." He put one in his mouth, took a large swallow of now cool tea and down it went.

"The dosage of this medication is very close to what would be prescribed for humans. Dogs have higher metabolisms. I think these will work for you." Claire said. "I also think you need to get into bed." Claire glanced at the clock. "It's 8:20 p.m.. We'll plan on another pill about 2:30 a.m., and then another one 8:30 in the morning. I have to open the clinic before eight. So you'll be on you own to take that next pill. I'll be home for the meds you must take at 2:40 p. m. tomorrow afternoon."

"If I wake up?" JD shook his head.

"Well, I'll leave you two to figure out the regimen for JD here. See you guys later." Suzanne picked up her shoulder bag, and let herself out the door.

CHAPTER ELEVEN

————— ✦✦✦✦✦✦ —————

IT WAS A fact. JD had pneumonia. Claire had treated extremely sick dogs with this kind of disease and JD was 'sicker' than a dog. A fever raged in his body. His cough sounded deep, and at first dry, but later became mucus filled. She had to shake him awake, to get him to take a pill and drink a glass of water. Monday and Tuesday she drove home on her lunch hour to check on him and get him up enough to swallow another dose of the meds. She vowed Monday evening if he got any worse she would have to take him to the hospital. Finally she called Suzanne to go and check on him before she went in for a shift at the morgue,

The most terrible experience was listening to him cough during the night. She barely slept. She now felt as if she were a mother nursing her sick child through a terrible illness. She hoped he wouldn't need oxygen. In a stroke of luck she went through the utility closet and found a humidifier. She cleaned and filled it and put it in his room. Wednesday morning, when she went into check on him, he was lying awake.

"How are you?" She touched his forehead and it felt cooler.

"I'm cooler, I can tell. Would you help me to sit up?" She helped him with two pillows behind his head.

"I must leave for the clinic, but there's a pitcher of cool water in the bathroom. Do you think you can get up?" She was still afraid to leave him.

He swung his legs over to the side of the bed and braced himself up with his hands. "Let me sit here for a few minutes. I need to get up on my own. You go to the clinic, and I'll be fine." He tilted his head. "At least, somewhat better."

"Okay, but if Suzanne comes and finds you on the floor, you'll be in trouble." She stood in the doorway for a long moment, but then went down the stairs.

As Claire drove to the clinic she wondered if her life would ever get back to normal. First of all she wondered if she would even get a full night's sleep. Since JD had entered her life, sleep had flown out the window.

When she arrived home that evening she found JD sitting at the kitchen table with a mug of coffee, and he was writing on a yellow pad. He glanced up and tried for a wan smile, and he looked like hell. Her brother's tee shirt that a week ago was too tight for JD now fit him. "Do you feel well enough to be downstairs?"

"The fact that I made it down here is a victory. I needed to write things down. They were swirling in my head, and so I came down here, warmed up the left over coffee and ate a muffin. I feel better, and I took my 2:30 p.m. dose of the meds." He slumped, as if just talking tired him.

"Tonight is Halloween. The doorbell will begin to ring very soon. I have some soup, and I'll put some on the stove to heat." She began to warm the soup. About ten seconds later the doorbell rang. She clicked off the stove and ran to the front door.

JD could hear Claire talk to the children. She was pleasant, asking about their costumes, and their ages. Listening to her wonderful laugh gave him strength. He decided he could stand and stir the soup. With some effort he went to the stove and turned on the gas burner. He felt familiar with this stove, as if he used one like it not long ago. The doorbell continued to ring, and Claire continued to give out candy and talk to the children.

JD managed to carry a bowl of hot soup to the table. He searched the small pantry and found a box of crackers. For a few minutes the doorbell was silent, and Claire returned to the kitchen.

"Oh you fixed some soup." She came to the table with a bowl of soup for herself. But the doorbell rang again. Then for the next few minutes the doorbell was quiet. She sat down at the table and ate some soup and crackers. She glanced over and noticed JD was writing on a yellow pad.

"What are you writing?" She asked.

"When I remember things, I write them down."

"What have you remembered?" She asked and leaned over to study the pad.

"First it was bank sorting numbers that filled my head. Later, the name Mac came into my mind. I think it's my name." He still scribbled on the pad.

The doorbell rang, and Claire ran to answer it. When she came back, she dropped unto the padded bench, and asked. "What things beside the name Mac have you remembered?"

"The bank sorting numbers are possibly for two off- shore accounts. And Mac is short for my last or possibly my first name. I need to search for things on your laptop. But if they are what I think they are, these are accounts somewhere in the Caribbean, and probably secret."

Claire's eyes widened. "You mean someone or a group, are hiding money offshore, illegally?"

"With no real memory- - - - -," He shrugged. "But my gut tells me, bad guys."

"Possibly the mob, or a cartel. Even terrorists?! She took a deep breath. "More and more you are sounding like FBI, Home Land Security, or CIA, or possibly a High level *wise guy.*"

"Any of those are possibilities." He said. But another name came to mind. He stopped and wrote down a name: *Theodore.* He frowned at the name, but circled it. Then he had an *ah-hah* moment. He glanced over at Claire. "I need one more favor. Please, will you buy a new bicycle tire for the bike in the garage? I know before, I used to ride a bike for exercise and pleasure. I know it will help me remember."

"You're in no shape to ride a bicycle." She frowned, but jumped up to answer the ringing doorbell.

"I know, but I'll take my meds and rest. And maybe in a week or so- - - - - - ? I'll be a good boy, I promise." He called to her and actually laughed.

She studied him. Even with the stubble of reddish beard, and deep circles under his eyes, he extruded an aura of little boy sexiness. She realized, right at the moment that whatever she could do to help him, she would. "I'm still not quite sure why I'm harboring you. It started out as a big adventure for Suzanne and me. And believe me at that point in my life I needed something adventurous."

"You'll have to tell me why you suddenly dropped out of veterinary college to return to this area and now have an animal clinic to run." He said.

"Maybe someday I'll tell you." She put her hands on her hips. "Are you finished with your soup? Would you like anything else to eat?" She reached for his bowl.

He finished with the soup and ate another cracker. "I think I'll go back upstairs. I'll take another pill before I crash. Have fun with the little Goblins, Princesses and the Storm troopers." He slowly eased up the stairs.

The next evening she brought home her laptop and set it on the kitchen table. He came downstairs soon after and asked her. "Why do you take this computer to work with you, when you have one there?"

"Because I'm doing a veterinary course and need it. When I have time, I work on it with this computer." She walked into the den and set it on the desk there. "If you use it in here, then I can have the table to set dinner on it. Then when you're through, I'll do some course work for a while." She knew canned soup and a cheese sandwich were boring, but she did not have the energy to do any real shopping. She called him to dinner, and he ate everything she put I front of him. He never complained.

JD went back into the den and about a half hour later he came back. "I found out where these two accounts are located. The Dutch Antilles, possibly Aruba. Is there another place that you know of that has a powerful computers?"

She stopped, but then kept loading the dishwasher. "We now have a university here, but the big computers are up at Cedar City in the

Bio lab. University of Southern Utah. I started a master's degree there, because my major was Biology, and I had access to those labs. That was over a year ago. I may be able to get back in there. Would a Krey computer that can split DNA strands be of use?" She raised her eyebrows and grinned.

"A Krey? How far is Cedar City?" He dropped unto the curved bench.

"From here about 50 miles north. Will you feel well enough to go Saturday?"

"I'll rest up and keep taking the pills and- - - - -whatever I need to do."

"Okay, I'll check on the activities going on up there on Saturday evening. Possibly a football game. On to another subject. Did my brother, Curt leave a sweater in his closet?"

"I believe so, why?"

"Because Cedar City is 5700 feet in elevation. While St. George ranges from 2300 to 3000 above sea level, *and* we're farther south. You're going to need something warmer than just a tee shirt." She said. "Oh, I bought a bicycle tire. It's out in the barn."

"Oh, thanks so much." He felt tears trickle down his nose, and dropped his head.

That night as he lay in bed, he decided that if he could hack into the Aruba accounts, he would use some of those funds for 'getting back to normal money'. It depended on the origins of the accounts and the dollar amounts in them. He also needed identification papers. A Social Security Card, or passport. Also a birth certificate. And enough money to open a bank account, with a new identity.

He felt better the next morning and went out to the barn. The first thing he noticed was the change in temperature. November seemed to bring in a real feel of autumn. It was cool and cloudy.

He fixed the bicycle, but then had to go in and rest. He ate lunch, took a nap, and returned to snoop around the barn. As he went through a pile of old magazines he found the perfect new name. The more he thought about it, he also might need to use still another name. The reason for this 'change of identity' was to protect Claire.

CHAPTER TWELVE

———— ✦✦✦✦✦ ————

T HE NEXT MORNING Mac alias JD went out into the barn with the plan of attaching the new bike tire to the bicycle. He noticed a short ladder and lifted the bicycle from its hook high on the west side of the barn. Just moving the bicycle left him weak and shaking. He stood there for a long time breathing in and breathing out. He leaned the bike on the wall and slowly walked inside. He sat near the kitchen table and rested, waiting for his heart rate to drop into some kind of normalcy.

It had been nearly a week since he felt the first effects of the pneumonia. He began to thank God and the medical profession for antibiotics. He had taken a class in college statistics and learned about the basic killers of Americans and for that matter the rest of the world a 100 years ago. Pneumonia was at the top of the list, and then there was the great flu epidemic of 1918. He'd never thought about the impact of those diseases until now. Probably the reason he was even out of bed today, was because of his age and general level of fitness. How old was he anyway? He knew Claire was 31, and he was probably a few years older than she was.

He vowed to improve his health. First thing was a nutritious breakfast, and he began assembling the ingredients of said breakfast immediately. After that he cleaned up, he and decided to watch the morning news on TV. There, on the sofa, he fell asleep, but woke after an hour or so and went back out into the barn to at least take the old tire off the bicycle. While he was working he had interesting bits of information flit through his head. He needed to find his yellow pad and write these down.

-------- ·•••••• --------

Claire arrived home an hour later than usual. He was upstairs and heard her car crunch the gravel drive. He eased downstairs and opened the kitchen door. She walked in carrying a large sack of groceries. "I was a little concerned, because you were later arriving home. Later than you usually are."

"We were low on many of the basic foods we usually eat. Since I had a good night's sleep last night, I had the energy to shop." She set the sack down on the counter.

"Is there more to bring in?" Mac asked.

She nodded and he went out to carry them in. "You take it easy. You don't need a relapse."

He set the sack down, and went back outside. He then went to sit down at the table. "See I'm resting now. I learned today that I have to take things easy for a while." He sat there and enjoyed watching her put the food items away. Then she pulled out two Subway sandwiches and set them on plates and brought them to the table.

"Do you want milk or soda?" She asked.

"I'll start with soda and have milk afterward." He said.

After they finished their sandwiches, he asked. "How close is Las Vegas?"

"Why do you want to go back to Las Vegas?" Claire asked.

"Because, I remember where I can buy some good identification papers. I thought of this guy's name and where he lives." It came to me as if I had read the information somewhere. However, to do this I'll need a loan of about $2,000 dollars. But I promise to pay you back with ten percent interest."

-------- ·•••••• --------

"I don't know." She frowned, took a bite of her sandwich and studied her plate. *I did decide to help him.* "Let me take a look at my finances. I did make a payment on the clinic for October. But my house payment is due in two weeks."

He sat back. "I know it's a lot to ask. If I can borrow your car say Saturday. I think I can buy a new identity. Then if we go up to the university in Cedar City, whenever. In a few days, I know I can pay you back later in the week." His words were soft, yet there was an intensity to them. "It all depends when I can open a personal account with my new identity."

"Okay, let me take a look at my finances." She sighed, and sipped her soda.

———— ✦✦✦✦ ————

Friday afternoon she came home with 2,000 in cash, a bottle of hair dye and some shaded green glasses. She set them on the kitchen table.

He came down stairs and stood looking at the money and her purchases. "Hair dye and glasses?" He asked.

"Think about it. So you manage to find this forger, and get the papers for a new identity. Then next you go into a bank and open an account. Your curly red hair is like a beacon. What will this teller or bank clerk remember about you? *Copper-red hair with green eyes, tall, with fair skin.* What we're going to do is ease your basic description into something more common." Claire said. "Tonight, we're going to change your appearance somewhat. But first I'm hungry, so I brought home food already prepared."

Claire had walked in with a roast chicken from Costco. She cooked some rice and they had a quick dinner. Next she coaxed JD upstairs to do the dye job on his hair. It wasn't black, but a darker brown shade. Once his hair was colored, she said. "Now put on the glasses."

He tried them on, and they muted his green eyes. "These are great. Where did you find them?" He asked.

"In a drawer, in the front area of the clinic. Someone must have left them on the counter." She said.

"Do you think they were Neil's?" He said with a faint smile.

"How do you know about Neil?" Hands on hips, she stepped back and frowned.

"I've been bringing in the mail. The Post Office is forwarding some of his mail, here. You'll have to tell me about Neil and why he left you his clinic to run."

"Someday, but right now, we have to get you ready to become Mister Average Guy."

·•••••·

The next morning When JD came down stairs he really looked different. He poured a mug of coffee and sat down at the table.

Claire came down and stood studying him. "One more thing we need to do to change your appearance. Come into the half-bath." Once she had him in there, she opened a container of make-up.

"No, I don't need any make-up." He grimaced.

"I don't mean cheek color or false eyelashes." A wicked grin spread across her face. 'We're just going to cover up your freckles. Women do it all the time to improve the appearance of their skin."

"You don't do that do you? Your skin is clear and smooth." He said.

"Well thank you for the compliment. I do the 'face' thing once in a while. I figure if the cats and dogs don't care why should I? Now come here and I'll show you how a little basic color will change your skin." She set to work smoothing the foundation on his face, hands and arms.

He squinted at the mirror. "Okay can I go drink my coffee and eat some cereal?"

She shrugged, and did much the same.

He drove her to the clinic. "Now you said that Las Vegas is about two hours away." He glanced at the clock in the car. "It's 8:20 a.m., I should be able to make it back here by 3:00 p.m. Is that okay?"

"Yes. I need to clean the clinic anyway. Especially on a Saturday it will take me at about an hour."

"Good. Boy I wish I had a cell phone."

She handed him her cell phone. "See you later."

He watched her go in the rear door. The door he walked out of nearly three weeks ago. *The dead man walking to his destiny.*

Once he drove into the north end of Las Vegas, he knew which exit to take to find an unassuming neighborhood and Ocotillo Street. He cruised down the street until he found the house number: 1009. Immediately he found himself thinking in Spanish! Up to that point he had no idea he knew the language. This gave him another clue to his lost past. He had lived where Spanish was a useful second language.

He took one last look at the dark brown hair and tinted sunglasses in the car mirror. Once he rang the doorbell and the young Hispanic man opened it, he spoke to him in the man's language.

Less than an hour later he emerged from the house with a Social Security card, a Nevada driver's license, and a U. S. passport all in the name of Jonathan David Mackay. The cost of all these papers: $1,560. In U. S. dollars

Our new Jonathan's next step was to set up an account at the Bank of Nevada, North Las Vegas Branch. They were branching out and had an office in Mesquite, Nevada, only 38 miles from St. George. This bank was accustomed to handling bank transfers from all over the world. He also stopped in Mesquite and opened a Post Office Box in the new name.

While he was there he called Claire. "I'm heading back to town. Mission accomplished." He could hear a dog barking and grinned.

"Good. Did you have any money left over?" She asked, a little hitch in her voice?

"Yes, I used it to open a bank account in Las Vegas and I filled up your car with gas. Next step, we need to go up to Cedar City, is it? Once up there I'll be able to enrich my new bank account."

"I've been thinking about that. I'll tell you at dinner." She said.

. He strolled into the clinic back door and had to watch where he stepped, because the floor was damp. "Claire the floor's wet."

"I know. I just mopped it. Can you tip toe to the chair by the door?" She yelled.

"Yeah, I put my feet on the folded rug." As he sat there and glanced around, he suddenly realized that taking care and running this clinic was a considerable amount of work. No wonder she fell asleep before 10 p.m. every night.

She poked her head around a corner, and pushed a mop bucket with her foot. "I think I'm finished." She picked up the bucket and poured out the dirty water into a large sink. She wore a large apron, and rubber shoes. She rinsed out the sink, and set the cleaning rags and mop on a towel by a closet. Her face was flushed, and she was a bit disheveled, but she smiled and leaned on the sink. "My idea for dinner is pizza. However, it's only three-thirty and I'd like to take a shower and clean up a little."

"Okay. Your chariot is waiting." He laughed.

CHAPTER THIRTEEN

H E DROVE BACK to Claire's house, and she immediately went upstairs. He slowly went up to his room. Soon he could hear a shower running. He realized he was tired, and dropped on his bed. When he woke the sun was dropping behind the trees. He flipped on the light and became aware it was quiet and nearly dark in the house. *Maybe she went to get the pizza?* He walked out into the hallway and noticed the door to her bedroom was open. He peaked in and could her lying asleep on a large bed. She was wearing only a terry cloth robe. A rumble of pure lust went through him. Right now, to him, she was *so* desirable, but also beautiful. He closed his eyes and forced himself to walk back to his room and shut the door. The best thing for him to do, right then was also take a long hot shower and then turn on the cold

He showered and dropped on his bed and surprisingly fell asleep. Later, there was a knock on his door. "JD it's after 6 p.m. We'd better go.' She called out. "The pizza place will just get more crowded, especially after the football game."

"Sorry, I fell asleep. I'll be down in a few minutes." He faked a loud yawn.

Claire and Mac sat in a cozy booth enjoying a Supreme pizza, salad and sodas. Suddenly she glanced over at the 'take out' counter and said. "Oh no, not her."

"Who are you talking about?" He carefully began perusing the group of customers standing in line to pick up pizzas.

"The blond woman at the take-out counter. She- - - - - -." Claire had no time to finish her sentence, because Sally Bradshaw looked their way and marched right over to their booth. She stood glaring down at Claire and Mac. "Well, well, you've managed to tear yourself away from the clinic long enough to grab a meal, I see." Her gaze burned down at Claire, but switched her gaze down at Mac. "And who might this be? Are you the new vet? I heard you hired a woman. Oh dear, I must have been mistaken." The venom in her voice was unmistakable.

"Claire cleared her throat. "This is a friend, John, ah--------."

Mac spoke up. "Jonathan David Mackay." He slid out of the booth and offered his hand. "And who might *you be?*"

To Claire's astonishment, Sally smiled. "I'm Sally Bradshaw, Neil's widow. Neil owned the animal clinic that Claire now-- - - - - - -."

"The clinic Claire inherited. Yes, I'm aware of your late husband's generous gift to Claire. 'Very kind of him don't you think? To repay her for all the hard work she did helping Neil to get established here in the Southwest, and help him build a large clientele." Mac turned a benevolent smile on Sally along with his soft words.

"I'm not so sure how appropriate Neil's gift was. He seemed to forget his wife."

"He left you penniless?" Mac spoke in mock surprise.

"Well, actually no. I have the house and the car and truck and all the household furnishings. But I'm finding it hard to deal with it all."

Claire watched in surprise as Sally patted her chest in mock distress.

"Perhaps you could improve your situation by finding suitable employment. Something that would fit your skills and talents. Look at the explosive growth going on in St. George. We see it all around us. Now is the time to find a good position that could develop into a fine career."

"I suppose I will eventually find a job. It's been difficult to recover from the shock of Neil's- - - - ah passing. It was so sudden." She pressed a hand to her throat.

"Mrs. Bradshaw." The man to the counter called out. "Your pizzas are ready."

"Oh, the pizzas for my son's cub scout group." She said.

"Well, it was very nice to meet you Mr. - - - - -?"

"Mackay. The pleasure was mine." Mac sat down and flashed an easy smile at Claire.

Sally stood for a long moment in seeming confusion. As if she wanted to keep talking to Jon Mackay. She nodded "It was nice to meet you, too Mr. Mackay." Sally slowly walked out clutching her pizzas.

Claire watched as Sally left the store. She turned to Mac. "You were amazing. I half- expected Sally to kiss you on the cheek."

He cleared his throat, to stop a cough. "She an interesting female. I can see there is no love lost between the two of you."

"Interesting doesn't half cover it. And you-- -. Your technique in flattery is really professional. You have the talent of a top interrogator. You must have worked for the government. But right now you need to eat some pizza."

"We can always take home the leftover food. I usually did that." He said and then frowned.

Driving back to Claire's house, she casually asked. "Have you come up with anymore revelations as to your actual name, occupation, and address? Other than the fact that you usually take home your leftovers."

"Yes, and no. When I used your computer, I located two off shore back accounts in Aruba. However, your computer isn't strong enough for me to hack into them. We need to go up to the college in Cedar City. Another reason is that I don't want to draw attention to your computer and your business. I honestly don't know what and who we are dealing with. And I won't know until I can do some research. People who have hidden bank accounts are usually doing something illegal. And these people can be very dangerous."

"Do you mean dangerous as in -------------?" She asked.

"National security, certain people, cities, and countries in jeopardy,- - - - dangerous." He said.

"More and more you are sounding and acting like a member of some national police organization. Do you remember anything significant?"

"I know my name is Mac, and I think it's what people call me. The Mac part of it sounded normal."

"And where did you get the name Jonathan David Mackay?"

"From a pile of old magazines I found in the barn. Mormon Church publications." He laughed.

"Oh those probably belonged to my mother. She was born into the LDS Church, but when she met my dad and he wasn't interested in converting. She married him anyway."

"The name of the man on the cover was David O. Mackay. He had such a kind face, so I thought. Why not be Jonathan David Mackay. A good Scottish name." The Mac part seemed familiar."

Claire pulled her car into the barn, because it was beginning to rain. When she reached the back door, Mac had a coughing spell, he ran into the bathroom.

"Are you okay?" She said as she stood by the closed bathroom door.

"Just a coughing spell." He cleared his throat, and wiped his face with a damp washcloth.

"You are better. But pneumonia is not to be taken lightly. It's going to take a few more days of taking it easy until you are your old self."

"I don't know what my *old self* feels like." He shrugged. "Maybe a cup of tea and some of that cough medicine will help."

"And don't forget your 8:30 p.m. meds. I'd like to watch the 9 p.m. news." She brought the tea and his medicine to the table. "Please go upstairs and get to bed, soon."

After they both watched the first segment of the news, she climbed off the sofa. "I can't stay awake much longer. But did you choose the name Mackay, because you think you are Scottish?" I can imagine you in a kilt."

"With your brown hair, brown eyes and pale olive skin, I would guess you're heritage is Southern Europe."

"I have an Italian Grandmother. You're good. On that note, good night." She left the room and Mac could hear her climb up the stairs.

———————— ⁘⁘⁘ ————————

The next morning Mac felt well enough to go down and begin some breakfast. He decided to make French toast.

Claire came down and was surprised. "You must be feeling better." She sat down at let him serve her. "You even fried bacon. Well, it is a Sunday. On Sunday I usually buy a paper and read it to see, if the world is crashing around us. The rest of the week, I don't worry about it." She shrugged, and grinned.

"How is it that you own a veterinary clinic? I did ask Suzanne about you relationship to the clinic, not being a vet, yet running the clinic. She told me to ask you." Mac said.

"When Neil died, he left it to me in his will. I was completely shocked. But when I went over to the building I felt so comfortable. It felt natural to run it. I had some help from Neil's attorney."

"So this Sally individual we met last night is or was Neil's wife. How long had they been married?" He asked.

"Maybe 18 months." She answered

"How long did you work for Neil at the clinic?" He asked.

"Eight years. I don't want to get into my relationship with Neil right now. When you can come and tell me what you have been doing for the past 8 years. Then we can share our past lives." Claire stood. "I'll clean up this morning. Perhaps you would like to go find a NFL game to watch." She picked up her plate and began to run water in the kitchen sink.

A few days later Mac returned to the garage and worked on the bicycle. The bike was old and needed to be cleaned, the chain oiled, and it could use a paint job. Or at least to be cleaned thoroughly. Something that he owned or used needed to be in top condition. He had a gut feeling about that. The weather was warm, and once he finished the work, he took it outside to wash it and oil the seat. He took it out on the street, but only rode it a block or two, because he had become fatigued.

He returned to the Claire's house, and put the bike into the barn and found an old tarp to cover it.

After lunch, he went into the den and began a search on Claire's computer for a place to buy paint for bicycles. It was several miles back into St. George. He realized he was bored, and began searching for something to read. He found a shelf in the den closet that had several older books on it. He selected a James Patterson novel. After about thirty pages he realized he had read it. On his yellow pad he wrote that he had read the novel before and liked the author, James Patterson.

Claire came bursting into the house that evening. "I think tomorrow evening will be a good time to drive up to Cedar City." The football team is playing an away game and so the campus will be fairly quiet. "Did my brother leave a jacket or sweater in the closet upstairs?" She asked.

"I believe so. Why?" Mac asked."

"Because it's mid- November and it's going to be much colder up there than it is here. So dress warmly."

"Okay, what did you decide on for supper?" He asked. "I'll help. Make a salad or something."

"You must be feeling better. Your appetite has improved. Go wash your hands and get out the greens."

CHAPTER FOURTEEN

——————— ✦✦✦✦✦✦ ———————

I T RAINED THE next day in Rawley, and the temperature dropped into the low 50's. Mac had been so used to the mild weather that he now knew he would need to wear the sweater left in his closet. If the weather cooled even more, he would need a warm jacket. That was an even a better reason to hack into those accounts. He needed money for clothes.

On the drive up to Cedar City, Mac noticed how they climbed in elevation for most of the drive. The topography changed too. Though it was dark, they left orange- red cliffs and desert for outcroppings for very different rock formations. Once they reach Cedar City, Claire drove onto the college campus and parked as close to Biology building group as she could. When she exited the car, she carried with her a small brown sack.

"You're correct, it's much colder up here, and I noticed snow on the tops of hills." He glanced at the sack in her hand. "May I ask what's in the brown sack?"

"When we get a little closer I'll show you." They reached the building and Claire stopped, and took a small bottle of bourbon from the sack, and a can of Coca Cola. "Could you open the bourbon, please?" She asked. She opened the can of coke, and let about the top third of it drain into a patch of bushes. "Hand me the bourbon." She poured a couple of ounces of the alcohol into the can of coke.

"Why the bourbon and coke?" He asked, and watched her mouth flash into a grin in the semi -darkness.

"It's the pass word." She laughed. "You'll see."

They climbed the six stairs into the building and took the elevator up two floors. Mac could see the building was not new, but it was well lighted and spotless. From the elevator they walked down the hall and were met by a large man in his early 60's.

"Hi there Missy. Haven't seen you for a while. Where you been?" He asked.

"I've been in Veterinary College in Colorado. How've you been, Gus? We need to get into the restricted lab. Is that okay?" She asked.

"Did you bring the pass word?" He grinned and showed a couple broken teeth partially hidden by his bushy gray mustache.

"Oh yes. I wouldn't forget that." Claire handed him the can of coke.

"An' this guy, who is he?" Gus pointed a finger at Mac.

"I'm a friend from school. Claire and I are together most of the time." Mac smiled at Gus, and put out his hand to shake. He noticed that the man carried a side arm.

Gus took a long swallow from the coke and nodded. "Missy here, really knows her pass words." He walked to a glassed in section of the area. On the door in big letters were the words. BIOLAB RESTRICTED AREA. Key access only. Gus flipped a group of keys he carried and entered one into the door, and punched in a four digit code.

"There ya go, Missy. You got about an hour. Don't forget to sign in. I'll be down in my office enjoying my beverage." She could hear the jingle of his keys, as he walked down stairs.

"Thanks Gus. I won't." Claire and Mac entered the world on high tech computers, desks and in another glassed- area it was lined with shelves holding bio equipment.

Mac eased around the room checking out computers. When he found the large Krey computer he stood for a long time staring at it.

"Wow. I've always wanted to use one of these." He promptly sat down and booted it up.

Claire signed in, and nervously wandered around until she found another computer and sat down. When the computer asked for a password she took a small slip of paper from her pocket and punched in the code.

Mac came over and watched her put in the code of letters and digits. Immediately he went back to the Krey and put in the same pass word. The screen changed to blue with the curser blinking. Within a few minutes he was into The Bank of Aruba. He put in the sorting code. Now the computer wanted a password the open those accounts.

He took a piece of blank paper and began to write various words he thought would work. Then he tried the word VICTORY/12/31, in various combinations in English, next Spanish, but finally French, and the first account opened up. His eyes widened when he read the dollar amount. $902,000.47. He debited that account and sent funds to the Bank of Panama, to another numbered account, the sum of $62,057.25 to Pedro and Sons Manufacturing: For Services Rendered

The amount in the second account was much smaller. $45,062.00. And there were regular withdrawals from this account. The latest was November 10th for $1,200.00 and it went to an address in Las Vegas. *Rent money?* Mac took out $5,000 from that account.

Now he sent the invoice from Pedro and Sons to the account of JD Mackay. Mesquite, Nevada. This time his deposit was for $55, 062. 25. He then moved smaller amounts of money into two other accounts. He shut down the Krey and wandered over to where Claire was sitting. He found her reading the campus newspaper on line on that computer. He touched her shoulder.

She gave a slight jump, and turned. "Are you finished already?" She flashed a questioning frown.

"Yes, for now. I'll think I've covered my computer path." He slid into the heavy sweater and walked to sign in-out book and glanced down. Claire had signed in as Diego and Dora Salazar.

He turned to her. "What I want to know is, are Dora and Diego husband and wife, or brother and sister?"

"Neither, they're cousins."

Mac waited while Claire ran down to Gus's office. She found him watching a small TV and sipping at the password. "We're finished for this evening. Thanks a bunch Gus."

"You make sure you get that degree from the Vets College, and come up and see me again." He said.

The next Tuesday Mac again asked to borrow Claire's car. He drove to Mesquite and went to the bank where JD Mackay had opened an account. He checked his new account, and asked if he could arrange to have a bank card to use from that account.

When the secretary pulled up his account and it had over $60.000 in it, she quickly gave Mac the paperwork to fill out. He also took about $3,000. dollars out in cash and drove back to St. George.

He located the St. George mall and walked into J. C. Penny's and began to buy clothes. As he strolled down the mall, he also noticed a ladies dress shop. In the window he saw a cream colored blouse in a silky fabric. He guessed her size and bought it for Claire.

When he went to pick up Claire, she glanced in the back seat and could see sacks and boxes of purchases. "My goodness it looks as if you went shopping. Did you find the mall?"

"Yes, and I also bought you something." When they reached Claire's house, she helped him carry in his purchases. They set them all on the kitchen table.

"First, I need to pay you the money you lent me." Mac fished an envelope from his jean's pocket and handed it to her.

In it was $2,150.00. She flipped through the money. "This is more than I lent you. My money returned with interest." A laughed bubbled from her throat.

"I promised to pay for the use of the money, and I have." he grinned. "I think we should celebrate. Think of a restaurant where you would like to dine and we'll go. Also, now that I have some decent clothes to wear." He gave her a lopsided grin, and picked up the box with the blouse in it. "See if this fits."

Claire held up the blouse to her chest. "Oh, this is so pretty. Thank you. I'll go try it on." She quickly returned to the kitchen. I thought of a great Italian restaurant; *Olive Garden*. Have you had dinner there?"

He thought for a moment. "Yes, I believe so. I'll go put on some decent clothes." He grabbed his sacks of clothes and hurried up stairs.

Twenty minutes later He came down stairs wearing a long sleeved, green shirt, dark brown slacks and new brown loafers. He sat down in the kitchen, but his wait for Claire was only a few minutes

She wore the new blouse, dressy navy slacks, and she had done the 'face' thing. She looked beautiful. "Let's go, I'm hungry."

✦✦✦✦✦

The *Olive Garden* lived up to its reputation. "Do you want a glass of wine to go with your dinner?"

Mac asked.

For a moment she frowned, but then said. Sure, a glass of red wine."

They talked about St. George, living in the Southwest compared to living in the Midwest. "Then you remember living on a farm? Was that farm in the Midwest?" Claire asked.

He sat back in his chair and frowned. "I remember a lot of acreage, and a house much like yours. You know, and house with two stories, bedrooms upstairs, and a big front porch. It was hot in the summer, and because of my skin and hair, I always wore a hat and a shirt with sleeves outside." He glanced at their partially eaten food. "Would you like another glass of wine?"

"One is enough. Besides I'm driving." She sighed and took a deep breath. "There was a time when I'd probably drink the whole bottle. But I found that alcohol doesn't solve anything. All that happened to me was a gain twenty-five pounds and became even more depressed."

"Did that happen after you stopped working for Neil?" Mac asked in a soft voice, his eyes on her face.

"How did you figure --------------? I suppose I'm easy to analyze, and the fact that you have an amazing talent for interrogation. Small town girl grieving over the end of a love affair, plus losing the job she loved."

"What changed in your life, because this is the first time I've ever seen you drink?"

"When I managed to become accepted into veterinary school, and moved away from the *new* Bradshaw couple. I got into something I loved to explore, and the Colorado weather is great for hiking and ski touring. I quit drinking, started hiking and in less than 4 months lost 25 pounds.

"You look great, just the right weight." He grinned.

"Thanks for the flattery." She sat back and tilted her head.

Just then, they heard a scream and a crash of dishes on the floor. Mac was up and ran toward the sound. He saw a man trying to pull a female server out the back door of the restaurant. Mac grabbed the guy's shoulder, threw one solid punch and the man dropped like a stone.

The manager ran to the girl and broken dishes with a cell phone to his ear. "Whoa Beth, who is this guy. Sir, do you know this man?" He asked Mac and his server.

Mac stepped back. "I just responded to her screams. Did you call the police?" As Mac spoke he lifted the girl up and noticed some small cuts on her arms and a larger one on her hand. He grabbed the towel she had dropped and wrapped it around the bleed on her hand. Next he rolled the attacker over on his chest and looked around for something to restrain him. On a high shelf he noticed a box of large twist ties use to tie up laundry. He used them as handcuffs on the perp.

By then Claire stepped in and gently eased the server away from the broken mess on the floor, and sat her down in an empty booth. She then grabbed Mac's arm and pushed him out the back door.

"You don't want to be questioned about this situation. She hustled him out to her car. "Let's go." She opened her car door. "Get in." She roared out of the parking lot and down the street to the main street back to Rawley.

CHAPTER FIFTEEN

⸱ ⬧⬧⬧⬧⬧⬧ ⸱

A S THEY DROVE out of the restaurant's parking lot, Mac asked. "Did you pay the check?"

"It was over 40 dollars so I left the 50 dollar bill you gave me this afternoon. Darn it. I wanted to take home the leftovers." She giggled nervously. "I can't believe how fast you responded to that situation. You must have been trained to react that way. You're definitely a Fed of some sort. Or ex-military. Special forces maybe?"

"Why did you guess special forces?" Mac asked.

"Because Gus is retired special forces, Gustav Meier is his name. That's why he got the job at the Bio Lab. He's a tough old guy."

"That situation in the restaurant- - - - - - - -, it was so weird, I just reacted. Now I know I have been trained to react like that. I'm glad I could help that girl."

"Before we go into the house, let's talked about these flashes you are now having."

"It's not that I'm trying to avoid them. Some of them are disturbing, and yet other times, I know I should behave the way I did."

"Give me an example." She said as she drove the car into the barn.

"I remember being in a crouch behind a big black SUV firing my weapon at a retreating blue car. I shot out the left tail light, And I had another memory, and a similar situation, but that time I remember it was practice. Shooting at a target, and it fell down."

"Okay, kick that around in your head. Let's go into the house. I want to see if they have something about your altercation with the bad guy and the server at the *Olive Garden* on TV."

They sat on the sofa and quietly watched the news. It began and then the channel showed the BREAKING NEWS logo. The reporter stood outside the restaurant in question. *"A man in his twenties went into this restaurant and tried to kidnap a female server. She was carrying a tray loaded with dishes, and as he grabbed her, she dropped the tray and screamed. A diner quickly came to her rescue, punched out the perp, tied him up, and then helped her with cuts that happened when she dropped the tray. The diner then told the manager to call the police. Strangely, his female partner grabbed him and they left the area before anyone could speak with them. We'll be following up on this shy hero later."*

Claire laughed. "Shy hero. I love it." The news program cut to a commercial.

Mac was now 'glued' to the TV. He turned to Claire and asked. "Where is this computer store they are advertising?"

"I believe the closest store is in Provo, at the South Town Mall. Why?"

"How far north is Provo?" Mac asked

"About three hours' drive. You want to buy something there?" Claire asked.

"I need a good laptop. Can we drive there next week sometime?"

"I have two college girls working for me, and my Vet comes in Monday Wednesday and Friday. We could go Wednesday."

"We also need a better router, one that will work for more than one computer, a WiFi." He said.

"Okay, let's watch the weather report. Wednesday may not be the best day to drive there. There are some low and higher elevation areas to drive through before we get to Provo. We could get into a snowstorm." They both were quiet watching the weather girl. Claire yawned. "I'd better go to upstairs before I- - -----------."

Mac took her hand and pulled her down on the sofa. He kissed it, and then leaned over and gently kissed her mouth. When he pulled away, her cheeks showed heightened color, and she smiled.

"That was- - - - - a surprise, and quite- - - - -lovely." She sat up and then eased off the sofa and stood. "I think I'd better go to bed." She turned quickly and knocked a cushion loose. But her smile was sweet, and she touched his shoulder for a brief moment before she ran upstairs.

He watched her leave, but he grinned. *She isn't angry, she liked the kiss.* He dropped back to the sofa. *Mac, you can't pursue Claire until you know exactly who and what you are.* He sat there for several minutes, but finally turned off the TV and went upstairs. He was falling for this sweet, competent girl. But first he had to find out what he had been and what he could be.

It was just after six a.m. when Geoffery Colson's telephone phone rang. At first he thought it was his alarm clock, and reached for it in the dark room. However the ringing continued. And in order to stop the shrill sound, he would have to find the phone. He hit the receiver and it fell on the floor, landing somewhere near his bed. He managed to reach the bedside lamp and snap it on. Now he had to find the receiver. He grabbed it and growled into it "What is it?"

"Dr. Colson, this is Zuhdi. I'm sorry- - - -."

Yes, Zuhdi. What is it, so early in the morning>"

"Have you withdrawn funds from the Aruba account?"

"No. not in the last three weeks or so. Why?" Colson sat up blinking the sleep from his eyes.

"Because we had to find an apartment. It has grown too cold at night to sleep in the house. I had no idea Las Vegas could be so cold."

"Okay did you take money from the account for an apartment?"

"Yes. $1,200, but when I looked up the balance there was another $5,000 missing. I have a notebook as you suggested, I keep track." Zuhdi said.

"The last time I used that account was to pay for property taxes to obtain the safe house. That was the last day in September." Colson was now up and pacing his bedroom. "The account was probably hacked. I have a man who is good with computers. I'll have him check the accounts. Thank you for alerting me. Good morning."

"Ah- - -, Dr. Colson, should we take more money out of that account? We will need more rent money and also for clothes for the winter weather coming to Las Vegas." Zuhdi said. "The newspapers say many of the hotels will need more workers for the Christmas and New Year's season."

"How's learning Spanish coming?" Colson asked. And anymore problems with the FBI?"

"We are practicing more every day, Sir. "No, all has been quiet."

"Good. I'll transfer more money into the account in two days. Good bye."

Dr. Colson frowned. The withdrawal on the account sounded like a hacker. He would alert Jeremy to the 'hack'. But first Colson must do his morning work-out. After a shower and dressing, he went to his kitchen for coffee and his normal nutritious breakfast.

Just after 7 a.m. that morning Colson called his student assistant Jeremy Ardmore. He let the phone ring five times as was ready to hang up, when Jeremy finally picked up.

"Hey man." - - - a beat "It's early."

"Jeremy, Professor Colson, here."

"Oh Professor Colson, I apologize for the way I- - - -- - -."

"Never mind, I have a small problem that came to my attention. And I'd like you to address it."

"Yes, sir?"

"Come into my office later this morning, and I'll explain."

"Yes. Sir!"

Professor Colson's first class at the university began at 9:10 a.m. It was *Advanced Middle Eastern Studies #391.* Only fifteen students were enrolled in the class. Although for the coming winter semester there was now a higher enrollment.

At the beginning of the semester, Dr. Colson was disappointed, because he thought the ongoing Iraqi- Afghanistan conflicts would have raised interest in the courses. Especially since the students on the Berkeley campus political leanings were heavily liberal. When the course had been approved, he thought students of both political camps would be interested and enroll.

One student in particular seemed especially interested in the material he taught. Her papers showed great insight, and she scored quite well on the two tests he had given so far. After only a few weeks he noticed her. She attracted his attention in a positive manner. She was blond, and rather tall with a trim athletic body. He had seen her jogging a few times around the campus in the early evening. He decided she was a little older than the average female student. She dressed rather conservatively and seemed quite a serious. When she spoke, she asked quiet, serious questions. Colson knew she had read her assignments

His curiosity caused him to check at the registrar's office. He found out that she was older than the average student: twenty-five. She had lived in Scottsdale, Arizona and attended Arizona State University, and her grade point was a 3.8. There were two two years between her last attendance at ASU and enrolling at Berkley This was because she had moved to Virginia. He wondered what she had been doing for those two years. She could have fled from an unhappy love relationship, or had problems with her family. "Is there any mention as to why this student dropped out of school for two years?" He asked the lady at the registrar's office.

"There's a note on her transcript. "Returned to her mother's home, prolonged illness. Cared for mother."

Her paperwork also said that she had a part-time job at the Bank of America, down town.

The information not listed on her university paperwork, or on any public record, was that Angela Biddough had spent those two years in FBI training. The bank building at which she 'worked' also housed the Bay Area offices of the FBI. Up until September first, Angela had been a field agent for the FBI in Virginia.

Later in the day, Jeremy came into Colson's office. "Come in Jeremy. I have two items to discuss with you. The first has to do with the paper grading you have been doing, for the course #115. *Middle Eastern Studies*

"Certainly Sir." Jeremy ran a shaky hand through his unruly mop of too long, dark brown hair. "I completed the paper grading on those tests Monday and gave them to your secretary." He glanced furtively at Colson's secretary in the outer office.

"Yes, she informed me of those tests. I am pleased with your promptness." Colson slid from his chair and walked to the open door of his office and closed it. He liked to have the desk between him and the student he had in his office. It kept the relationship under his control.

"Jeremy, we have a little problem with the off shore accounts. There are some funds missing in two of the accounts, and I believe someone has hacked them. Please see what you can discover about this situation and come to see me, ASAP."

"Yes sir, I'll get right on it." He jumped up grabbed his overstuffed back pack and grimy sweater and left, banging the door.

At 7 a.m. the next morning, Colson's phone rang. This time he was already up and working through his morning exercise routine. "Good morning." He answered.

"Sir, its Jeremy. "I traced the withdrawn funds to a new account at the Bank of Panama. So far I haven't been able to trace them any further. But- - I did find out where the computer is located, where transactions originated."

CHAPTER SIXTEEN

———— ✦✦✦✦✦ ————

C OLSON HEARD THE rattle of paper, and the sound of Jeremy's heavy breathing.

"Sir, the computer used in this transaction is Southern Utah. And I believe it is on the campus of that University there. The computer used must be new and very powerful. The hacking on both accounts was done quickly and the guy/hacker is an expert."

"Both accounts? Are you also speaking about the larger of the two? How much was taken from that account?" *Damn it, I didn't want Jeremy to find out about the larger account.*

"Over $60,000 in, US Dollars, Sir. And the smaller account, $5,000." Jeremy said.

"Once you arrive on campus, come over to my office sometime before lunch. Thank you. Goodbye." Colson stood gazing out the window. *Money in the larger account had come from many middle-eastern donors. Sixty-five thousand is a significant amount missing. This hacker must be well trained or just plain brilliant. It's unfortunate he doesn't attend school here.* Colson mused

Jeremy came into Colson's office right before the first afternoon class.

"Sit down Jeremy. Do you know how far Cedar City is from this part of California?"

"No sir."

"Let me show you." Colson put a map on his desk. There are two routes to reach Southern, Utah. I believe that the best route now is longer, than the more direct route. It's mainly because of the weather. You would be forced to go through high mountain passes if you take the central route. And this time of the year you could run into a heavy snow storm." Colson shook out a road map and spread it on his desk. "It would be better if you took this freeway, by passing Los Angeles, but this way you can go through Las Vegas, and then north to Cedar City.

It is a long drive, however you can stop a night in Las Vegas. From 'Vegas, Cedar City is only three hours north. On your return trip I have some paperwork I want you to deliver to some friends. I'll phone you as to where you should to meet them." Colson put a pen on the map.

"Pick up highway105, going southeast. Take the turn-off to Bakersfield. You can pick Interstate-15 at Barstow. I-15 will take you to Las Vegas. and all the way to Cedar City." Colson drew a line on a California-Nevada road map.

"I found a motel in Las Vegas for you in the northern, older section of the city, and it is close a famous street called Fremont Street. I believe you'll enjoy it. Warning: don't gamble. Have a nice dinner and go on to your destination the next day. I have booked two nights for you at this motel. You'll need to stop at the address I'll phone to you. So keep your phone on."

Jeremy's eyes widened. "You're sending me on a field assignment?!"

"Don't forget the reason I'm sending you on this trip. Find out who hacked those accounts."

"Jeremy, don't worry about the Friday class you teach. I believe I have an individual to cover for you. Now, today is Wednesday. If you leave Thursday morning, you can be in Cedar City easily by Friday afternoon." Colson said. He pushed an envelope to Jeremy. "I've contacted the motel you are to stay in, and paid for two nights' lodging. The funds in this envelope, along with these instructions, are for meals and gasoline. Have a safe trip. Enjoy your field assignment."

After Colson's Middle East class, he stopped Angela Biddough as she left the classroom. "Do you have a few minutes to come to my office? I have a special request to present to you."

"Of course, Professor." She smiled graciously.

"Friday my graduate assistant Jeremy Ardmore must be away from his class. It is: *Beginning Middle Eastern Studies*, #115. Is it possible that you could fill in for Jeremy?"

"I'm not sure Professor? When is the class held?" She asked. She opened her notebook and checked her schedule.

"The class is held at 10 a.m. The materials are all prepared. There is s quiz and then a lecture. I'm sure you could handle the assignment easily. Pick up the materials from Ms. Grayson."

"Thank you for your confidence in me. I'm glad I can be of assistance to you." She stood and smiled down at Colson. "I'll pick up the materials right now." She quietly left his office and went straight to his secretary.

A few minutes later Colson sat staring out his window. Suddenly he could see Angela come into view. She walked quickly toward the parking lot. Perhaps she could be groomed to be a member of the cell? He would need to find out more about her, and her personal views concerning Middle Eastern politics.

Angela drove straight home. The place she now occupied was part of her 'cover'. It was a small apartment over the garage owned by her sister and brother-in-law. Her boss: director of the FBI: Bay Area Division had given her the assignment over a year ago.

James Hafen had been with the FBI for 20 years, and had served in the Army before that.

Before this assignment, Angela had live in a fairly decent apartment with a room-mate. However to become Angela, the student with limited funds, she had to live the part.

Now she carefully changed her clothes for her 'bank job' and took the teaching file with her down town. During her two years in Virginia, she had spent in FBI training, Bak then she had worked some 'lighter' assignments. Now she was a 'plant' in Dr. Colson's courses. Reason: He had been on the FBI's watch list for six months.

She took careful notes at his lectures hoping to find something incriminating. Now she sat at her desk in FBI headquarters and began going over Jeremy's notes, and then the textbook, and lastly: the quiz. She came across a piece of paper clipped inside his notebook. It was a strange little notation high on the margin next to the last page of his notes. It was in pencil and he had written a 12 digit number, plus the word: (VICTORY/12/31) in French. Could this be a hidden bank account? She took out her cell phone and snapped a picture of it. Then she gathered all the paper work and dropped it into her bag.

Next, she went straight to Hafen's office. On her way there, her normal cell phone rang. It was from a woman named Julie. "It's time you came downstairs and become a bank clerk. There's a man, nice looking, around 50 or so, to see you."

She *knew* it was Professor Colson. She knocked on Hafen's door, marched in and dropped her phone on his desk. "There's a picture on it you should take a look at. And Julie called. I believe Dr. Colson came to the bank, and he's asking for me."

Director Hafen was talking on his office phone, but he glanced up at Angela and nodded.

When she reached her desk in the bank's front office Angela set her bag on the chair and quickly slid it under the desk. Without breaking stride she moved along the area for secretaries and went to the front where Julie was chatting with Dr. Colson.

She pasted a smile on her face and walked next to Julie. "Dr. Colson, what a surprise." She gushed. "Did you come down to my workplace to open an account? Sorry, I forgot to make myself a lunch this morning, so I went to the lunchroom to eat and study a bit. Am I late for work, Julie?"

"No, right on time. The woman glanced at her wristwatch." I'd better get back to my desk. It was nice to meet you Mr. Colson." Julie flashed a pleasant smile and walked back to her desk.

Colson frowned slightly at the 'Mr.' rather than 'Dr.' but he turned to Angela and his face morphed into a smile. "I'll have to admit. I contacted the registrar's office to find out where you worked. You have a demanding schedule. You must work hard to maintain your high grade point average."

Angela nodded. "Yes, it does keep me busy. But I decided that working hard for a few years now, will be of benefit later. Did you want to include some other instructions for the teaching assignment, Sir?"

"No. I had some free time, and my curiosity got the best of me. Perhaps tomorrow afternoon after the classes you and I teach, we could go for some coffee?"

"That would be very nice," She smiled. "However it is my sister's birthday tomorrow and I'm helping with a surprise dinner. I could meet you around 2 p. m. for perhaps an hour. Would that be okay?"

Colson frowned, but then looked up at Angela. "Coffee around 2 p.m. will be fine. Just come into my office and we'll go from there."

Jeremy Ardmore's car was old and battered, but the ten year old Honda Civic did get pretty good gas mileage. He stopped and filled the tank, using some of the money from the envelope Dr. Colson had given him.

What he did not do was prepare for changes in the weather. If he had watched the weather channel on TV or listened to his car radio, he would have come better prepared with an warmer wardrobe. He knew he was going to stop in Las Vegas, so he dressed for the heat. Everybody knew Las Vegas could be very hot. He wore baggy shorts, a tee shirt at the last minute he threw in a light weight jacket for cooler nights. At least he wore his walking shoes and not flip flops.

He drove south as instructed, until he turned to go east to Bakersfield. Once he began to drive up out of the valley he encountered stiff winds, and a twenty degree drop in the temperature. He would be forced to buy gas soon, if he had to drive into the wind for most of the trip.

When he stopped to buy gas in Barstow and it had begun to rain. His car heater was not giving off very much heat, and the windshield wipers sitting in the California sun all summer were not very effective either.

By the time Jeremy found the King of Cards Motel in North Las Vegas it was dark. One thing the place did have: a parking garage. Once in the building, it took Jeremy nearly an hour of standing in line to register and then wait several minutes for an elevator be free to go up to his room on the sixth floor. The first thing that Jeremy noticed when walking in this room in this old motel that it was very, very small. *Colson, you're such tight fist.*

No, small didn't describe this place. It was tiny! He set down his duffle bag and it barely fit into the tiny closet closet opposite the bathroom. There was one double bed, an old night stand and an ancient table holding an old TV. He picked up the remote, but the TV did not come on. "Oh my god, Colson. this is a rat trap not a motel room!" At least there was a decent sized bed. Jeremy dropped across the bed, and covered his eyes with his arm.

Much later, Jeremy sat up and glanced at the bedside clock. 11:45 p.m. He could hear music. Is that a rock band? He could hear the music coming from down, out in the street. Scrambling across the bed he glanced out the window. To the left, a group of musicians had set up on a corner stand below. *Hey. Colson did mention that this 'dump' was close to Fremont Street and I'm starving. Let's begin to enjoy this trip.* Jeremy thought.

After scarfing down a whole pizza at a coffee shop type restaurant, Jeremy wondered up and down Fremont Street. *Hey this place really rocks for a Thursday night. I wonder what it would be like on a Saturday night?* Finally, the band quit and the crowd began to thin. Jeremy returned to his and room dropped into bed. *This bed is pretty comfortable, I'm going to sleep- -- - - - - - -.*

CHAPTER SEVENTEEN

———— ✦✦✦✦✦ ————

W HEN JEREMY WORK it was after 4 p.m. *Man, I was really tired. But I'd better get moving.* After a shower, Jeremy dressed and looked out the window at Fremont Street. Across the street he could see a waffle house. *I wonder if they are still serving breakfast?"*

He left his bag in the motel room, because he would be driving back here tonight. The food at the waffle house was okay, and the waitress that flirted with him was pretty hot. But he realized it was time to get on the road. Once he left Las Vegas, he drove through a desert that stretched endlessly north and it turned cloudy and there was a south wind. Soon it began to rain.

Since he not watched TV, or listened to a weather report. He did not know that a heavy low pressure was moving across the whole area of Southern California and was spreading north through Nevada and into southern Utah. The wind and rain intensified, and driving through the desert of northern Nevada became difficult.

Once he reached the south end of Mesquite, he had to stop for gas. When he got out of his car the stiff wind nearly knocked him down. And it was cold, really cold. When paying for the gas, he grabbed a mug of coffee and a frosted cookie.

The woman at the cash register warned him. "Hey kid, take it easy driving through the Arizona Strip In this weather it can be rough."

"Arizona Strip?" Jeremy asked.

"Ah, I can see you've never been here before. Once you leave Mesquite, a few miles later the road goes through the corner of the state of Arizona, and the Virgin River. Over the years the river has cut a deep winding gorge through the mountain. Watch what you're doing."

Jeremy walked around the convenience store. Do you sell wind shield wipers here?" He asked.

"Go look on the back wall over there." She pointed to the back wall by a sign. REST ROOMS. She moved around the counter and looked outside. "What you got out there, a Honda Civic? I believe there should be a package of the wipers that'll fit your car."

Jeremy located the package and forked over another $15.00 for the wiper blades.

Once he had them installed he was wet and cold. But it was nearly six o'clock. He'd better get moving.

The Virgin River Gorge was every bit as tricky to drive as the convenience store woman had said. And Jeremy was never so glad to see the sign: ST. GEORGE, Six Miles.

Twenty miles north of St. George the rain turned to snow. The tires on Jeremy's car were in need of replacement, and it was a constant climb in elevation. He fought curves and shared the road with big semi's. The roadway became slick.

Jeremy had lived in California his whole life, and had no experience driving in snowy weather. Yet he knew if he stopped the car he would be stuck and not be able to go any farther. He finally got behind an '18' wheeler and was forced to drive the speed of the truck-trailer.

Finding the University in Cedar City was the easiest task of this assignment, so far. He easily found a parking place and followed the signs to the library. Walking around the campus was much more difficult than driving to it. The walks were covered with heavy wet snow, and the big flakes continued to drop from the cloudy sky. He shivered, and his wet feet felt like lead. His tennis shoes were soaking west and his feet were going numb. He finally found the library, and sloshed to the information desk. "Where are your computers?" He asked a bored girl behind the main desk.

"Go back to the private desks. Each one is equipped with a computer. Follow the instructions if you want to print anything."

He searched for the newest one, and sat down to type. After typing a page and a second page with the bank numbers on it, he realized these computers were not powerful enough to use to hack anything. He went back to the girl. "Where will I find really powerful computers?" He asked.

She shrugged. "Probably either the Material Science Building, or the new Bio Lab in the main Bio- building. You'd better hurry, 'cause the campus shuts down in 20 minutes. Hey, you owe me thirty-five cents for the two pages you printed."

Jeremy searched his damp shorts' pockets to come up with two quarters. He slammed them down on the desk and stalked outside the building. It was hard to read the signs in the snow. As he tried to run across campus, his head was now being assaulted by snow dripping off the trees along the walkway. Finally he stopped and pulled up the damp hood, on his wet cotton jacket. He stopped and took a breath, and his hand touched the 'persuasion' he had borrowed from his brother. A 38' Caliber hand gun. Jeremy was frustrated and miserable enough to use on the first person he encountered.

"I need it just in case." He had told Jackson. "I promise I won't need to use it."

He found the building and dashed in leaving a wet trail on the marble floor. He didn't even reach the elevators before a rheumy old guy dressed in a security guard's uniform stopped him.

"Too late. Come back tomorrow. Building closes in ten minutes." The guard, though old was big, well over six feet.

What should I do? I'll try being nice. "I just need to get into the Bio lab. I need to find out who used one of the computers- - - - -." The word came out shaky, because he was so wet and cold.

"Hey kid, I said, come back tomorrow, and you'd better know the 'password'. Are you even a student? It's my job to keep out the riff raff. Now leave." Gus put his hands on his hips and glowered at Jeremy.

Password? What is he talking about? Jeremy pulled out the .38. "I just need to see that sign-in book. Now you and I are going to go get it." Jeremy screamed

"Hey boy." Gus raised his hands a little above his head. "Waving that little pistol around will get you nowhere. So put it back in your pocket and get the hell outa here."

"I need that book, Now go get it!"

Gus put his hands on his hips, but as he did, he eased out his firearm.

Adrenalin flowing in Jeremy's veins, frustration fogging his brain, sent im over the edge. *He was in charge now. He blinked. This jerk reminded him of his father. Had he come back to teach Jeremy a lesson?*

Gus eased back close to the outside doors. His weapon tucked down against his right side.

Jeremy gazed at Gus's gun and literally saw 'red'. He fired, but the bullet lodged in the wall next to the door. He fired again, but Gus had dropped into a crouch, and the bullet grazed Gus' scalp. He slumped, but managed to fire his own weapon, and the bullet slammed into Jeremy's right side, just below his waist.

The shock and burning pain in Jeremy's side knocked him down. He lay there for several seconds, and couldn't seem to take air into his lungs. Then he heard a scream and he managed to crash out through the outside door, tumble down the six stairs leaving a trail of blood. *Get up. Run, back to the car.* But he had fallen down the stairs and landed near a small pine tree, and tangled his jacket in the tree. The pine needles snagged his jacket and scratched his hand. It began to bleed.

Jeremy staggered to his car. Just opening the door took what strength he had. He slumped there for several minutes. Then he heard sirens, and knew he had to leave or be charged with attempted murder or worse.

Two students had just stepped into the elevator and were planning to go down to the main floor, when they heard the three shots. Brittany Michaels and Jim Stanton turned toward the stairway. Leaving the elevator, Brittany stared down and could see Gus sprawled on the floor and she screamed. Jim pulled her back. "Stop. If those were gun shots, we don't want to go down there." Jim already had his cell phone out and dialed 911. He listened and then began to report the possible gun shots. "We're afraid for Gus, the guard who works here." He listened again. "Okay, we'll stay up here."

Once the campus police arrived, they noticed the floor smeared with blood, and found Gus slumped near the outside doors, unconscious. They realized they had an actual crime scene.

Henry Johnston, campus security, knew who to call: Dr. Parklin, dean of the Biology department. The biologist was in the process of designing, and planning to teach several courses in Crime Scene Investigation.

"Dr. Parklin, this is Henry Johnston, Campus Security. 'We have a possible shooting in the lobby of the Bio Building. Gustav Meier is lying here unconscious."

"I'll be over as soon as I can. Call the Iron County Police, tell them about Gus. They'll be able to transfer him to a hospital. I'll be over there, soon."

Jeremy was in more pain, than he could ever remember. His whole body shook with the cold, and he fought dizziness and nausea. He looked in his back seat and could see a beach towel. He managed to grab it and wrap it around his side, and then start his car. He eased down off campus and took a long road that led south to the freeway. Once on the freeway he noticed a large shopping center less than half mile on right the side. He managed to pull off the road and park near the group of movie theaters.

He sat taking in the cold damp air, and finally had enough energy to fumble with his cell phone and call Colson.

"Hello?"

"Professor Colson?" Words tumbled out of his trembling mouth. "It's Jeremy."

"Oh Jeremy, what did you find out?"

"Professor, There's a problem."

"What kind of problem?"

Then the words came out dis-jointed, along with sniffing and crying. "Had to shoot him!"

"Shoot him? Shoot the guard?" Colson took a deep breath. *My god, what has Jeremy got himself into?* This time it was Colson, up and pacing, who had to take a deep calming breath. "Where are you?"

"Shopping center, - -- - - -outside of town,- - - - - south. Parked by movie theaters. Shot, Guard shot me." More crying.

"I'm going to hang up now. Don't turn off your cell phone. I'm calling someone to help you. I'll call you right back." Colson disconnected.

"Oh god." Colson rubbed his hand through his short gray hair. It was after 10 p.m. in Utah, but earlier in Las Vegas. Sooner or later the local police would stop when they saw Jeremy's car. *I've get to get him back to Las Vegas.* He called Zuhdi's cell phone. "Zuhdi?"

"No sir. This is Ali. Zudhi is suffering his malaise tonight."

"We have a situation. I sent my associate to Cedar City, Utah yesterday morning concerning the hacking of the Aruba accounts." Then he explained Jeremy's situation. "I need you and your brother to drive to Cedar City. Jeremy has parked his car by the theaters showing films. This shopping area is a few miles south of the city close to the freeway. I know it's about three hours' drive from where you are, but the police patrols will soon be driving by. One of you will have to drive Jeremy's car back to Las Vegas. One of our donors lives in Henderson. He is a doctor. These are the directions to the motel. Do you have pencil and paper?"

"Yes, Dr. Colson. I'll bring my brother with me, Jahreal."

"What are your orders, Sir?" Ali asked.

"As soon as possible drive to Cedar City." Then Colson explained that Cedar City was north of St. George. "I'll call the doctor, and then Jeremy. Have a safe trip."

Colson held the receiver in his hand for a few seconds. *Yes, it was time to get the doctor involved. To see if he was really loyal to the cause. To see if his actions will speak as loudly as his words, and even the money he has donated.* Colson dialed the number in Henderson, Nevada.

Even though it was late, the phone was answered in two rings. "Hello, Walter here. What are your needs?"

"Yes Walter." Geoffrey said. "We have a situation. I sent one of my assistants to Cedar City, Utah on an important errand. It has turned out badly." He went on to tell Walter of Jeremy's actions and the result.

"Where is he?"

"Right now he is in his car. He drove a few miles south of Cedar City. It is a large shopping area, and he parked near the movie theaters. I sent two of the Sons of Islam to pick him up. I booked him a motel room at The King of Cards in northern Las Vegas. He stayed there last night. I'll phone you the room number when they call me back."

"I know the place." Walter chuckled. You really went cheap, Geoffery."

"I thought he would enjoy Fremont Street." Colson answered with irritation.

"How long do you think it will take the 'Sons' to get him into the motel?" Walter asked.

"At least six hours." I called them a few minutes ago."

"Is the room you booked for him in your name or his?" Walter asked.

"I suppose both. I had to give them my credit card. Damn stupid of me." Colson sighed.

CHAPTER EIGHTEEN

———— ✦✦✦✦✦ ————

"**P**ERHAPS I WILL be able to get in there and set things up. I hope the boy doesn't bleed out before he reaches the motel room. Have them call me on my cell when they are 20 minutes away."

Dr. Parklin soon arrived and a graduate student accompanied him. The police had arrived with a gurney, and two of the men were loading Gus onto it. Dr. Parklin went over to check on Gus. He pulled on latex gloves, and noticed the blood on the man's head. "It looks like a head wound. I believe a bullet grazed Gus's scalp." He checked the man's clothing. "I don't see any other entry wounds. Maybe the head wound is it."

"There is a trail of blood leading out the door." Parklin's assistant, Maria Sanderson said.

"Grab the camera and start shooting, then get some samples. Check the bloody hand print on the door. Photograph that too."

The two of them worked together, taking samples, and finally 'lifting' the hand print from the door. Maria went outside and tried for photographs before the falling snow erased them. As she opened the door, a tall man caught the door and held it for her.

Dr. Parklin turned and noticed the man. "Lt. Reston, good to see you again."

"Ah, Dr. Parklin, you made here before me, and you're well into the case, I see." Paul Reston smiled. "What can you tell about the crime scene?"

"A shooting. The perp shot Gustav Meier, the guard, and Gus returned fire. And I believe the suspect got the worst of it." Parklin was bent over digging a bullet from the wall near the door. As he stood up, he rubbed his back. "Not as young as I used to be." He frowned.

"The ambulance taking Gus to the hospital, pulled out into the street just as I pulled in. "Was Gus shot too? What's his situation?" Reston asked.

"He was unresponsive, but breathing. He has a head wound. And I think I just dug out the bullet that caused it." Parklin showed Reston the metal slug in a plastic bag. "Maria, can you dig the other bullet right here?" Parklin pointed to a mark in the wall close to the right double door. "We're close to doing what we can, here. There are two students in the classroom down the hall. They heard the shots and called 911."

"Thank you Glenn. It's good to have you here on campus, as well as the other crime scenes we've worked on. I'll go take their statements and talk to you tomorrow. Reston clapped the doctor on the back and disappeared down the hall.

A half-hour later, Paul Reston escorted Brittany and Jim out the door and walked them across the campus. "You two have a good evening. Thank you for your statements. I'm sure we'll need to talk to you two again."

Paul rubbed his whiskered chin. *Why do people always decide to break the law at night?* He yawned and hurried to his car.

It was still dark when Walter Bellamy drove into the underground parking beneath the King of Cards Hotel. He grabbed his big black bag as well as another sack loaded with items he would need to do surgery.

Colson had called with the room number, and luckily or a security breach on the part of motel security, allowed him to take the elevator straight up to the sixth floor. He knocked softly on the door. A clean shaven young man with black hair answered the door.

"Dr. Bellamy?" He asked, and stepped back to allow the doctor to enter. "I'm Jahreal."

Jeremy was lying on the single bed in the room, curled up in the fetal position.

Bellamy turned to Jahreal. "How is he?"

"He has lost a large amount of blood, but his breathing is steady, and I estimate his heart is about sixty-nine beats per minute."

Bellamy widened his eyes in surprise. "Have you studied medicine?"

"No." A voice came from the chair near a small table. "My brother hopes to be an animal doctor, and reads many books. I'm Ali."

"Right now let's set up an area for surgery." Bellamy went to the large sack and shook out a large water proof pad. "Jahreal, push the bedding away and help me slide this under Jeremy. Take off his clothes from the waist down. I'm going to wash my hands."

Snapping on latex gloves, the doctor first took a vial and filled it with fluid from a small bottle. Next he injected the drug into Jeremy's arm. Then he listened to Jeremy's pulse. When he rolled Jeremy toward him, he found a small towel packed into the wound. Looking up at Jahreal. "Did you do this?"

"Yes sir."

"Do you want to assist me?" Bellamy asked.

A smile creased Jahreal's face. "Yes sir!"

"Then go wash your hands a put on the latex gloves. Next go to the sack and pull out the tray. There's a bag of medical instruments. Put those on the tray. Ali, bring that lamp from the corner over here and plug it in by the night stand." Bellamy waited until the lamp was properly placed. "Good, now we begin."

The wound was not life threatening. Walter probed to find the bullet, but found it had torn through, and probably would be found lodged in the wall or floor. He stitched up Jeremy, and wrapped him in a tight, wide bandage. Walter backed away from his make-shift operating area. "Why don't you two go find us some breakfast? I'd like coffee and a muffin, if you can find one."

Once they brothers were gone. Walter dropped into the lone chair by the small desk and wiped his face with his hands. *I'm glad now I had medical battlefield experience in Iraq,* He jumped up and began to clean up the room. He pulled out the water proof sheet, folded it and dropped it into the sack, along with his instruments, Opening the door he eased down the hall few doors down to a storage room. He took a set of sheets and towels and went back to the room. Soon he had pulled the blood soaked sheets and towels away from Jeremy and all the towels in the bathroom. He returned to the storage closet and stuffed them in a canvas bag with other soiled items. Next he took some vials from his bag and prepared another injection for Jeremy. The first one was an antibiotic and the second a sedative.

The brothers returned with sacks of food. Jahreal handed Walter a sack with coffee and blueberry muffin. For a few minutes the three of them ate quietly. Then Ali's cell phone rang.

"Yes?, Doctor Colson." He listened. "Yes sir. The phone is for you, doctor."

"Take him with me? What should I tell Denise?" Bellamy scowled at the phone and listened. "Well, putting him the pool house might work, but only for day or two. Then the 'brothers' will need to come and pick him up." Bellamy glanced up at Ali. "He wants to speak with you."

"Ali, how is Jeremy?" Colson asked.

"He has a gunshot wound in his side, and really not that serious. It took some stitching, but the doctor closed it. He is sleeping now. We'll need to move him in a couple of hours."

Walter took the phone "With the brothers' help I can put him in the rear of my SUV. The problem is: Jeremy's car."

"Let me again speak to Ali."

Walter waved the phone at Ali. "He wants to talk to you."

Ali took the phone and listened for a moment. "Yes, we could drive the car and leave it at the 'safe house' Yes Sir. We're glad we could help. Good bye."

Walter noticed the deferential tone of voice Ali used when speaking to Colson. It irritated him. Money, he decided. Colson controlled the money.

"I'm going to search for a wheelchair. That will be the easiest way to take Jeremy to the parking garage." Walter ate the last of his muffin and walked out the door with his black bag and sack of instruments.

After depositing his belongings in his car, he walked around the parking garage searching for a wheel chair. *Good, someone pushed this one into a corner rather than returning it upstairs.*

When Walter knocked on the room six-seventeen, Jahreal opened it almost immediately.

"The maid knocked on the door about five minutes ago. We'd better hurry."

They strapped Jeremy in the wheelchair along his bag and shoes.

Walter found the gun in Jeremy's jacket and slid it into 'his' pocket. Then they all went down to the parking garage. The three of them managed to load Jeremy in the rear of the SUV. Walter had grabbed the blanket from the bed and used it to wrap around Jeremy.

For a moment, they stood quietly. "Give me your cell phone number." Walter said. "When Jeremy is well enough to travel, I'll take him to you? Do you have an apartment?"

"Yes, we barely moved in." Ali said. "We have room for Jeremy, but no bed."

"When Jeremy is ready, I'll call you, and see what you people need." Good bye." He shook Jahreal's hand and climbed into his luxury SUV

That same morning, one hunred fifteen miles north of Las Vegas, Claire began cooking breakfast before Mac came down.

"You're cooking breakfast. Are you staying home from the clinic?" He asked.

"No Caroline, one of the college girls who works at the clinic, is opening up. We have no surgeries today, and I could leave about noon. This afternoon we could drive to Provo and find the computer store."

Mac grabbed a plate and filled it with bacon and eggs. As he had begun to feel better, his appetite had improved. "Okay. You go to work and I'll clean up, and be ready to leave when you come home."

Shopping in this computer store was to Mac, like a kid in a candy store. Finally he settled on a pricy laptop, a good WiFi router and printer. When he stood at the check-out desk, Claire came over to look over his purchases.

"Are you sure you need all these pricy items?" She asked.

He nodded. "And now I need some special software." The salesman ringing up Mac's purchases came around the desk and stood close to him.

"There's a shop in the next block with some pretty good spyware." The young guy pulled out a card from his wallet, and handed it to Mac. "Tell him Travis sent you. I don't think you will be disappointed."

"How do I get there?" Mac asked.

"Go to the end of the parking lot. Take a right and then another. It's in the middle of the block."

As Claire walked around the spyware shop, she was astonished, and then appalled. "Look at this stuff. Listening devices, phone plugs, tiny cameras. It's like walking into a James Bond Movie."

"Yeah. What's even more interesting, it's all legal. With this stuff, I could hack into your bank account and move funds in and out." He grinned.

"That's terrible!" She huffed.

He glanced at the wall clock. "It's nearly 5 p.m., and I'm hungry."

As she drove from Provo and picked up the freeway, she said. "I'm hungry, too. The next town south of any size is Payson. I'll find a good place to eat there."

While they ate at a new hamburger emporium, Mac glanced up. "Darn, I planned on shopping for a wrist watch, and I need a warm coat."

"You're also going to need a cell phone, too." She said and finished off her sandwich. "How about this? What if we go to Costco tomorrow, and you can shop for those things? Maybe even a cell phone."

"You think a can find a good watch at Costco?" He asked.

"Absolutely." She laughed.

"You know, you're going to make some lucky guy a great wife." He grinned and touched her hand.

A look of astonishment on her face surprised him. "Thank you, but where did you come up with that idea." Her face took on that rosy blush he enjoyed.

"You're practical and careful with your own money, as well as mine." He flashed a teasing smile.

He picked up the paper plates, cups, and napkins and deposited them in the trash receptacle. "It's getting late. We'd better go."

When they walked in the Claire's kitchen, it was after 9 p.m. "I want to watch the 9 p.m. news program." Claire said and dropped onto the sofa in the den.

"The top story of evening is still the shooting at Utah's Southern University. The shoot-out in the lobby of the Bio Building has left campus guard, Gustav Meier in critical condition and the suspect has yet to be apprehended. Much evidence has been gathered, and authorities tell us that they will soon have more knowledge of the suspect."

Claire turned up the volume on the TV remote. "He did say Gus was shot, - - - - - -, didn't he?"

Mac nodded and put a finger to his lips.

The announcer went on with the details of the story. *Friday evening, just before 10 p.m. Gus the guard in the biology building was challenged by a guy wanting to get into the restricted bio-lab. When Gus refused, the suspect, an intruder, shot at Gus twice, One bullet hit Gus, but he managed to shoot back and wounded the perp. The suspect escaped leaving a trail of blood. LT. Paul Reston of Iron County PD is the primary in the investigation."*

"Do you think this has to do with our using the Bio-Lab computers?" Claire asked.

"I don't know." Mac frowned and took a deep breath. He continued to watch the newscast, his mind sorting out the information he just heard.

"You know what, it's cold in here." Mac jumped up. "I'm going to check the furnace. He went down in the basement, and sure enough the pilot had gone out. A few minutes later he returned, and he took the thermostat in the hall apart, and next he went out into the barn and brought in a box of tools.

Claire came over and watched him. "I'm glad you know what you are doing, because if I were here alone I'd have to call a repair man."

After a few minutes Mac closed the thermostat, and set it. Within few seconds, Claire could feel the warm air circulating out of the hall vent. "You're amazing." She kissed him on the cheek.

He turned and took her mouth against his in a long, more than friendly kiss. He stepped back. "Anytime, I'm just your friendly, handy man, house guest." He grinned.

She stared and then blinked. "I'll keep that in mind." She turned and rushed upstairs.

CHAPTER NINETEEN

W ALTER BELLAMY'S IRRITATION with this stupid kid, Jeremy had 'hit the top of the charts'. Walter had returned to his house in Henderson, and just trying to get Jeremy out of his car and into the pool house took him at least twenty minutes. First Jeremy decided he couldn't walk through the main house and out to the small cottage next to the swimming pool. He swore he couldn't walk.

Finally, Walter drove the car into the garage, and left Jeremy there while he checked on the cottage. Luckily for Walter, his wife was still out of town. Their oldest daughter, living in Texas had just given birth to a baby. Denise, Walter's wife had gone down the week before to help their daughter with the new baby boy.

The cottage was clean, though a bit chilly. Walter turned on the gas fireplace, and turned down one of the twin beds, so as the place warmed up so would the bed covers. Walter went back to the garage, and found Jeremy sitting in the front seat of the SUV.

"You left me." Jeremy whined.

Walter stood and stared down at this unhappy house guest. "See, you can walk. Now we're going out of the garage and to the pool cottage. It's all ready for you." Luckily, Walter was tall and strong, because of daily exercise, and he managed to get Jeremy into the cottage and into bed. He brought a glass of water to Jeremy, and had him drink it. "Our goal to hydrate you, so drink the water, and rest.

"I'll bring you some breakfast in a hour or so." Walter went to a closet and located a pair of shorts and a baggy tee shirt for Jeremy to wear.

"Why can't I stay in your big house? I'm sure it has lots of bedrooms." Jeremy pleaded.

"You're a suspect in an attempted murder. This is a better place for you. Besides it's November, and the pool will not be used now." Walter scowled down at Jeremy and left closing and locking the door.

Saturday morning the phone rang at the North Las Vegas Police Precinct. The dispatcher took the message. The police team who had come on duty that morning was Andy Freeman and Brock Jackson.

"Hey, Jackson, Freeman, they got a situation up at the King of Cards motel. You two better get up there and see to it."

Brock grinned down at Lola, the dispatcher. "What kind'a situation?"

"They just called. Those ladies who clean the rooms came upon some blood stains and such. And they also found bloody sheets, too. Go check it out."

When Freeman and Jackson reached the motel, they went from the parking garage to the check-in desk. The name on the plate read: Wendy Dickson. "Which room did your people find blood stains and the blood soaked sheet?" Jackson asked.

"Go up to room six-seventeen. There's a maid waiting for you. Then come back down and I'll show you the check-in cards for that room." Wendy said.

At a little after 8 a.m. the motel was quiet. Most of the people were still asleep, or had checked out the day before. A maid met them. "I'm Marissa Gomez. I'm started cleaning the room about an hour ago." She led the policemen into the small room. "What is strange is that there were clean towels and sheets left on the bed. Whoever was last in here went to the linen storage area and got them, but stuffed the soiled sheets and towels in the laundry bag".

"You still have the soiled sheets?' Freeman asked.

"Yes sir. But also what I found in the room was this." She showed them the blood drops on the carpet, and on the pillows. "This room is a single, but there was breakfast trash in the basket for at least three people. I'm sorry, but I cleaned real good in here, I know now I washed off fingerprints. I watch cop shows all the time. But down here, I kept the bloody sheets. And the blanket is missing from the bed." Marissa turned and led the two policemen to a linen room five doors down.

They walked into a storage area with shelves stacked with sheets, towels, other bedding, plus soap, small tubes of lotion and shampoo. There was a table counter height, and she pulled a blood stained sheet out of a sack and spread it on the counter.

"That's quite a bit of blood." Jackson commented.

She also pulled out a top sheet, and two towels. "There's more." She took a small plastic bag and dumped the contents on the counter. There were soiled cotton swabs, a cotton gauze pieces, and two pair surgical gloves.

"We'll need these," Freeman said. "As well as the sheets and towels." He turned to his partner. "Ya think some sort of surgery was done in that room? Now we need to go down and see who paid to stay in it."

Once they reached the check-in Ms. Dickson was just checking in a couple. "I'm sorry, but you won't be able to use the room until one p.m. In the discount packet I gave you, there are some restaurants you could get some lunch or breakfast. Or just take in the sights on Fremont Street." She smiled at the couple.

"Ah, Las Vegas' finest, you're back." She grinned. "These are the motel cards showing who checked into room six- seventeen. I also took a photo of his driver's license." She pushed the motel sheet across the counter to Freeman and Jackson.

On one sheet of paper was a picture of a driver's license and below it a signature. It was hard to really see the picture. On the California driver's license it Listed: *Jeremy Ardmore, age 21 address in Los Denis, CA Automobile Honda Civic.*

"Did he pay with a credit card or cash?" Andy Freeman asked.

"That is the interesting part. The room was booked for two days earlier, by a man in the Bay Area for Thursday and Friday evening. The name on this credit card is: *Geoffrey Colson*

We ran the card and it was an Amex with a high credit limit. $15,000. The guy has excellent credit."

"We need copies of this paperwork." Jackson said.

"Yes, of course." Wendy went to the computer and soon two copies slid out of the printer. "My daughter works at the waffle house out on Fremont Street. I called her when you came in. She should be over here soon. She thinks she waited on Jeremy Friday afternoon."

About five minutes later a young girl came bustling through the gambling area and over to the check- in desk. She was blond like her mother, slim, but taller. She came right up to the two young policemen.

"Hi," She put out her hand. "I'm Beth Dickson. My Mom told me about this situation in room six-seventeen."

"She told us you work at the waffle house?" Freeman asked.

"That's right. Last Friday this white guy, young, came in late afternoon and wanted breakfast. Well we serve breakfast 24/7. Anyway I remember him, because he said he taught at a big university in California; Kind. of bragged about it. After I talked to my Mom, I decided he could be the guy staying over here. He was in his early twenties, lots of unruly dark hair, not too tall. Medium height, maybe."

"Did you talk to him again?" Jackson asked.

"Yes, I try to ask questions of my customers. Like, where are you from, etc. He said he had to drive north for about three hours, because he was searching for a particular computer." She shrugged. "I hope that helps you guys." She grinned, backed up and waved. "'Got to get back to the waffles." She turned on her heel and disappeared through the maze of slot machines.

"Thank you Ms. Dickson, you and your daughter. We'd better get back to work." Jackson turned with Freeman right behind him. "We'd better get this evidence back to the division."

Mac woke up Sunday morning, and went straight to the barn to work on the bicycle. He had tuned and cleaned it. It was ready for a good, long ride.

By noon the rain had stopped, and the sun was peeking through the clouds. He went into the house and found the breakfast Claire had left for him. He ate enough to give him the energy to ride several miles.

She came down stairs in old jeans and a sweater. "I'm going over to the clinic to check on the animals and clean up a bit. I'll be back in a couple of hours. Think about dinner. We could go over to Costco and look for those items you were looking to buy, and grab some food there."

"The bike is as ready as I could fix it for a long ride, I'll see you later." He said and finished his coffee. He opened the door for her and watched, as she backed her car out from the barn.

He changed into shorts and long sleeved tee shirt. The athletic shoes he had recently purchased would have to do for 'bicycle' shoes. The air was cool, and somewhat damp, but perfect for a long ride.

He rode west into the Snow Canyon area. As he rode, along flashes of his former life came to mind. One was of another bike ride up a winding canyon taking him out of a busy city. He could feel the air rushing into his lungs. And though it was cool, he began to sweat.

A half- mile later he stopped at an intersection and glanced down at the bike he was astride. *Something was wrong.* This bicycle did not resemble his precious Tarmac. It should be navy-blue with white trim. He heart thudded in his chest. He closed his eyes, and felt panic rise like bile in his throat. Where was he? He gazed north and saw red desert peaks with a dusting of snow on them. There was never any snow riding up this canyon.

He picked up the bike and turn around, looking back where he had come. The flat red buttes of St. George were visible in the clear, cool air. *This is not the Las Angeles basin.* He stared down at the reddish dirt under the bikes' wheels. He blinked, and wiped his sun glasses on his shirt. *What and where was this place?* He stood for a long time. Now he remembered: Southern, Utah.

He wanted, needed to go back to his apartment, to his computer, to his bicycle. Where was his car? All these thoughts jumbled around in his head as he stood there. Cars whizzed by, and one honked at him. As if on automatic pilot he began pumping back to where he had come. Back to Rawley, to the red hills and to Claire house.

As Mac rode, he envisioned his apartment, the street it was on, and the city where it was located. Costa Mesa, California. He must return there as soon as possible. He rode in a smooth rhythm concentrating on getting back to where he started. Yet old memories invaded his thoughts, old shadows lurked far back of his consciousness.

Once he reached Claire's house, he stored the bicycle in the barn and covered it with the tarp. When he went in, he stood for a long time holding onto the sink. He felt dizzy and weak. Water! He needed water. He filled a large glass of cool water and drank it down. Next, he needed a shower. As he dried off, he knew he must return to Southern California as soon as possible. After dressing he came down and searched for a phone book.

Claire had finished the last of the cleaning chores. She was ready to return home. Suddenly the clinic phone jangled. When she picked up she heard Suzanne's voice.

"Hi Suzy. What's up?"

"'Haven't talked to you for a while and thought we needed to catch up. How are you?"

"Muddling through day by day. No actually the business end of the clinic is improving." Claire said.

"Is JD still with you?" Suzy asked.

"Yes, he's still around." Claire sighed.

"I thought so. People have seen you two around and have been asking questions?"

Claire felt a sudden irritation rise into anger. "What kind of questions?" She growled.

"Ah, come on. People are curious. And for all its growth, St. George is still a small town."

"Let them talk. Tell them he's my cousin."

"Oh, that's a *good one.* Claire."

"Okay then why else did you call? Suzy?"

"To invite you to Thanksgiving. It is Thursday, you know."

"With you mother giving me the 'third degree', I don't think so."

"My mother is going up to Ogden to spend Thanksgiving with good 'ole sister Karen and her family."

"My blessings on Karen. Who's minding Justin?"

"I found a college girl to come while I work the swing shift. Anyway, Andy is coming up from Las Vegas, so please bring JD." Suzy said.

"Ah ha, with no Mom around, invite Andy, great idea. We'd love to come. Okay what shall I bring?" Oh by the way JD is now Jonathan David Mackay, and he has identification to prove it."

"That's his real identity?"

"No, but he has the paper work and driver's license saying that's who he is. So what so you want me to bring?" Claire asked.

"How about hot rolls, a vegetable dish and a pie from Marie Callender's". Suzanne suggested.

"It will be good to see Andy again. What time?"

"Oh, around 4 p.m. That will give me time to cook the turkey."

"Sounds like a plan. See you Thursday."

When Claire walked into the house, she found Mac setting up his new computer, printer and the WIFI. He barely raised his head. Suddenly he jumped up and said. "I have to go home."

She backed into the sofa, dropped down and stared at him. *Oh no, he's leaving me. Oh god I knew he would.* She coughed, trying to breathe normally. "Where is home?" she asked and tried for a neutral tone of voice.

"Costa Mesa, California." He sat next to her. "Sit down on the sofa.' He took her hand. "I remembered who I am and where I live. I'm an FBI agent and my name is Dexter MacCandlass. Those people who left me in a ditch in St. George, I need to find. But right now, I can't remember that. But now I need to go back to my apartment, and see if I can find my car."

She stared at him, but then a small smile teased her mouth. "I *knew* you were a fed or cop. Are you coming back or going back to your job there?" *Please say you'll come back.*

He stood and pulled her into his arms. "I have to return to St. George, because- - - -because of you, Claire Talbot. He pulled her close and held her for a long moment. "But I need to leave today. I called, and there is a Greyhound bus leaving tonight at 7:15 p.m. and it will stop in down town Costa Mesa. I called and bought a ticket. Please, will drive me there, the bus depot, I mean?"

"Okay, I'll drive you in town on one condition. You have to be back for Thanksgiving dinner. That's Thursday."

CHAPTER TWENTY

--------◆◆◆◆◆--------

A S MAC SAT in the rear of a less than crowded bus, He thought about these new memories, but also he envisioned his apartment, and where it was: *Willow Street, the Willow Glen Apartments.* He closed his eyes and tried to remember where he left his car. How did he travel from California to Las Vegas? But the movement of the bus made him sleepy, and lolled him into a light sleep. When he awoke he remembered where his car was: In the parking garage under the building where FBI headquarters were located.

He and his partner had driven to 'Vegas in a 'company' car. His partner? He thought on that for several minutes. Theodore! Theo Kastanis. What happened to Theo? He also remembered Dan Forester, a good agent. Why were they all together with some other agents or policemen? When he tried to recall the reason they had gone to Las Vegas, his heart beat hard in his chest and a wave of fear made his mouth dry and his hands shake.

Calm down, think of Claire. Little things. The way she brushed back her hair, when she was impatient. The interesting 'white lock' in her hair. Was that genetic? How hard she worked in her clinic. And she was a good cook. But more importantly he owed her and Suzanne his life. Was he just grateful? Absolutely! When he sat next to her on the sofa and watched TV, it felt normal and made him happy. He wanted her to love him, and see that he was worth saving, a guy worth loving.

The bus stopped for a bathroom break in Jean, Nevada. He bought a sandwich and a soda. Once back on the bus he dozed for a while, then he dreamed: A warehouse, a firefight, and a bullet whizzing by his shoulder, and then nothing.

Another stop outside of Las Angeles, and then the bus continued on to the Costa Mesa, Greyhound building. It was 4:50 a.m. early morning when Mac went to the inside counter. "Can I get a cab this time in the morning?" He asked an older man.

"Where do you need to go?" The man asked. He wore a name plate on his shirt. It read: Robert Leads.

"I'm off at 5:a.m. this morning. If you can wait for another ten to fifteen minutes, I'll be off duty. A cab will cost you ten bucks. I'll take you home for the ten." He rubbed his blood shot eyes, and tried for a weary smile.

"Okay, sounds like a deal." Mac said, walked over to a bench against the wall, and dropped onto it.

Robert was a good as his word and stopped in front the Willow Glen Apartments. Mac gave him fifteen dollars and grabbed his duffle and wearily walked into the center of the apartment complex. He had hidden a set of car keys holding the key to his apartment. He had placed them under a rock in the bushes near the east side of the pool.

At 5:40 a.m. the apartment area was quiet. All he could hear were the roof mounted cooling/heating systems. The air was damp and quite chilly. He shivered as he dug around the bush, but finally he lifted the rock and in a heavy plastic bag were his keys. He took them and put the plastic bag back into the dirt and the rock back in its place. Quietly he climbed up the one flight of stairs and opened his front door. The apartment was cold and dank. Had he left the air conditioning on?

I was dark with the shutters and drapes closed across the sliding door in his bedroom. He remembered where there was a flashlight. He found it and went back to the thermostat and turned on the heat. The bedroom was cold and the bedding damp to the touch. He stripped the bed and draped the sheets and quilt over the four chairs near the kitchen table. He also checked the water heater. He had turned it down, but not off. He adjusted the temperature of the water, too. He went to the den. And found his computer missing, but his bicycle was still there. Obviously, the FBI had been in his apartment. He checked the James Patterson novel, and the disc he had copied was still there. Mac looked around his den, but he was *so* tired, he couldn't focus on anything. He crawled onto the living room sofa, and grabbed the fringed blanket-throw and wrapped it around him. He closed his eyes, and sleep came instantly.

When he awoke the apartment was warm, but still quite dark inside. He peaked out through his kitchen window and noticed the usual morning clouds. He went to his closet and took out some clothes he could use in Southern Utah. He also found his bicycle riding clothes and shoes. Next he showered, and went to the kitchen and made coffee with five week old beans. Searching his freezer, he found a loaf of frozen bread and also some jam and peanut butter in the tiny pantry. At least he wouldn't starve. The next thing he did was go to the false bottom shelf he had built in his den closet. In it were his personal files. They were of his graduation from Kansas State, his college major and minor, and his files from FBI training in Langley. He sat at the kitchen table, ate his food and studied these files.

As the day wore on, from time to time he heard people climbing up and down the stairs, and brief snatches of conversation. He needed to go down town to pick up his car. He waited until dark, and casually walked to the bus stop and took the correct bus to FBI headquarters. As he walked down into the underground parking his heart beat faster, and he worried that someone had moved his car. Yet as he walked around the corner to his parking slot, there it was, his Subaru Outback. Dust and dampness marred its pale gray surface, but amazingly no one had disturbed it. He climbed in it and sat for long enough to calm his racing heart.

It took four starts to keep the car's engine running, but finally he eased out of the garage, and was careful to stay within the speed limit, to reach his apartment. He carefully drove the car into his designated slot. and sat there for a moment. He was hungry, so he drove a block away to a convenience store and bought some food. He ate his dinner in the darkened apartment, put the bed back together and at about 10:30 p.m. took the risk of turning on the TV, but kept the sound down.

He climbed into his bed sometime after 11 p.m. and tried to sleep. After four hours he gave up, packed his car, changed back the thermostat and water heater as he had found them and left.

Mac listened to the car radio for the latest news, stopped for coffee and donuts in Pomona, California and began the long drive across California to the Nevada border. Once he crossed over to Nevada, he found a motel, drove around the rear of the establishment and parked his car. It seemed that the motel was nearly full, but he stayed in his car in the parking place. He lowered the front seat, wrapped up in his sofa blanket, and slept for a few hours.

After all, tomorrow *was* Thanksgiving, and people were traveling here and there to enjoy the Holiday with friends and family. Wasn't that his plan? To have Thanksgiving with Claire and her friends, and of more importance meet Andy Freeman of the LVPD.

Mac drove into Claire's barn and parked his car on the other side. Her car was absent. He went in the house, drank some water, ate an orange and went upstairs to his/Eric's room. He pulled down the bedspread, and quickly fell asleep.

It was dark when Claire stomped up the stairs and stood in the doorway of his bedroom. "I'm glad you made it home. I mean back here." She quickly amended her words.

He rolled over and squinted up at the light she had flipped on. "Hi, good to see you, too." He sat up and reached for her, pulling her down on his lap, and kissed her. For moment she resisted his kisses, but then wrapped her arms around his neck and they tumbled together. The kisses became intense, and soon he sat her up and pulled off her scrub top.

She stood up and slipped out of the rest of her clothes.

He came up and held her close. "You are so beautiful." He said. He stood and allowed Claire to strip him of his clothes. Soon they were lying together skin to skin.

When they came together joining they bodies, Claire felt as if her heart was singing. Later as he held her close, she could not stop the tears from dripping down her cheeks.

"You're crying. Did I hurt you?' He moved away from her and sat up.

"Oh no. It's just that having you- - - - -here with me." *How can I explain to him the great joy I felt with him inside of me?*

He rubbed her back and pulled the bed spread up around them. Then his stomach growled loud enough for both of them to hear. "Sorry." He said and touched his mid-section.

"You're hungry. When did you eat last? Come on, there's some pizza left in the refrigerator." She slid from the bed and hurried to her room. She quickly returned wearing a white terry cloth robe. By then he had taken his navy blue robe from his duffle bag and slipped it on.

He watched her bounce down the stairs, and followed. They sat down at the kitchen table and ate pizza, and apples. They cleaned up together.

"Wow, it's after eight." Claire said. "If you want to continue the activity we began upstairs, I'm inviting you to come into my bed. It's larger, and it's fun to sit in the dark at night and gaze out the windows."

He wrapped her into his arms. "Claire you never stop amazing me. A few minutes ago you were crying, because of the wonder of our coming together sexually. Now, you invite me into your bed as if we were buddies having a sleepover together." He shook his head, but smiled down at her and kissed her nose.

"I guess I was thinking you are my friend, and now even better, my lover." She touched his face.

"I'm thrilled with you invitation. "I'll be right up." He stopped to lower the thermostat, and snap off the kitchen light.

That same evening Denise Bellamy stood silently in the darkened family room of her expansive house in Henderson, Nevada and watched lights go on and off in the pool cottage.

Walter had been called in to the hospital, because of one of patients had fallen out of the bed, and Walter had performed spinal surgery on him yesterday morning.

Walter had picked her up from (name of airport) Las Vegas airport earlier that day. After twelve days in Houston, Texas with her daughter and new grandson, she decided she had been there long enough. She had fallen asleep in the late afternoon, and now had come down stairs to find something to eat.

She stood and watched the flickering light from the pool house and decided that is was the TV, *and* the fireplace. Someone was staying in there watching TV, and moving around the place. Who was in there? But of more importance. Why?

Walter had made reservations for Thanksgiving dinner with some friends at the *Charter House* tomorrow. This relieved Denise of worrying about cooking for Thanksgiving. Yet, she needed something to eat now. She searched the refrigerator and found eggs, milk and bacon. She would make an omelet. Her curiosity about the pool cottage continued as well into a rising anger. Why hadn't Walter told her about someone staying in the cottage? I'm going to text him right now. *Walter, I'd like to know if some criminal is living 40 feet from our house. If you don't get home pretty soon I'm going to check it out, armed with my pistol. I want some answers, Denise.*

A few minutes later the phone rang. Impatiently, Denise picked up. Hello?" She growled.

"Denise, I'm glad you've arrived home. Walter was beginning to sound like a grumpy old bachelor without you." Goeffery Colson said.

"Well thank you. Geof. As you know we have a beautiful grandson. However, I arrived home to a little problem. Walter has someone living on the pool house. Knowing Walter, it's probably some derelict he's picked off the street and brought home to feed."

Geoff cleared his throat. "Actually the individual in the pool house is of my doing."

"What?! What had you two been up to?"

"The young man in the cottage used to be a student of mine, and he had an accident, and needed some minor surgery. He was on his way to a college in Southern Utah, when I heard about it. I asked Walter to step in. He should be out of your place tomorrow or no later than Friday. I'm sorry we have inconvenienced you, Denise."

"Thank you for easing my fears. I'll let Walter explain the whole situation when he comes home."

"I'm sorry you were worried, Denise. Just have a Happy Thanksgiving. Good Bye."

Colson set down the phone, and paced back and forth in his den. "Now I'd better call Walter, and get our stories straight. Next I must make a call to the 'brothers' in Las Vegas. They'll have to come and move Jeremy in with them." Walter's next call was to Zuhdi's cell phone.

"Yes, brother Colson. What message do you have for us?"

"I'll be sending an address to you now." Colson typed in Walter's home address. "Tomorrow during the day, you must go there and take Jeremy to your apartment with you. He'll be your responsibility from now on. Now, what do you need to be comfortable in the apartment?"

"We have only the five cots we moved from the 'safe' house."

"Okay, I'll bring you some furniture this weekend. You do have two bedrooms, correct?"

"Yes, room for the other 'brothers' when they arrive next week."

"Good. There are many used furniture stores here in my area. I'll pick up a truckload and be there by Sunday. Be vigilant. Have a good evening." Colson hung up, and went to his desk, and located the telephone number of Angela Biddough.

CHAPTER TWENTY-ONE

———— ◆◆◆◆◆◆ ————

I T WAS JUST after 8 a.m. when Claire stirred from her deep sleep. She sat up and stared and this body sleeping next to her. She yawned and lay back down. Then she lifted the quilt and lightly touched this naked man in her bed. She pulled her hand back with a start. *Who is- - - - - ?-then it all came flooding back. Mac and I spent most of the night making love.* She eased from the bed, and felt stiff in places and tender in others. As if she had climbed some mountain the day before. She hurried to the relief of a hot shower.

She dressed quickly went downstairs for coffee. She had to make a casserole, pies and rolls to take to Suzanne's. She better start fixing the food. But first she needed coffee.

As she was assembling the green bean casserole, a long muscular arm reached around her for the carafe of coffee.

"Morning." Mac said and snagged a mug from the cupboard above her head. "What are you preparing?" He asked.

"Green bean casserole. Next I must bake the two pies I bought. One pumpkin and one apple." She answered.

"Will the four of us eat two pies?" He asked.

"We always want leftovers. That's part of Thanksgiving. Besides, Justin will eat some of the food, too." She teased. "You're on your own to find something for breakfast."

"No problem. I'll manage." He kissed her cheek and went to the pantry.

When Claire and Mac rang the doorbell at Suzanne's family house, an excited Justin answered the door. Andy, deeply involved in a NFL game slowly followed his son to the door. "Here, let me take that." He took the plate of rolls and one of the pies from Claire's hands, and Mac followed Andy to the kitchen with the second pie and the casserole.

Suzanne met them in the kitchen. "Just set everything on the table. We're eating in the dining room."

"Andy, this is Claire's friend, ah- - -, what do I call him. I mean- - - - - -?"

Mac amused by this little confusion about his name, put out his hand to Andy. "I'm Jonathan David Mackay. You can call me Mac."

Andy, with a lift of one eyebrow asked. "What does she call you?" He angled his head at Claire.

"JD. Short for my first and middle name. I suppose."

Suzanne nodded nervously. "I like JD too, more familiar to me." She turned to Claire. "Come help me in the kitchen."

Justin, hanging on his father's arm, gazed up at Mac and said. "I like JD, too. Sounds 'portant."

"You like football Mac?" Andy asked. Mac nodded. "Good. The Forty-Niners and the Broncos were tied in the in the beginning of the third quarter. Let's see if anyone has scored in the last few minutes." He led the way to the family room and the large screen TV. The three males settled down on a large brown leather sectional.

When there was a commercial break, Andy called out. "How soon is dinner, Suzy? Can you give us a few minutes?"

"I'll give you fifteen minutes." She called back. "Which means a half-hour." She said in a low voice.

Mac studied Andy. He was physically impressive. He had at least two-to-three inches over Mac's height, and he was least fifteen to twenty pounds heavier. Wide shoulders, long muscular arms long lean legs. Mac would *not* relish a confrontation with this guy. He also noticed now close Justin sat with his father. From time to time Andy would pat or ruffle Justin's blond hair. A few shades lighter than his own. The affection between the two was obvious. Mac decided father and son needed to live together.

Suzanne glanced at Claire, and then really looked at her. "Ah ha. You and JD are 'getting it on'." She chortled.

Claire's color heightened. "It's just warm in here." She turned to Suzanne and laughed. "You've got that 'glow', too."

"But Andy and I are married." Suzanne put her hands on her hips.

"True. But did you make sure you won't be having another little Justin next year?" Claire asked. "I protected first, then acted. Here, taste this gravy. Do you want to add more salt?" she handed a spoon to Suzanne.

"Okay. Enough talk. Let's dish up the potatoes and gravy. Men, it's time to eat." Suzanne yelled.

"The last play. Hang on." Andy yelled. Mac went into the kitchen and picked up the turkey platter.

The five of them sat down in the dining room. The food was the best Mac had eaten in his recent memory. It was a challenge not to overeat. When the eating slowed, Suzanne stood and said. 'Let's save the desert for later. Then we'll appreciate it more."

"Okay girls, you put the food away, and Mac and I will wash the dishes." Andy said.

"Okay, Mac. Let's get to it." As the men were organizing the dish washing chore, Mac turned to Andy. "Claire tells me that you are with the Las Vegas PD. How long have you been with them?"

"Since the first of the year. I applied and went through their training program for three months; A short version of Police College. Then I was assigned a partner in May."

"How do you like it there?" Mac asked.

"It's a good organization, and the pay is much better than in St. George. I was a deputy-sheriff for three years here. There just are not the opportunities, or the salary, or chances for advancement in this county."

Why do you ask?" Andy said.

"It's because I have experience in law enforcement. I majored in computer science and criminology in college." Mac said. "I heard about the combined FBI-LVPD raid on the suspected Islam cell that happened over a month ago. It went bad didn't it?"

Andy stopped washing a large platter and pulled away from the sink. Frowning he asked. "How did you hear about that?"

"There are all kinds of information on the internet." Mac answered blandly, and continued to dry a large pot and place it on the kitchen table.

Andy eyed Mac warily. "What else do you know?"

"The information I found mentioned there were some fatalities." Mac said.

"Yeah, it was a *bad* scene. We lost Roberto Valdez. And the FBI guy, MacCandlass went missing, and presumed dead. Theo Kastanis was shot twice and had a stroke during surgery. He's in some medical facility in California, and Dan Forester was shot. We did get one of them. We call them Sons of Islam or *sob's* for short." Andy said.

"Was it a set up?" Mac asked.

"They're not sure. It could be Kastanis, and we haven't found MacCandlass. Or perhaps someone else."

"Is there any trace of the terrorists?"

"No, they never found them. The FBI believes they've moved, somehow gone to ground, or moved to another area."

"At least you did get one of them. But I don't believe they have moved on." Mac said.

"Do you have any hard evidence that they are still around here?" Andy asked frowning.

"On to another subject." Andy laughed. "I have to tell you about a crazy situation my partner and I investigated last Saturday. There is this old motel in North Las Vegas. We went in and found blood stains in a room, bloody sheets and towels and used surgical gloves. Someone did surgery on someone, possibly the guy registered in that room. We won't know until the blood and finger prints are analyzed."

"Hey, did you know there was a shooting in the Bio building at the college in Cedar City, Friday evening. Maybe there's a connection. It was on the evening news here last weekend."

"You're right. There may be a connection. I'll call it in tomorrow morning." Andy grinned. It's been good talking to you."

"You know. You could get pictures of those terrorists from Interpol. Hanging them up in your squad room, might jar someone's memory. Possibly one of your officers could spot one of them."

"That's great idea. Good talking, I'm glad we met."

"Hey you guys, did you finally finish up.?" What have you two been up to anyway?" Suzanne asked.

Andy glanced over his wife's head at Mac. "Just trying to save the world, Honey. One city at the time."

Colson called Angela and she answered on the second ring. "Hello?"

"Good evening, Angela. This is Geoffery Colson. I hate to disturb you on this Wednesday evening. But I'm about to ask you to help me. It's a large favor, I'm afraid."

Angela rolled her eyes, but answered sweetly. "Whatever it is you need, and if I can be of any help. I'll do what I can."

"I have been helping some immigrants. They have gone to Las Vegas to find work, especially this busy time of year. One of them called me and said they had moved into an unfurnished apartment. There are five of them. They need just the basics in furniture. I could use a woman's touch in picking out some used items to take over to them. I know its Thanksgiving tomorrow. And I'm sure you will want to be with your family. But since there are no classes on Friday, do you think you could accompany me on a search for some used pieces of furniture they'll need. They are ready to go work Friday morning."

"I should be at the bank at 1:30 p.m. Friday afternoon. However, I'd be pleased and could help you Friday morning. Oh, by the way, do you want me to continue teaching Jeremy Ardmore's class Monday morning?"

"Yes. Jeremy's had an accident, and will be laid up for a week or two. I'll make sure you have the class materials to continue on Monday. You are officially on the payroll for the class you are teaching. Don't worry about that." I'll pick you up at, say 9 a.m. Friday morning. Perhaps we can go somewhere for brunch, after we shop."

"That would be fine, Doctor Colson. See you Friday. Good evening."

Angela sat at her desk and mulled over Colson's latest request. She searched for Director's Hafen's number on her cell phone. She was excited to inform him of Colson's request.

CHAPTER TWENTY-TWO

———— ✦✦✦✦✦✦ ————

D IRECTOR HAFEN OF the Bay Area FBI sat in his den reading
another transcript of a fraud case he had assigned to two agents.
He squeezed his eyes shut for a moment trying to clear them. Just then
his cell phone rang. "Director Hafen here."

"Director Hafen, this is Angela Biddough I just received a phone
call from Geoffery Colson He has asked me to assist him with buying
furniture for some 'immigrants' he is setting up an apartment for, in
Las Vegas, no less."

"Las Vegas, Great. That just confirmed some 'whispers' we have
heard that whatever attack these hostiles are planning is aimed at Las
Vegas. I'll let our people know that the 'bad guys' plan to go after some
site in 'Vegas. Those numbers you photographed are off shore bank
sorting numbers. Our computer experts are at work on them now.
It sounds as if Colson is planning to furnish an apartment for these
people? He did call them immigrants? Perhaps he will let it slip as to
other information about them."

"He said there were five of them." Angela said.

"Last I heard we killed one of them. Maybe they picked up another
one." Hafen said.

"I've been thinking. This Jeremy Ardmore, the fact that Colson gave
me Jeremy's materials so I can take over his class to teach, and suddenly
he's unable to teach it any longer. I asked why? Then Colson said that

Jeremy had an *accident*. Maybe he's the fifth one. But knowing Jeremy, I can't see him being a combatant. He's more like a 'wimpy kid'."

"Go ahead and go shopping with him, but be careful. Be sympathetic for the 'poor immigrants'. He's thinking he can *win* you over to the cause. Stay non-committal. Again be careful." Thanks for calling. This is a good break in the investigation."

Hafen looked up private cell number for Las Vegas Director V. R. Strickland. Hafen now was sure the terrorists were in Las Vegas.

After a late evening snack of pie and some ice cream Claire had in the freezer, Claire and Mac went to bed in her room. "Explain to me why you have a king sized bed in this room." Mac asked as shook out the pillows and slid into the large bed.

"Look around the room. The bed back matches the dresser and chest and the night stands. It's a matching bedroom set. When my parents sold me this house nearly two years ago, Mom wanted a more contemporary style bedroom set for their condo near San Diego. They moved there for Mom's arthritis. Anyway, I bought the bedroom set." Claire explained.

"Okay, actually, I quite like the big bed." Mac reached over at touched her shoulder. "Are you ready for lights out?" He asked.

"Yes." She lay there in semidarkness, a little stiff, until he reached for her, snuggled close and kissed her. "I'm a little new at this sharing a bed, really sleeping with a man. It's been a long time since- - - - -.

"I know. But it seems to be the next step in our relationship. If you'd rather I go back to Eric's room, I could do that, but- - - - - - -,

"No, stay." She hugged him and laid her head on his chest. I want you here with me."

Claire woke to see Mac standing near the windows looking out.

He was dressed, turned to her and said. "I have return to California. About an hour ago, I woke up and must have been dreaming about the shootout we had in Las Vegas. I now realize that Theo Kastanis was the 'mole'. For his 'trouble' he was shot, and nearly died. I would have, too if you and Suzanne- - - - - - -. You know the rest." Mac came back and sat on the bed next to Claire. He touched her face. "My body and mind want to stay with you, but my head says go clear up this 'mess' if it's at all possible."

Claire reached over and clicked on a bedside lamp. "So you don't want to leave me. So don't. I'll come with you." She climbed from the bed and took hold of his arm.

"What about the clinic? Can you leave it? I don't want your business to suffer because of me." He paced and stood staring out the window, but then turned back to Claire.

"I gave everybody the day off Friday. I can close on Saturday, too. But we have to be back by Monday, because I must open the clinic then."

"If we leave as soon as possible, we can get a jump on the Holiday travel. What do you want me to pack?" We should take some of the food." He suggested.

Claire was up grabbed some clothes and headed for the bathroom. "Soon as I dress I'll come down and choose what we can take. If you're packed, make coffee and some toast. Oh, I think we should take my car. Put your stuff in there."

Claire and Mac stopped for brunch of sorts at a new Denny's close to the California border. With the two of them sharing the driving, the trip didn't seem nearly as long as it had been for Mac a few days earlier. One or the other could nap while the other partner could drive. It was dark when Mac drove into his parking spot at the Willow Glen Apartments. This time it didn't take too long for his apartment to warm up, and they ate Thanksgiving leftovers for their mid-night supper.

Mac got on his new computer and found out which assisted living facility listed Theo Kastanis as a patient.

"I think I should go with you to see Theo. When do you plan to go, and how long will it take us to drive there?"

"We have one stop before we drive north to the 'Desert Oaks' assisted living facility. We should be ready to leave by 10 a.m." Mac said. On a Saturday we could drive there in a little over an hour."

"What stop do you need to make?" Claire asked, as she finished up her slice of apple pie.

"The Post Office. Before I left to drive over to Las Vegas, I had the post office to hold my mail." Mac said.

"Good idea. Clair said. "Do you think they held it all these weeks?" Mac tilted his head and shrugged. "I guess we'll find out tomorrow."

That Friday morning at precisely seven a.m., the four Sons of Islam stood outside the Tri-Corp Hotel on the Las Vegas strip. It was the basement entrance to the conference room. There was a crowd of people, most of them men, and many of them were Hispanic. The 'Sons' had shaved off their beards, trimmed their hair and tried to copy the dress as they had seen many of the men who lived in their apartment complex. Each one of them had new identity papers, new names, but with the apartment address where they now lived.

Jahreal's new identity gave him the name of Jose' Escobar. Ali Hakim's green card read Arturo Escobar. Aukmed had a card reading Hector Lopez, and Zuhdi had a driver's license with his picture, and the name Zachary Sanchez from California. Soon the doors opened, and they were ushered in and told to sit and one by one they would be called up to fill out forms for the hotel chain and given a specific place to work in the buildings.

Our new Zachary and Hector were given a place to report to later that afternoon. Outside the unloading docs they had the job of delivering various supplies for each hotel in the group. Arturo and Jose' were assigned to trash collection, which was what the four of them had planned. This would give them access to trash cans on all the levels they were told to work. When the specific *day of attack* came, they would wire all the trash receptacles each with a bomb and a detonator. The explosion would be controlled by a single cell phone.

They spoke little that day, answering with *Si or No* in most cases or a shake or nod of a head. A about a half-hour after 4 p.m. that afternoon, they returned to their apartment in an older Northwest section of the growing city. The apartment was a drafty, old, one level, and built of cinder block painted gray and yellow on the outside. It consisted of a living room, kitchen with just enough room for a small table, also two bedrooms, and one bathroom. The carpet was neither gray or beige, but something close to a 'dirty snow' tone. Zuhdi had an excruciating head ache. He told Ali and Jehreal to go out and pick up something for supper.

Just before the brothers left, the cell phone rang. Aukmed picked it up. "Yes?"

"This is Colson, May I speak to Zuhdi?"

"Zuhdi is suffering from his affliction at present. May I take the message?"

"Yes, this is for all of you. I'll be in Las Vegas tomorrow with a load of furniture. Right now I need two of you to go Henderson and pick up Jeremy. He must continue to be hidden, so please bring him to your apartment. I sent the address and co-ordinates to Zuhdi yesterday. I will see you sometime Sunday evening." Be vigilant. Colson." The call ended.

The next morning Mac and Claire were up and dressed for their drive to the Desert Oaks facility. Claire had brought bacon, eggs, milk and oranges. While Mac checked their route to visit Theo Kastanis, Claire cooked breakfast. They ate quietly, but Mac reached around to Claire, and picked up her hands. "Traveling with you is certainly more fun than without you." He kissed her hand.

"Now you're getting all romantic on me." She laughed. "I love you, too."

"You love me Claire? I so hoped you would." Mac pulled her out of her chair kissed and held her close.

She gazed up at him. This man she knew so well, yet didn't know much about him. "Let's save all this romance for tonight. Right now we've got places to go and things to do." She cleared the table and began a quick clean up.

As they walked to Claire's car, she said. "You look very nice in that leather jacket and khaki slacks."

"I like it that you brought a skirt. I don't often see you in a skirt. And along with the black skirt and beige jacket, you seem very businesslike."

"Well, I thank you, sir" She hugged his arm, and he opened the car door for her.

The drive to the local U S. Post Office took 15 minutes, and Claire sat in the car for nearly that long. People kept streaming into the building. *There are just too many people here. I suppose I'm spoiled living in a rather small town.* Her reverie ended as she watched Mac carry out a large canvas bag and drop it into the trunk.

When he climbed into the car, she asked. "Is all that your mail?"

"Yep, most of it third class stuff, but there is some items that I am glad to receive like pay checks. That's why I put it in the trunk. It's going to take a while to sort through all that stuff."

About an hour later they reached their destination. The building had a long drive way leading to the rear of the one story structure. There was a back door which Mac tried and found it locked. The two of them were forced to walk around to the front of the building. Mac walked up to the front desk, and an older woman sat behind it wearing s pale green uniform. She glanced up at him, but seemed more interested in Claire and smiled at her.

"I'd like to see Theodore Kastanis." Mac said.

The woman pushed a clip board with a sheet on it and said. "Sign in, please. Both of you."

Mac wrote: Jon and Claire Mackay.

The desk lady glanced at the clip board and said. "Room 349. Go to the right."

The door to the room was like those in hospitals. It had a long handle that could be reached by an individual sitting or standing. As Mac touched it, the door swung open easily. The light from a large window made the room pleasant. Along the bottom of the window a sofa had been built against the wall. It was long enough for an individual to possibly sleep on it. Next to the window seat there was an easy chair. This is where Mac found Theo.

Theo was casually dressed and siting in the large chair. Mac sat down on the sofa close to his ex-partner and asked. "Theo, how are you?"

Claire watched as Mac put his hand on Theo's shoulder.

The man did not move his head or seem to look at Mac.

Claire moved closer and now she could see Theo's face. The only recognition was a change in his eyes. For a moment they focused on

Mac. But Theo blinked and quickly they showed only a lifeless stare out the window.

Mac moved closer and put a hand on Theo's knee. "It's me, Dexter MacCandlass. Tell me how you are."

Theo made a small sound. Something like a sigh. For a brief moment his brown eyes met Mac's green ones. Then he dropped his gaze.

"Come on Theo, old buddy, talk to me. Remember we were partners." Mac put his hand in Theo's and squeezed it.

There was a change in Theo's breathing. "Shot me, wasn't- - - - - - -'posed to."

CHAPTER TWENTY-THREE

———— ✦✦✦✦✦✦ ————

"YOU WERE THE 'mole'. Why? What did they offer or how did they threaten you?" Mac asked

"I can tell you why." A definitely feminine voice came from the doorway.

Both Mac and Claire turned and stared at the woman as she stepped into the room. Mac stood and took a step toward this young, pretty woman standing there dressed in Muslim garb.

Claire studied this girl. She wore a long sleeved, navy blue dress that touched her ankles. A navy blue and white head scarf covered her hair and neck. "Who are you?" Claire asked the girl.

Mac stood transfixed for a several heartbeats. "You're Theo's daughter. He carried your picture in his wallet."

The young woman turned to Claire. "The sign- in sheet says that you are Mac's wife. Are you two really married? I'm Mira Kastanis or used to be before I was dumb enough to get married." She scowled and dropped her eyes. "Dad *turned* so I would be allowed to leave Syria." She glanced down at the floor, but raised her head and met Claire's eyes. "It's my fault Dad's like this." The girl waved her hand at her father.

Suddenly Claire understood. "You married a terrorist, or a Muslim who became one."

"Yes, I married Khalid Marcos. Later he radicalized and joined the Sons of Allah. We met at UC Berkley. He had been in the U.S. for nearly four years. He talked of staying here. But when we moved to Syria, he changed. I lived with his mother and sister, and he went into training for months. When he returned his whole behavior changed toward me and even his family. He forced me to wear a veil when we went out. He read my mail, so I stopped writing to my family. But I found a café, and I used the internet. Because we married in California, a friend wrote to the U S. State Department on my behalf."

"How did you get out of the country?" Mac asked.

"I loved Khalid, at least at first, but when he changed from being a kind loving husband, to one who gained pleasure in domination and control and especially controlling me, a well-educated American woman. For over a year I was trapped in his village in Syria."

"When Khalid found out that Dad was an FBI agent, he bartered, actually, blackmailed to get his 'help' in exchange for an Italian passport for me."

"Italy? "What was the connection?" Mac asked.

"You see Khalid was born in Milan, Italy. He has dual citizenship. Someone in our state department located the paperwork of his birth. So I have citizenship in Italy, because I became Mira Marcosa. Because of some paperwork filed with the Syrian government, I was allowed an Italian passport. And the fact that we had no children, Khalid's uncle bought me a ticket to Milan."

"How did you manage to return to the U. S.?" Mac asked.

"It took me nearly three months to earn enough money to fly back to California. "I worked as a maid for two Italian families, and taught the children English. I had help from Khalid's aunt in Milan."

"Then why are you still wearing the Muslim mode of dress?" Claire asked.

"Because the divorce will take another five months. After that I can renew my American citizenship. The FBI has been helpful, in exchange for 'picking' my brain. One of their theories for a while is that you were the 'mole'. But when they discovered my connection to Dad, now they think you're dead."

"Hasn't Theo been able to explain all this to them?" Mac asked, frowning.

"No. The stroke he had limits his speech. Two agents come to visit him every Sunday. A Ken, and a woman named Jeri. Mira said. "What happened to you?"

"Though I have no memory, I believe I was kidnapped by the 'cell', dumped in Utah and left for dead. Claire and a friend rescued me."

"It seems to me you've made a full recovery." Mira smiled,

Mac realized she was a very pretty woman. He glanced at Claire. "I think we'd better leave. Claire must open her business on Monday morning in St. George. We'll have to get an early start driving back."

"A word of warning. Khalid and two or perhaps or three others are scheduled to come into the U.S. soon. They are part of a destructive operation aimed at a U.S. City. The plan is to inflict as much damage as they can. Khalid spent four years in the U. S. and is savvy to our ways. He is fluent in American English. I tried to listen to his phone conversations. Sometimes I didn't understand their language. I think at times he spoke in Farsi. His group is bringing in bomb making materials and plan on assembling them after they arrive here." Mira said.

"Thanks for the warning, but some of them are already here." Mac said and turned and took hold of Claire's arm.

Darkness was closing in that Saturday evening. The fog from the Pacific had rolled in blanketing the area with chilly dampness. There was also a stiff breeze along the San Pedro docks.

An old contractors' trailer stood close to a group of warehouses that had been recently sold, and now were marked to be renovated. Only a dim light shown from the small windows within the trailer. Otherwise the docks were dark and quiet.

A black Lincoln Town Car moved slowly down the wide lane along the waterfront. It came to a stop next to the trailer. The driver jumped out, and opened the rear door for a large man to exit. He was wide of shoulder, heavy build, and formidable. He wore an expensive gray suit with a black cashmere overcoat. A large diamond and ruby ring were on the 'pinky' finger of his right hand. For an instant the security light high on one of the buildings, flashed an icy glitter of light from the ring.

The driver went up the metal steps of the trailer and banged on the metal door. An olive skinned, black haired man opened door and stared down at the two visitors. The man directed his words to the larger man. "Are you Alphonse?"

"That's what people call me. Are three of you here?"

"We arrived this morning and have been waiting for you since then. Why did you not come to pick us up earlier? You promised to be here by noon." He asked harshly.

"When a body is found in a boat listing off one of the large slips, the law enforcement and soon the Coast Guard become involved. Especially when the boat has Mexican registration, and the owner of the boat is found dead in the hold. I did not feel my presence would aid the investigation overmuch." Alphonse gave all three men a hard stare.

The first man scowled, the other two moved away and seemed uneasy.

"The facts seemed to lead to you people, to be the killer or killers. What was the purpose of the murder anyway? Khalid? It is Khalid is it not?" Alphonse growled.

The taller, younger man called Khalid spoke softly, but with menace in his voice. "He became too curious."

"Oh, curious? About what?" Alphonse asked.

"Our cargo." The second man stepped away from the single desk in the trailer and revealed a brown packing box about three feet square.

"What is in the box?" The driver asked and frowned.

"It is better you do not know. Just transport us quickly to the safe house you promised. We need to eat and rest. You said you would have food for us. We will pay you when we arrive there. We will also need a vehicle. One large enough to transport us, our belongings, and our cargo to our destination."

The driver spoke up. "That will cost you people another 15 to 20, K."

The second terrorist came forward "I am Hassam, the banker." What is a K?"

Alphonse spoke slowly as if he were teaching them the local language. "A K', in Toby's words, is American slang for a thousand. In your case thousands of dollars, and that will be added to the $21,000. you already owe us."

"I do understand, and the money will be yours when we reach the safe house." Abdul answered.

Toby pulled a large gunny sack from the rear of the car and went around to each of the men. "We'll be on our way as soon as you surrender your weapons. That is if you choose to ride in the Lincoln." Toby held the sack open for each man to drop in his knives and guns. Then he frisked each man for hidden weapons, and walked to the car and opened the trunk.

"Well now, I believe we are ready to leave." Alphonse held the door open for the first man. "Bring your cargo." Alphonse continued to survey the men as they carried what seemed to be the heavy box and loaded it into the large trunk. He clicked off the interior light in the trailer, closed and locked the door. He resumed his place in the rear of the car next to Abdul and Hassam. Khalid climbed up in the front passenger seat.

Toby drove several miles inland to a modest neighborhood. There were many modest older houses on the street, and he drove down a driveway to another house behind the first. It was a cinderblock structure, dark inside and rather small. He stopped the car, but it was Alphonse who climbed out and searched his coat pocket for a set of keys. With the light from his cell phone, he found the correct key and opened the door. He stepped in and flipped on an interior light. "Gentlemen, this is your shelter for the evening."

Toby released the lock on the trunk and watched as Hassam and Abdul lifted the box and carefully carry it inside. The way they were handling it, the box seemed quite heavy. They chose a spot in a corner of the small living room and set it down.

Abdul waited until he watched the Lincoln leave. Then he pulled his cell phone from his pocket. "We are now here in Los Angeles. Turn on your GPS to find us." He paused and listened to the speaker on the phone.

"Yes tomorrow, we will be able to find you." The speaker said.

"Allah be Praised, we have managed to bring in the explosives without incident. We have a few detonators, but we need a supply of timers and switches." He listened for another moment, and closed the phone.

"Is there room for us to be comfortable in this house?" He asked Khalid.

Khalid walked back to the entrance to the house. "Come in and close the door. I turned on the heating system. There are two bedrooms with two beds each. We will manage."

"Now let us see what the Americans have left for us to eat. We must eat well and be rested to begin our drive tomorrow." Abdul said.

Khalid opened the refrigerator and found an extra-large cheese pizza with black olives and mushrooms. There was also six pack of Pepsi. "Pizza, you will enjoy it. However, I'll go find the beverage that really enhances the taste of pizza. I'll be back soon." *As he walked to the closest convenience store he chastised himself. I know I should not indulge, but it has been over a year since I've had a beer. Allah, be praised, please forgive me of this little sin.* He walked out of the store with a six pack. When he returned, Hassam had figured out how to operate the microwave oven.

"Khalid. You are correct. This American dish is excellent. Also they left cookies, oranges and something called breakfast sandwiches."

CHAPTER TWENTY-FOUR

———————— •✦✦✦✦✦• ————————

ARLY THE NEXT morning, not too many miles from Mac's apartment, two automobiles returned to the neighborhood. The same Lincoln traveled to the street evening before. Both cars motored down the driveway to the small house behind the larger one. The second car was a ten year old Ford Explorer and Toby was behind the wheel. The Ford had rust spots on the hood and rear fender. The license plates were from a dealer in East Los Angeles. Also across the wind shield a large sign read: NO WARRANTY, AS IS. Toby removed the registration and walked to the front door of the house and banged on it.

Khalid answered it "You brought the car?"

Toby nodded. "It's out here, a Ford Explorer, four-wheel drive. All the 'bells' and 'whistles'. It's an older model, but runs well, and it is large enough to hold your cargo."

"The car should meet your needs." Alphonse said as he strolled from the Lincoln and stood by the house.

Khalid stepped outside and walked around the car opening and closing all the doors, kicking the tires, and lastly unlocking the rear lift door and found it locked securely.

Abdul came outside and inspected the car, too. A gust of wind blew rain into his face. "When did it start to rain?"

"Let's go back inside, and we will pay you." Alphonse came in and they all walked into the kitchen. Abdul came to the kitchen counter, took a large envelope from his coat and began counting out one hundred dollar bills.

The five men stood in the small kitchen eyeing each other warily. "Because the Ford is not new, we found a bargain for you. Only $11,000. dollars." Toby handed the car keys to Khalid.

"Thank you." Alphonse said as he took the money and dropped it into a manila envelope. "It is good we could do business together." Alphonse and Toby left the small house richer by $32,000 in U.S dollars.

A half-hour later there was another knock at the door. Abdul opened it allowing a tall, dark haired, olive skinned man to come in. He carried a long box that could have held a dozen roses.

"We have your delivery, Sir." The man said politely, but began to laugh. Another man carried in a similar box into the living room and set it on the floor.

"How many in each box?" Abdul asked.

"Thirty-six each, timers and detonators. Will that be enough?"

"I'm sure it is sufficient. Thank you for bringing them here." The man stood quietly until Hassam counted out payment in hundred dollar bills.

The two men walked to the front door, but as Hassam opened it, a gust of wind whipped the door against the wall outside. "There is a storm coming." The first delivery man said. "Be prepared, but we say good bye until you return. Allah be Praised, there will be more work for you to do." The two delivery men walked out and slammed the door.

Khalid turned to the other two men. "We have everything our brothers in Las Vegas will need. The Americans in 'Sin city' will find their Holiday Celebrations to be sad ones. And they will spend their Christmas Holidays in mourning. I'd better call Zuhdi to expect us."

"Yes." Hassam said. "It is sad we will not be there to witness the destruction. But we have duties, other contacts to make."

On the return to Mac's apartment, the evening before, Claire and Mac passed a large supermarket. "We need something for dinner. I noticed you had a jar of pasta in your pantry. Let's go in the store and find some meat to go with it." Claire found shrimp, and shrimp flavored canned soup. She shopped for vegetables and a carton of half and half.

While Claire made dinner, Mac sat down in his den and began sorting through his mail. Then he wrote a letter to the management of the Willow Glen Apartments. *Rent for the month of December. Enclosed a check.* He put these items in an envelope and wrote: From Dexter MacCandlass. Apartment 219. He went downstairs and dropped his letter into the mail slot for the management. The apartment complex was quiet, except for sudden wind gusts. He did not see anyone.

Walking into his apartment, he returned the scent of something very tasty teased his nose. He came up behind Claire and peered over her shoulder. "What are you cooking?" He asked and kissed the back of her neck.

"Shrimp and pasta in a sauce." She began to wash some fresh vegetables. "It should be ready in five to ten minutes. After we settle down for the evening, you may kiss my neck - - - - - and other places." She turned around and gave him a hug. "Set the table."

As they sat down to eat, a huge of wind rattled the building. "What a changed in the weather." Claire commented." Is this normal for Southern California in late November?"

With a mouthful of delicious pasta and shrimp, Mac shrugged. "I've only lived here for a little over two years. Last year we were in a drought situation. Then we dealt with forest fires. I guess while living in California you should expect anything."

After dinner the wind gusts grew stronger, and the apartment heating system had trouble keeping the place comfortable. Mac turned on the gas fireplace in his living room. Claire crawled into his lap on the sofa, and they wrapped up in his sofa blanket. Both of them fell asleep.

Later on as the wind died down, it began to rain. Claire got up and pulled down the bed. Mac wandered into the bathroom and brushed his teeth and climbed into bed, next to Claire. She curled up next to him, and again found sleep. Mac loved snuggling next to her, but his mind was going in a myriad of different directions. Finally, as the rain pounded on the roof, Mac fell into a fitful sleep.

When he woke, Claire was up and in the shower. He glanced at the clock. It was nearly 8 a.m.

He began to pack while she was still in the bathroom. Quietly they readied for their trip back to St. George. As they were carrying some of their belonging out to Claire's car, a flash of lightning hit a utility pole on the corner. And just across the street and the wires snapped and sizzled. Within a few seconds, there was another flash of lightning, but not as close. Mac and Claire ran for the apartment.

"Wow, this is a wicked storm." Claire exclaimed, catching her breath, as she ran up to the second level. The rain seemed to be everywhere. Soaking them even in and the covered walkway. They burst into the apartment. "Are we going to be able to drive in this?"

"How good are your windshield wipers?" Mac asked in a dead pan voice. They both burst into hysterical laughter. "We *have* to leave. Maybe as we drive east the storm will ease. But I'm afraid it's going to be nasty until we drive up and out of the LA. Basin."

A few minutes later, Mac eased the car out into the morning traffic and drove toward the freeway.

At about the same time the three terrorists carefully loaded their cargo into the Ford Explorer and left the small house in Torrance. "Abdul you must drive." Khalid ordered. He handed the car keys to his comrade terrorist, as they climbed into the car.

Khalid had a fierce headache and a queasy stomach. He had over indulged in the beer, he had purchased the evening before to *enjoy* the pizza. He had become quite intoxicated. Even after two cups of strong coffee that morning, he still felt terrible.

"Something in America has already defeated you." Hassam laughed. "American beer!"

"You are much better at driving these many wheeled vehicles." Abdul whined.

"I'll take over the driving later. When we leave, drive around the right corner and stop at the convenience store, I'll buy some aspirin. Perhaps in an hour or so I'll feel better." Khalid said.

As they drove east searching for the onramp to I-5, Hassam looked out at the leaden sky. "Does it often rain in the winter in California?"

"Sometimes it rains heavily, and many times causing mud slides. This year it will be worse, because of the wild fires this past summer. California is not the 'golden' state they brag it to be." Khalid said.

"The desert of Nevada is more to my liking."

Khalid dozed, and they came upon the exits to the city of Corona. He sat up and glanced out the window. "Stop in this town, Abdul, I'll find some more coffee and perhaps a sack of donuts." When he came back with the treats and cups of coffee, he took over the wheel.

Abdul sat in front and sometime later, picked up the cardboard box that the coffee had come in. He took some wires and a blob from his coat pocket.

The winds had become stronger blowing east up the canyon. Khalid was negotiating. The road was not running with rainwater as when Abdul had been driving, but the steering on this car was tight and jerked slightly. The road now narrowed from three lanes to two, because the right lane became a truck lane: Marked :*LARGE TRUCKS ONLY.* For a moment Khalid glanced over at Abdul. "What are you doing?"

"Building a bomb." Abdul grinned. On his lap he held the cardboard box, and in it he had a blob of plastic explosive, a coffee stirrer, and other components of bomb making. "You see, I take a small amount of the plastic explosive, stick in a wire, and wrap the explosive around it. Hook it to a detonator and I have a little bomb."

Kalid scowled and shook his head. "What you are doing is very dangerous. A small spark, a lighted match or a flame from a lighter, and you, me and everything in this car would be in one hundred pieces." He waved his hand in the air. "Put that away, where it will be secure."

"Uh oh, all right. If you pull off at the next town, I will put it in the back, and put this little box inside a larger one." He tucked the little box under the seat.

"Soon, in a few miles, I must change to the I-15 freeway, perhaps I will see a place to stop there." But the present road they were on narrowed to two lanes and truck lane was still to the right. Although the traffic was light, at least every other vehicle on the freeway was a large truck. Large cabs pulling trailers, what the Americans called 18-wheelers. Khalid thought about the richness of the United States. Its wide variety of foodstuffs and other goods being transported across the vast country every day. Someday all of this could be controlled by his people, and everyone would bow down to Allah.

CHAPTER TWENTY-FIVE

———— ✦✦✦✦✦✦ ————

EVERAL CAR LENGTHS behind, Mac handled driving the steep road with quiet skill. Claire had played with the radio, and found more static that music or news. "I guess we won't have any stations to listen to until we get out of this canyon." She sighed.

"Your radio is tuned to Utah stations. We may begin to pick up some Nevada stations once we get out this canyon and up on the desert. The wind and rain doesn't help either. Believe me, driving in this storm is not fun," He shook his head. "We'll stop, once we reach Barstow. By then I'll be ready for some lunch."

"I'm glad you are the one driving. This road is tricky on a sunny day, and the weather today is awful, just plain bad." Claire straightened her seatbelt.

Once Khalid reached the highest point of the road, it turned and began to wind down in steep curves. As the curves flattened out, traffic picked up speed, and Khalid, still suffering from a headache became sleepy, and had to close his eyes from time to time. Hassam had already snapped off his seatbelt and curled up in the back seat. Abdul fell asleep leaning on the passenger side window.

Now the road began to climb. And on the far right side there were deep drop-offs. On the far right edge, close to the truck lane the desert canyon had deep embankments. Many of them were at least twenty to thirty feet straight down, and yet on the other side, ridges rose above the highway.

The rain poured at a steady rate. The wind shield wipers continued slashing at the rain swamping the windshield. Keeping up their rhythm, steady, hypnotic.

Khalid had to gear down to slow the car for another down curve; and had trouble dropping it in gear. It seemed stiff. He was forced to ram it down and it dropped into low, The car sputtered, but he managed to shift back to second gear. Fighting with the gear shift, he allowed the car to drift into the pass lane. The automobile behind him, honked loud and long. Khalid now nervous and shaky, fought to shift the car back into drive, but over corrected and it slid into the truck lane.

Now the road climbed again, and Khalid barely cleared out of the way of a large truck carrying lumber. At the moment they reached the summit of the hill, the truck right on the Explorer's tail started down the hill. Khalid could hear the trucker trying down shift, and the Explorer was still in second gear, yet it was moving too fast. As he fought to shift into low gear, the truck clipped tail of the Ford.

In a panic Khalid slid into the second lane, and another passenger truck, hit the Explorer, and sent it spinning sideways. The big truck grinding down the hill slammed into the front end of the Explorer and sent it spinning over the edge on the far right side. It crashed through the guard rail and barreled end over end, and came to rest at the bottom of a deep ravine. Khalid hit his head on the steering wheel with his foot still on the accelerator. Then the rear end bounced and crashed into a huge boulder.

For a moment nothing happened. Then the gas tank exploded setting small plant growth on fire, until the rain sputtered it out. A moment later the whole car erupted into a huge fireball, one and then another and another. Traffic that reached the summit kept going. But all the traffic on the hill below the summit had to slow and then stop. A shockwave of superheated air knocked cars closest to the drop-off into each other. Those cars' tires melted from the heat. The sound was deafening. It reverberated bouncing off the rock walls of the hillside.

The rain falling on the explosion sent a huge cloud of steam up, across the freeway and into the air.

The truck that hit the Explorer continued around the next curve, but managed to slow and then stop a half-mile down as the curve straightened out. Another car managed to pull over behind the truck. A few moments later, a woman climbed from that car with a cell phone. She pulled a raincoat to put on from her car. She managed to duck back in just a large rock shattered her windshield. Now rocks and medium sized pebbles began peppering the cars and the road.

Mac was in the center lane about a hundred yards away from the blast. He felt the concussion of the explosion as a hot wind coming through the air vents. Then the sound slammed into his ears, for several moments, deafening him. He managed to ease Claire's Honda over to the right side near the guard rail and stopped. He glanced over at Claire. She grimaced. Her eyes were closed, and her hands were tight over her ears.

She had this shocked expression on her face. "What was that?" As she spoke, she wondered if Mac could hear her, because she couldn't hear anything Rocks and debris rained down along the road and onto to roofs, hoods and windshields of cars and trucks.

Mac thanked God or fate that he and Claire had been a good distance away from the explosion. He touched her shoulder and asked. "Are you okay?" Her eyes were wide.

Suddenly, one medium sized rock hit the roof, and bounced down onto the windshield. He closed his eyes, and shook his head. At that moment, he knew he would have buy Claire another car.

She let go of her ears. "Was that an explosion? It must have been close." Her ears still rang, but she heard the rock crack the windshield. "Dammit, my windshield." She winced. Then another rock slammed onto the roof of the car. Smaller rocks continued to pepper the car and other vehicles in front and next to them.

The wind shifted and began to blow the steam and clouds of smoke more to the north. Very slowly most of the steam cloud drifted away from the road.

"Claire, may I borrow your cell phone. I think I need to get some pictures of this mess." He reached in the back seat for his rain coat and ball cap.

"Okay, you're back thinking like an FBI Agent again. I knew it would happen." She reached into her purse and handed him her cell phone. She said. "When we get back to St. George, we're going shopping. You need your own cell phone."

"Yes we are. And that *is* a promise." Mac gingerly climbed from the car. He began weaving between cars and trucks. Trying to find a place where he could see the smoke and flames. He was not the only individual out taking pictures. He began snapping pictures, but stopped and dialed a familiar number.

"FBI, Michael Shaw." A text began across the screen of his phone, along with some pictures of a disaster, an explosion? He picked up the official FBI line.

"Connect me with Director Velois. Director, someone is sending pictures of some kind of, - - - -looks like an explosion. I'll text back and see who it is and where this is happening."

Another text came: Explosion just happened, I-15. East of Pomona, CA. Sending pictures from a cell phone."

Michael Shaw found the cell phone number, and in a few strokes on his computer. had a name: Claire Talbot. He texted back "Claire talk to me. Do you have any idea of what exploded?"

Mac texted back. "Mile marker 78, l-15 going east. Sorry, I didn't see the car, but the way the explosions came in waves, I'm betting there were explosives in it. And they were probably the plastic variety." Then Mac began to talk to Michael. "For now, freeway is shut down going east. I suggest you send a crime scene team here as soon as possible. I just saw one California State Highway Patrol car. More will come, and they will contaminate the scene. A helicopter would be the quickest way to get up here." Mac suggested

"You voice is very familiar. Who are you? Why did you call?"

"I had to. This is amazing. It's MacCandlass."

Michael put down the phone, A wide grin creased his face. *"Well, my god. MacCandlass is alive. And who is Claire Talbot? But first things first.* He had to organize a crime scene team and go up there, ASAP. He walked down the hall to Velois' office and the director had just thrown open his door and yelled. "Get Michael Shaw in here. The he bounced out into the hall, and yelled at his secretary, "Call the air field and get a chopper up here, fast."

"I'm here, director. I'll get a team organized right now."

Now Velois followed Michael into the lab and watched as the tech survey the pictures Mac had sent. How did these people, now victims of the crash, manage to obtain, bring in to the U.S. these types of explosives? Velois began to pace, and run his hands through his thinning hair.

Why hadn't Mac just walked in here and told us where he has been for nearly six weeks. Yet, he *knew* why. The FBI knew it was Kastanis, not Mac who was the 'mole. Mac, poor guy, would just get bogged down with red tape from the bureau, because he had been missing all that time. Now as a free agent, he could come and go as he pleased. Investigate where the next lead would take him. *Please Mac, just keep us in the loop.*

Mac stood transfixed, watching the clouds of smoke and steam rising from the explosion at the bottom of the drop off. From time to time, though the drifting clouds, he could see sections of the car. Bent, smoke blackened. Now he thought he could see a boot. Was there a part of a foot still inside it?

Many emotions, thoughts bounced around in his head. First there was horror, then amazement at the power of the explosion. How much 'plastic' had been in that vehicle? What if those explosives had been planted in a high rise hotel or shopping mall? The damage they could have done to the structure and the people inside it? The death toll would be unthinkable. Now he was grateful he and Claire had been a football field away from the explosion. He continued to stare down in the abyss that had once been a simple embankment. He tried to find twisted parts of a car, and its contents, and continued to snap pictures. The Crime

Scene Team would search the carnage and find only bits and pieces of people lying at the bottom of this area of the desert.

The rain kept up a steady beat on his cap and the water ran down from his rain coat to his legs and feet. His body began to shake, and he shivered uncontrollably. He turned and slowly made his way around the cars and trucks stalled in the freeway, and back to Claire and her car.

When she saw him she said. "You're soaking wet. Get in on the passenger side. Or get in the back seat or front, 'Cause I'm going to drive. If you catch pneumonia it will be worse than before." She railed at him.

"Yes, you'd better drive." He said and ducked around to the passenger side. Wisely he took off the soaked coat, cap, shoes. He dropped into the back seat, and wrapped up in the sofa blanket they had brought along.

"The police are starting to clear the road." Claire said and turned up the heat in the car. A front loader was up ahead, and scraping the road of rocks and debris. Claire glanced back at Mac. He was still shaking, but working to take off his socks.

The traffic finally began to move. Slowly it wound down the hill, around and up again. A few minutes later the speed of the traffic picked up and Claire began to read road signs. Her goal was to get to stay on I-15 East.

As Claire drove up to the flat of the desert, Mac's mind took him back to another procession of cars: Automobiles following a hearse to a cemetery. He sat in a limo following the hearse, which carried the body of his mother. From time to time he would glance at his father, who sat red eyed, stony faced, and clutched a large white handkerchief.

How many years ago, and how old had he been back then? 20? No 21. His little sister sat next to him holding another white handkerchief, and wiping her eyes. His mother's illness had been so sudden, and she never told anyone until it was too late.

When his sister called, so distraught, he had been a student at Kansas State, and had left quickly to return home. She could barely get the words out, when she told that him their Mom had died. Then, too, the day they had buried his mother, it had been raining.

He shook his head as if to shake away the memory. He didn't want to feel that gut wrenching pain ever again. He closed his eyes, and managed to doze for a few minutes. As he slept, and his body relaxed, and when he awoke his thoughts turned analytical. He felt the car gain freeway speed, and he was so grateful that other people, FBI technicians would take over the crime scene. He was glad he wouldn't have to dig through that pit. What would be most interesting is how the FBI would 'spin' this explosion in the desert to the media. He decided he would keep in touch with Velois.

CHAPTER TWENTY-SIX

———— ✦✦✦✦✦✦ ————

C LAIRE REMEMBERED THE drive to California, and the place they had stopped for dinner on the way down. She glanced at the car's clock. Mountain Time, it was just after 3 p.m., and she was hungry. She spotted an *In and out Burger,* and pulled the car into the parking lot. She turned to Mac. "I'm going to the restroom. Do you want to change clothes here in the car or inside?"

He blinked and stretched as much as rear seat would allow. "I'll be in in a minute. See if you can find us a booth or table."

Soon they were sitting in the large restaurant eating hamburgers, fries and drinking soda. "How much farther is St. George from here?" Claire asked.

"About 350 miles. Mac pulled Claire's cell phone from his pocket. He downloaded a miles and temperature app. "The weather is moving north, but the rain seemed to be letting up. I'll drive to Las Vegas and you can take it from there. I know we need to get back to Rawley, so you can open the clinic tomorrow. I'm sorry this trip turned out the way it did." He touched her hand and shook his head.

"Hey, it's not your fault that terrorists or other 'crazies' decided to transport explosives on the same road and at the same time we were driving home. We'll just have to get my car fixed later this week."

"I plan to take care of that." Mac said.

The rest of the way home they just drove, and only stopped for gas and coffee. They managed to reach Claire's house a little after 11 p.m. With quiet team work, they carried all their belongings into the house, The rain had caught up with them, and looked like the Monday after Thanksgiving in St. George would be chilly and wet.

Late that same evening, Geoffery Colson drove a rented truck full of furniture down a shabby street, into an older neighborhood of Las Vegas. The area was a mix of older apartment complexes, small stores, some boarded up, some older houses. At the corner he noticed a boarded up factory. Stopping at a red light, he read the directions Jeremy had given him on his phone an hour ago. *"Turn left at the intersection of Frontier Road and 1580 West. In the middle of the block you'll see two sets of four apartment groups. The apartment number is 12-B*

Though it was windy and raining, Colson peered through the truck windshield, decided that he had located the correct apartment. Since the driveway was at the far end of the apartment group, he parked as close to the curb as possible.

Wisely he had watched the weather channel before leaving the Bay Area. He took the chance of taking I-80 east through the mountains of central California, and across the Sierra Nevada's past Reno. It was a long drive, but he found an alternate route to take him around Salt Lake City, and stopped at a friendly looking motel in Provo, Utah. The storm that hit Southern California, Las Vegas and even as far as north as Cedar City, but had not reached to what people in Utah called the Wasatch Front. It was the most populist area of the state.

Now he had arrived in Las Vegas, and climbed out of the truck. He slouched across pools of water on what once used to be a lawn. It had given up to weeds. When he knocked on the door, Jehreal flung open the door.

"Professor Colson how good it is to see you." The young man glanced out the door. "Is that your truck?"

"Yes. You and the others can come out and empty it. It's full of furniture." Colson glanced around the small apartment. *This is really pathetic.* He stood in the doorway, because there was no place to sit.

Jeremy came out of a bedroom. "Professor Colson, I'm glad you made through this storm. Jeremy gazed out the door. "Okay, I see Jahreal has gone out to help empty the truck. I'm still healing, but I could perhaps carry in a chair or two." He slowly walked out to the truck and stood as Jahreal opened the double rear doors of the truck.

Ali and Aukmed also followed Colson out to the truck, and began to empty it. As they set up the kitchen table and the four chairs. Jahreal asked the professor. "Where did you find this yellow table with strong metal legs and padded chairs? It is a bright, cheerful color."

"This is all used furniture, and I purchased the table for its strength, and it will be easy to keep clean." Colson said as he gazed around the dismal apartment with a frown. Aukmed and Ali brought in single beds that could be bunks, and went out for the mattresses.

Once the truck was emptied Colson came in and handed Jeremy five twenty dollar bills. "What is this for, Professor?" Jeremy asked.

"You are in charge of keeping this apartment clean. This money is for trips to the Laundromat, and for other cleaning products."

"Aren't you driving me back to the university?" Jeremy asked, surprise on his face.

"No. I can't take you back. You are a wanted fugitive. Remember, you tried to kill a guard at the college in Cedar City. You are fortunate to be alive."

"But what about my teaching assignment?" Jeremy whined, and dropped his eyes to the floor.

"I have found a very adequate substitute. After all, the semester has only a few weeks left." Colson said. "Oh, follow me out to the truck. I brought your computer."

Colson turned to the other men in the apartment, and gestured at Jeremy. "He can be a great help to you. He can shop and keep the place and your clothing neat and clean." He turned to Zuhdi and handed him an envelope. "If you need more funds, call me. I am driving to a motel I am familiar with, and will rest for the evening. I must be on the road early tomorrow." Colson walked out and closed the door.

Monday morning, Lt. Paul Reston called Las Vegas Police Headquarters. "I'm inquiring about a call I received from one of your officers. He mentioned a hotel in the area North Las Vegas. Something about blood soaked sheets, and a possible surgery there?"

"You're calling from Cedar City, Utah? Stay on the line, I'll connect you with North Las Vegas Precinct." A few seconds later Paul heard: "North Las Vegas, How can we help you?"

"This is Lt. Paul Reston, Iron County PD. Southern Utah" He repeated his request.

"Yes, Lt. Reston. I'll connect you with my captain." This connection took a few seconds longer.

"Captain Redding, here. I see you are calling about the situation we had last week at the King of Cards motel. I have been informed that you had a shooting at the university there in Cedar City. As I read over the report from my officers, I believe there is a connection. Were you able to find any finger prints or DNA?"

"Yes, our crime scene team was able to harvest fingerprints and blood samples." Reston said. "Would you send us your information, and we can send you ours."

"Fax it to us and we will fax our evidence to you. How is the victim of the assault?" Captain Redding asked.

"He is recovering. Thank you for this trade of evidence."

"I realize that we should be more aware of connections between crime scenes happening in other cities." Thank you, Lt. Reston."

Paul Reston sat back and read over the paperwork from North Las Vegas Precinct. DNA had been identified from the blood on the motel sheets. It matched the blood stains on the wall and floor of the Bio building at the university in town. LVPD sent the perp's name, and address, the picture of his driver's license, and age. Had he returned to the Bay Area? How critical was he wounded? Who did the surgery on him in a motel room? And Why?

Reston put out an APB on Jeremy Ardmore, and sent it to California and Nevada. He was limited in man power, and funds. Right now that was all he could do.

Monday morning Mac got up and began breakfast for Claire and him. He knew she was tired from their trip. And he also knew her car needed repair.

When she came down stairs, she gave him a kiss. "You made breakfast. Thank you." By her place at the table he had set a mug of steaming coffee, and soon served her a plate of French toast and bacon. She began to eat. "What are you going to do this morning?" She asked between mouthfuls of food.

"I'm taking your car in for repairs. You drive my car to the clinic. I'll bring you some lunch. What would you like?" Mac asked, setting his own breakfast on the table.

"A chicken salad. Wendy's has a good one." She said. She finished her breakfast, and set the plate and mug in the sink. "I am really enjoying the 'butler' service around here."

He pulled her into his arms and gave her a long kiss. Then reached into his pocket and dropped his keys in her hand. "See you about one p.m."

While cleaning up the kitchen, Mac began thinking in FBI mode. *If the exploded car in California proved to be driven by terrorists, and it was loaded with bomb making materials, what was their destination? How did they get into the country? They were driving east. They could have come into the country from Mexico. But how? Cross the border, or by sea? His gut told him there was still a terrorist 'cell' in or near Las Vegas. What was their target? The Christmas Season had begun. Hotels, shopping malls, anywhere there were large groups of people, explosives could cause many casualties* Mac went to his computer and began checking news casts, especially in California. There was news of the Explosion, the FBI investigating. Another news story caught his attention. Last Saturday, a Mexican fishing boat found near the San Pedro docks, the owner found dead.

Is that how the terrorists travelled into the United States?

But for now, his responsibility was to help Claire. He looked up the Honda dealership and drove her car into St. George.

Mid-morning Director Velois asked technicians who had flown up to search through the explosion site for an update. "How are you people doing? What have you found?"

Michael Shaw wiped his tired face. "There are literally mountains of debris, hundreds of pounds of evidence to collect. We have been photographing as we inch through it. It's going to take days to process all this stuff. The actual hole in the ground is at least fifteen feet deep. We worked at it until we lost the light, sundown. We stopped then, because we were tired, wet, cold and hungry." He grimaced. "The damage to that little drop-off is unbelievable."

"Take your time. Velois shrugged. "The evidence will still be there tomorrow."

"We posted a guard, and five of us are ready to go there in an hour. At least today the storm has moved on. We did bring in several sacks of evidence." Michael Shaw said. "We sent it to the lab."

One of the agents, Jeri Fox walked into Velois' office as Michael walked out. She set a folder on Velois' desk. "We got a hit on some of the fingerprints from the Mexican boat."

"Thanks Jeri." He opened the folder. There were three individual sets of fingerprints lifted from the boat, The prints were from cigarette butts and hand prints from the on the railing of the boat. Even some wet shoe prints, and a 9 mil. shell casing was found. *Checking the fingerprints through Interpol, they should have results tomorrow."* Velois sighed. "Who are these people, and what was their objective?" He wondered if there was a connection between the murder on the boat and the explosion in the Mojave Desert

CHAPTER TWENTY-SEVEN

―――――――・・◆◆◆◆・・―――――――

W HEN MAC FOUND out what it would cost to repair Claire's car, he next cruised the used car lot and examined late model Honda sedans and drove three of them. There was one only two yours old with low mileage and had some nice features. He would need to take Claire shopping with him, but he planned to purchase a car for her outright. Using JD Mackay's Mesquite account he could easily afford one of these cars.

He picked up two salads and one double hamburger and walked into the clinic about one p.m. The vet Olga and Claire had just finished a surgery on a dog. She came out into the front office and flashed a big smile when she saw Mac.

"I need to clean up. Give me a few minutes." She disappeared back in the clinic.

One of the girls who worked for Claire walked in about then. She came over to Mac and asked. "May I help you?"

"Ah, no. I'm waiting for Claire."

"I'm Natalie Jacobs. I'll tell her you're here." She went into the rear of the clinic.

Then Mac could hear Natalie and Claire talking and then she came out front. "Shall we go?" She smiled at Mac and they went out to his car.

"It's a warm day. Let's go over to that park." Mac said. They settled down at a picnic table, and began to eat. "I took your car over to the dealership. The repairs on the car are going to run at least $1,500 dollars." Mac explained.

"What! The car's 10 years old." She frowned and stabbed at her salad.

"Um, I found that out earlier. I shopped for another car for you. I've picked out two, that I think you might like." Mac said and took a bite of his hamburger.

"I don't want you to buy a car for me. It's my fault I suggested=------."

"No, it was my trip, and so I'm responsible. I've funds enough to purchase a modest car. So eat your salad, and then we'll go over to the car lot and you can pick one out. Even if we repair your car it's only worth about $3,000 and less than $4,000." Mac sat back and ate his food.

"Okay, I'll go look at a car maybe even two different ones." Claire shrugged and smiled."

Less than an hour later, Claire had chosen one the cars Mac had picked out. It was a medium blue sedan with *blu-tooth*, and an extra channel for satellite radio. They arranged to pick it up the next afternoon. The repair technician and the dealer negotiated with Mac a price for Claire's old car.

When Mac took her back to the clinic, he asked if he could help start dinner for her.

"Wow, you are already behaving like a hus- - - - partner." She corrected, and color flared in her cheeks.

Before she climbed from the Mac's car, she reached over and kissed him. "I guess, right now we are partners."

"I want it to last, Claire. I meant it when I said I loved you." Mac watched her run into the back door of the clinic. It occurred to him it had only been six weeks since she had helped him from that rear door of the clinic and into her life.

Tuesday morning V.L Strickland, Director of the Las Vegas FBI office called Dan Forester in for a new assignment. "Sit down Dan. How is your case load?"

"Right now I can handle it. I have lots of small situations I'm dealing with, or at least to investigate. Dan sat back and studied his boss. V.I seemed relaxed enough, but he juggled a pencil rapidly in his hand. *Something's come up*

"I received a phone call yesterday from Velois, Southland office. He was enquiring about the Holiday attractions we had coming in to 'Vegas for Christmas."

Dan nodded. "What particular area is he interested in?"

"Outdoor attractions, or those usually attracting large crowds." Strickland continued to jiggle the pencil.

"His office is the one working on the explosion in the California desert."

"Wasn't that less than a hundred miles from the L.A. Basin?" Dan asked.

"Yes. Although the teams working the explosion site are really just getting started, they have found some evidence of bomb making materials. So the theory is that all of those explosives were meant to be used somewhere in our fair city. There has to be a terrorist cell operating somewhere in Las Vegas. How would you like to go on a man hunt?" Strickland said, sat forward and grinned.

"A man hunt, sir? What man?"

"There is evidence that MacCandlass is alive, well, and probably in the area. He was driving near the explosion, and managed to send several pictures from a cell phone. This phone is registered to a Claire Talbot of St. George, Utah. We ran her background, and she doesn't even have a recent traffic ticket.

She owns a house in Rawley, and runs a Vet's clinic in St. George. She is 31 years old and is single."

"I see where you are going. Find Claire Talbot, and I'll find Mac." Right now, Dan wanted to be the one jiggling the pencil. He was relieved that Mac was alive, but felt his temper flash. Why hadn't Mac 'come in'? On the other hand he wanted to be the first agent to find Mac and ring his neck. *I liked the guy, and possibly he had been kidnapped. I want to know his story.*

"The teams working the explosion site will be at it all week. Luckily the weather has improved. I'll hear more from Velois tomorrow. I understand why MacCandlass hasn't come in. He would be embroiled in miles of red tape. And since he all but witnessed the explosion, I'm sure he wants to investigate. If he's living with this Claire Talbot, they must have some sort of relationship. They are the right age to be attracted to each other, and both are single."

"Your assignment is to find him, and find out where he's been, what he knows, what the 'hell happened to him," Strickland said. "Give some of your work to Janice Hansen. 'Stuff that she can do here, in the office."

"Okay. I'll start looking for Mac today."

⸻ ·✦✦✦✦· ⸻

After she closed the clinic Claire asked her employee to stop at the grocery store for a few fresh food items. She had them when Mac came to pick her up. When Claire walked into her kitchen she picked up the delightful scent of roast beef from the crock pot.

"What did you fix? Ah, beef. Did you get out the beef roast from the freezer? What else did you put in the crockpot?" She grinned, and hugged him.

"I found some potatoes, carrots and onion soup mix. Pretty easy." He seemed pleased at her comments.

"Where did you learn to cook?" Claire asked.

"College. Well, actually before. I watched my Mom- - - - - -.'" He shrugged. *Someday I'll talk about Mom, but not right now.*

"Well, I'll get busy with some salad greens, then let's eat." Claire said and went to wash her hands.

As they sat at the table, Mac took Claire's hand. "I need to go to Las Vegas, and I need Andy Freeman's address. I know there are terrorists in 'Vegas and I suspect the explosives that went up in flames on the freeway were meant for Las Vegas to be used sometime around Christmas week. The bad guys like to make their 'dirty work' memorable. I want to warn the 'Vegas police. I'm sure the FBI, once they analyze the bits and pieces left from that explosion, they'll find all kinds of bomb making materials. Would you call Suzanne and at least ask for Andy's phone number?"

Claire stared at him for several beats, and then sighed. "Okay, but please be careful. When are you going back to 'sin city'?"

"We can pick up your new car tomorrow at lunch time. I'll drive down in the afternoon tomorrow."

"I'm thrilled that you bought me a new car." Claire squealed.

"Well, they wanted $1500.00 plus to fix your car and it is nearly 11 years old. To fix that car would be a bad investment. Besides you work hard and deserve a better car." He sat back on the padded bench. "I want you to know that I love you Claire, but I have to do what I can to protect innocent people from crazies like the 'Sons of Allah.'"

⁘

When Mac reached the outskirts of Las Vegas it was nearly dark. The storm of a few days ago had passed, but it was cold. He stopped at a convenience store and called Andy. Freeman picked up on the third ring.

"Andy? This is JD, I am passing through Las Vegas and wondered if you had any dinner plans for this evening."

"Hi, I'm just leaving the North 'Vegas Precinct." Andy said. "I haven't given much thought about dinner yet."

"Do you have any suggestions? Somewhere we could meet." Mac asked.

"Yeah, there's a pretty good café south of the racing track road called Lil's. It's east on Frontier Road about 3 miles from the Precinct."

"Thanks Andy." Mac scribbled the address in a little book he took from his pocket. "I'll try to get there in 20 minutes."

⁘

Lil's Diner was built in the shape of an old railroad car, but much larger. By the number of cars in the parking lot, it seemed fairly busy on a Tuesday evening. As he walked in, Mac found it noisy, warm and inviting. The lovely smell of food broiling, baking or frying made his stomach growl.

He spotted Andy at the front of a line of people waiting for a table or booth. Mac sidled up and stood next to him.

Andy looked over at Mac. "You made good time."

They were shown a booth by a server, and handed each a menu. "What can I bring you guys to drink?"

"I'll take coffee and a glass of water." Mac said.

"I'll be okay with the same." Andy said. He opened the menu and glanced at it for a moment, then gazed at his dinner mate.

Mac studied the menu. "What do you recommend?"

"I'm having the meat loaf and mashed potatoes. But the roasted chicken and potatoes are good, or even the salmon." Andy recommended.

From the corner of the room the mounted TV began a newscast. Andy could see it, but Mac could not. "Man, they're showing more of the explosion site in the California desert. They now have found evidence of explosive materials."

Mac got up and stood by Andy's side of the booth and watched the TV coverage. "I was there." Mac said softly.

"You were? How close? What did you see?" Andy stared up at Mac.

Mac sat back down and leaned across the table. "Claire and I were about 100 yards back, but the sound alone was deafening. Plus smoke, but luckily it kept raining. That's why I wanted to speak with you."

The server came over to their table and asked what they wanted for dinner. A minute later she brought coffee cups and glasses of ice water.

Andy and Mac ordered and sat back, Mac began sipping his coffee, and Andy downed his water.

"I felt you, as representative of the Las Vegas Police force should know about these terrorists. I'm pretty sure their target is or was somewhere in Las Vegas. My gut feeling is that the original cell we tried to catch is still in the area." Mac said.

"Are you working under cover, for the FBI or homeland security?" Andy asked.

"FBI. It's a long story, but you can ask Suzanne, because she knows about me. Actually she and Claire saved my life." Mac spread his hands on the table, and eyes never left Andy's face.

Andy shook his head. "That sounds like Suzy. She fearless, and deviant and I love the pants off her. Anytime, I get the chance." He grinned.

Mac laughed. "You 'guys' need to be together."

"I know. She says she loves me, but it's her *mother*. My apartment here is in a good neighborhood, and there's an elementary school a half a mile away. Suzy did fill out an application for a position at a hospital's ME department here in 'Vegas. We'll just have to wait and see. I'm going up there for Christmas whether her mother likes it or not."

Their food came and they both started to eat. Both quiet for several minutes. Finally Mac stopped, sat back and toyed with his fork. "Thanks for listening to me. I just feel these individuals represent a great threat to the people here in this area."

"So what's going on with you and Claire? Are you living with her?"

"Ah, - - - -yes. You could say we are a couple." Mac grinned. "I've had girlfriends before, but Claire is amazing, and I love her. I just worry, that she will become involved in this situation. I don't want anything to happen to her. And in a way she's like Suzanne. Gutsy."

"Oh, by the way. That tip you gave me about the shooting at university in Cedar City. We shared the information. The guy who shot the guard up was identified. Call me tomorrow, and I'll give you the info. For all we know he may still be in the 'Vegas, too." Andy said.

CHAPTER TWENTY-EIGHT

J EREMY BEGAN CHAUFFEURING the four terrorists to their jobs at The Tri-Hotel Corp. Afterward he would take their laundry to the local coin operated laundry, and found a good market to shop for groceries.

When he picked them up, Zuhdi voiced concern over the fact that their group had not heard from Khalid. They were waiting for the delivery of the explosives. "Still, I am worried." Zuhdi said.

"That was a wicked storm last Sunday. Maybe they were delayed, or perhaps they didn't make it to California as soon as they planned. You know what, without a TV we don't know what's going on in the world." Jeremy said. "You control an 'expense account' don't you? I'll bet there's enough money in there to buy a small TV."

"What amount of the funds would you need?" Zuhdi asked.

"Less than $500. Oh, and I have another concern: This car that I'm driving. It has a broken left tail light. When did that happen?"

"The first FBI raid in California." Jahreal said. "We were afraid to have it fixed."

"Well then we need to 'ditch' it and find another car." Jeremy suggested.

"What would another car cost?" Aukmed asked.

"I'm not sure. I could shop around and see what's available." Jeremy said.

When they reached the apartment, Jeremy told them to 'wash up' because dinner would soon be ready.

Jahreal came into the small kitchen and watched Jeremy stir something in a fry pan. "It smelled good, "What is in the pan?"

"Just some ground beef. We're having tacos. Hey Jahreal, grab the lettuce and tomatoes from the fridge." On the kitchen bar, there were plates lined up with a soft tortilla on each. There were also other foods to add to the lettuce and tomatoes.

Once the food was prepared, Jeremy brought out sodas and milk. "Choose what you want to drink. I also made coffee." He said to the other men. They sat down to eat. Afterward, Jahreal come to help Jeremy to clean up.

"You are doing a great service for us." Jahreal patted Jeremy on the back.

"Thanks Bro. A little appreciation goes a long way. I didn't get much from Doctor Colson."

"Hmmm, The Professor provides us with funds, but I believe he likes to control us, also." Jahreal said.

"Do you know how much money we are talking about?" Jeremy asked.

"No. only Zuhdi has the account information. But sometimes there is more money than other times. When we were living at the 'safe' house, it was not good. Cold and windy. We needed warm clothing, and Zuhdi asked for funds and then we could shop for clothing and food."

"That's good to know." Jeremy nodded his head. "Yep, good to know."

In his hunt for MacCandlass, the first thing Dan did was find out where Mac had an apartment in Southern California. He called the Southland office of the FBI and spoke to a girl named Jeri Fox.

"Sure I know Mac. He was in on the first raid we made on the 'Sons of Allah'. In fact he shot at their car, an old blue Mercedes. I believe he shot out the left taillight."

"I'm supposed to find him. What is his address there in Costa Mesa?" Dan asked.

"Hang on. Here I'm sending it to you now. When he was missing for so long, Ken and I visited his apartment and took his laptop, and some other files when we suspected him of being the 'mole', but it turned out to be Theo Kastanis. However that's another story. Anything else I can do for you?" She asked.

"No this does help me for now. Thanks. Oh, while I have you on the line. Where did MacCandlass bank?"

"That information we don't give out without a court order. We just send the paychecks to the individual's address, or they can pick them up downstairs."

"Thanks for your help." Dan closed his laptop.

Now let's check out Jonathan David Mackay. Dan began checking out banks in St. George. There was nothing there in the name of JD Mackay. Next he checked the banks in Mesquite, Nevada and second bank he checked he hit 'pay dirt'. However, the bank would not give the account information without a court order.

I suppose I'll need to drive up to St. George. Dan drove back to his apartment and grabbed a gym bag with some fresh clothes. *This assignment might turn out to be an overnighter.*

⸺ •✦✦✦•• ⸺

Mac sat in Claire's den and worked on his computer. He hacked into the previous off shore accounts. He wanted to see what if any activity had taken place. The larger account showed money withdrawn in the form of a credit account to a used furniture store. The company listed three locations in the bay area. The amount of the debit was nineteen –hundred, sixty dollars. Another credit transaction was to a car/ truck rental place for $460.00, in the name of J A. Sutherland.

Mac printed these out and hid them in Claire's closet in the den. *Suddenly there's activity on this account also showing an influx of funds. Where is this money coming from? I'll check on this account tomorrow.*

Then he made his own withdrawal in the amount of $25,660. Again in payment for services rendered to Pedro and Son's Automotive. This withdrawal made its way into J.D. Mackay's account in Mesquite.

After all, there was nearly a million dollars in this off shore account. Next time he would try and trace where the inflow of funds was coming from.

++++++

Dan Forester drove around St. George looking for somewhere to eat lunch. Close to the freeway off ramp was a resturant called *The Golden Corral* He knew it was a buffet restaurant and he went in and took his laptop with him. The food was pretty good, and while he sat alone in a booth, he snagged a local phone book. In the 'yellow pages he found the address for The Southern Utah Dixie Animal Clinic. He studied the map in the advertisement and figured out where it was located.

He drove around the rear of the establishment and parked. He sat there for a moment trying to decide whether to go in and confront this Claire Talbot, or not. As he sat there he watched two cars cruise into the parking lot. One was a late model blue Honda, and the second was a silver gray Subaru SUV. The driver of the Honda parked, climbed out and walked over to the driver's side of the Subaru. She leaned in and said something to the driver for a moment, and then it looked like she kissed him. She walked to the rear door of the clinic, waved at the driver of the Subaru and went in.

Dan only saw her for a moment, but he decided that she was attractive, rather tall and had short brown hair. The driver of the Subaru was a young man, but he had dark hair and wore glasses. Nevertheless, Dan decided to follow him.

The drive took Dan west out of the main section of the city to a more rural area. He had to hang back so as not to tip off the driver he was following him. Suddenly, the Subaru turned into a place between a white house and a barn. Dan could do nothing put keep driving. He went to the next cross street and turned around. When he drove slowly back the way he had come the Subaru had disappeared. The next house to the east was at least a block away from the white house. Dan parked by the side of the road, about halfway between the two houses and walked back. He decided that the barn could be used as a garage.

Mac had gone into the den and to his computer. That room had no front facing window, but it did have a large window to the east. A man walking along the road caught Mac's attention. It was unusual for an individual to walk along the road, And Mac watched, he recognized the man: *Dan Forester.* He shook his head and laughed. Then he walked into the living room and stood by the large window and watched Dan walk up onto the porch.

Just as Dan stood there, Mac opened the door. "Come in Agent Forester."

"I'm looking for-------------. His eyes widened in surprise. "Mac, you've dyed your hair."

Mac laughed. "Yeah, it became necessary to get some good new identity papers."

Dan entered and glanced around. This is Claire Talbot's place?"

"Yes, it's an older house, but quite comfortable. You figured out I would be living with Claire. Good detective work. Since you're here you may as well come in. I assume that you were sent on this 'seek and find visit'." Mac laughed.

"You're correct. Strickland sent me to find you. First, how did you manage to get those pictures you sent to the FBI in Southern California? Were you following the vehicle those explosives were in?"

"No, just 'luck'. Claire and I were driving back to St. George, and were on the freeway when all 'hell broke loose'. It was quite an experience to be on that road at that particular time."

"Were you driving that Subaru?" Dan asked.

"No, we were in Claire's car, and it was damaged."

"I saw you and Claire at the animal clinic. The car she drove into the parking lot looked new."

"Almost new. We just picked it up from the dealer." Mac grinned.

Dan settled down on the sofa. "Now let's get on to the reason why I hunted you down. I want to know what happened to you and why you didn't 'come in'." Dan Frowned.

"I suppose you thought of me a 'mole'. One of the reasons why Claire and I drove back to Costa Mesa was to visit Theo. There, we met his daughter. Her name is Mira Marcosa. First of all she was wearing

Muslim garb. Second she is the reason that Theo tipped off the 'Sons of Allah', about the Vegas raid on the warehouse. She had married a Muslim guy while in college, and ended up a 'captive' in Syria. Her husband was most likely in the vehicle that exploded. She warned Claire and me about him. His name is or was Khalid."

Dan raised his eyebrows. "I knew you'd have some information we didn't. But I want to know what happened to you. Where have you been for over six weeks? Well I surmised you've been with Claire Talbot. How did you meet her?"

Mac frowned down at the floor, but then raised his eyes. "I'll tell you what I remember, but it would be better hearing the whole story from Claire. When we 'hit the warehouse in 'Vegas I ran upstairs to grab the computer. Someone shot at me, hit me on the back of my head. The next thing I remember was waking up in Clare's clinic basement, sort of shackled to a sofa bed, listening to feminine voices and dogs barking.

She found some old clothes for me, and took me to this house and took care of me. I was pretty sick for two to three weeks, and at that time couldn't even remember my name. But as I began to feel better, I started to remember some details about my life. Anyway she had help from one of her friends. Claire's an amazing girl, and we are - - - - -close." Mac smiled and glanced down at his empty coffee mug.

CHAPTER TWENTY-NINE

"HEY, WOULD YOU like some coffee?" He gazed over at Dan's frown.

"Sure." Dan blinked as if had been in deep thought. He followed Mac into the kitchen. For a few minutes they sat in the curved booth and sipped the brew. "I noticed you have a computer in that room we passed. I know you are known for your expertise with the internet. These terrorists must have taken you to some sort of 'safe house', before they dumped you, what, here in St. George? Is it possible that you would recognize it, if we found it?"

Mac shrugged. "I don't know. What are you thinking?"

"Can you break into the Clark County, Nevada records of property abandoned or sold for taxes?"

"Possibly. Let's find out." Mac sat down at the computer and began to type, opening up various screens. He turned to Dan. "You live in 'Vegas. Think of a password."

They tried various passwords, until Dan said. "Try something about old, abandoned, taxes, empty."

Finally Mac tried: 'CCmoneylost/2018'. The screen changed and a list of properties sold in the last quarter of the year came up. "Where is West Mountain road?"

"That is a road about 15 miles north of Las Vegas. It leads up into the mountains to the west of the city. There can be some snow up there in the winter and it gets pretty cold. There are a few old cabins, and really old houses up there."

"Okay." Mac said and began scrolling down lists of properties asking only the amount of back taxes to own the piece of land. "Here's one. 10.2 miles west from I-15 north. Sold to J.A Sutherland for $8,460. How about this one? Well, what do you know? Someone named J. A. Sutherland had some other charges on certain items I found."

Dan jumped up and peered over Mac's shoulder. "You can tell me about those other activities on the account later. This property you found is a possibility. I'm going to call Strickland. He'll want to know that I've found you and this possible safe house."

Thursday morning Jeremy drove around in a better neighborhood, just getting a feel for the Las Vegas most people never see. He came to a corner lot, and on it sat a middle class, single family house, where a white Jeep Grand Cherokee was parked. A sign sat on the windshield. 2013, Jeep, four wheel drive. 52,000 miles. Must sacrifice. $11,500. Jeremy studied it. "Hmm."

He glanced down at his old worn jeans, and he knew his hair needed a good cut. He wrote down the address and phone number and drove away. *That could be a good car for a number of reasons. Especially, if we need to buy and transport bomb making materials.* He drove back to the apartment and unloaded the groceries he had purchased.

He had watched the morning news, there was mention of the explosion site in California and how the FBI was still working there. He had a strong hunch that Zuhdi's comrades had 'gone up in smoke' along with the plastic explosives and bomb components, they were supposed to deliver/

As he put away the food and a cheap set of dishes he had purchased, Jeremy figured they needed them. He had seen them for 'sale' at the supermarket. They were wasting money on paper plates. If these guys were going to carry out their 'mission' he would have get on the computer and find some bomb constructing information. *We'll need at least 19 grand for the car and for the bomb components. I'll call Colson tonight.* Jeremy mused.

-------------·•◆◆◆•·-------------

Later on that evening Jeremy called Colson on his private house line.

When the professor picked up Jeremy said. "Professor Colson, I noticed that you have an account in the name of J.A. Sutherland. The guys and I are in need of another car. The Mercedes has been recognized by the authorities, and we need to hide it. We could use about $25,000 in the Sutherland account."

"Twenty thousand! What are you planning to buy a Cadillac?" Colson choked.

"No. The car I've picked out is much more modest than that. They *need supplies* for their mission.

I've shopped around and found one. We'll take the Mercedes up to the 'safe' house and hide it. Also I am doing the cooking, and we bought a TV. "Have to have a TV to keep up with the changes in the world. Thanks for your involvement, Professor. Good bye."

The 'good' professor stood in his den in his lovely home and shook with fear. *How did I come to be involved with these terrorists? When I started out to help the Middle Eastern people it was to enlighten them. I'll put twenty-five thousand in the Sutherland account, and be done with it.* But he knew where the large amounts of the money came from: *The mortal enemies of the United States.*

Thursday afternoon Velois called another meeting of all those involved in the car explosion investigation. They all sat down in the conference room.

"Okay people what have you 'uncovered' so far?" Velois asked. There were a few chuckles at the word 'uncovered'.

Mike Shaw, who was heading the investigation, had a stack of paperwork by his place at the table. "We've found DNA of three separate individuals all showing North African ethnic groupings. We found them on databases through Kodex, Interpol, and even domestic sources. For example, Khalid Marcosa, we found on a U.S source, because he had been a student at UC Berkley. He was in California for four years, until 2018. While here, he married a U.S citizen Mira Kastanis, Theo Kastanis' daughter. There was a divorce a few months ago, and Mira was allowed to immigrate to Italy. She managed to return to the U.S 3 weeks ago."

"That's substantial proof then, that Theo was the 'mole'. He still resides at a care center in Anaheim. Jeri and Ken have been visiting him." Velois said.

Jason Garn spoke up. "Then MacCandlass is innocent and a free agent. Do you have any idea where he is and what he is up to?"

"Strickland in 'Vegas sent Dan Forester to find him. And if anyone can find him, it will be Dan. Let's get back to the evidence. Go ahead Michael."

"On a section of the dashboard we recovered a set of finger prints. They belonged to Abdul Rasheem, a Syrian. The DNA from a partial foot in a boot was from Hassam, no authentic last name. He listed Jonas as a last name. He had been picked up for speeding in Alberta, Canada a few weeks ago. Somehow he obtained a Canadian passport." Michael said.

"We're sure the explosives were meant for Las Vegas. We have found several e-mails mentioning people in that city would suffer loss and sadness at the time of the Christmas Holidays. I would imagine terrorists' time table has changed.

The four remaining cell members probably are already employed in or near the place they have chosen to plant bombs. Knowing how they love a flair for the dramatic. They would have picked an American Holiday such as Christmas or New Years as their target day. Now that their bomb materials have 'gone up in smoke', they must find other ways to cause chaos. We still have much evidence to examine." Michael Shaw said. "We'll get back again tomorrow."

"Thank you for all your hard work." Velois said. The group filed out of the conference room and went back to their work areas.

Late that afternoon, Suzanne called Claire at the animal clinic. "How are things between you and JD?" She asked.

"We're fine. Why do you ask?" Claire said. Somehow she knew Suzy would say something to irritate her.

"Well,- - - -the reason why I called is that Mary Ellen Frawley called my mother to tell her that you and JD came into the Honda dealership, and you two left with a late model car. And that JD paid 'cash' for it."

Claire closed her eyes, and touched her head. Already she was ripe for a migraine. "Can we meet and talk about this, not on any phone."

"You can tell me now. None of my *clients* can hear what I say, or whatever you tell me, for that matter." Suzanne said. "I'll share a secret with you. Will that work?"

"Okay, I'm all ears." Claire began to giggle.

"Andy and I are going back together. He found a larger apartment in the same complex he now lives in, and offered the smaller apartment to JD. Apparently my husband and your boyfriend are investigating some crime together. One more little question before I hang up and, you rush home to your 'significant other'. Where did JD get the money to buy the car?"

"He had three paychecks from his work place he hadn't cashed, and he's been living with me and not paying for any rent, so - - - - -." Claire hoped that sounded even remotely plausible.

"The short answer is that he has a source of cash." Suzanne said. "I'll support that premise, Bye." The line went dead.

When Claire arrived home she found Mac had a guest. "Claire, this is Dan Forester. He is FBI from the Las Vegas offices."

Claire studied this man, tall, strong, and obviously someone who 'worked out' He had short brown hair and brown eyes, and he was someone from Mac's past. "It's good to meet you. Have you come to recruit Mac back into the "Vegas office?" She asked.

"No, not yet, I've come to pick his brain, and speak to you about how you and your friend rescued this guy you refer to as JD." As he gazed at her, she felt as if she were in a room with a very skilled interrogator.

"I think we all should sit down and eat some supper, first." Mac said. "I called *Superior Pizza,* and the pizza will be ready in 20 minutes0-. We could start with a salad. Is that okay with you, Claire?"

Claire stared at these two guys, and nodded. "Let me go change, and I'll see what we have in the fridge." She dashed upstairs; slipped out of the scrubs she wore to work, and pulled on some old jeans and red sweater.

Down stairs, Mac had pulled out salad makings from the refrigerator and a large glass bowl from the cupboard.

"You seem familiar with this kitchen, Mac. Do you cook, too?" Dan asked humor in his voice.

"Claire worked, and for some weeks I didn't. Sometimes I would start dinner." Mac said, and began to cut up vegetables for salad. He glanced at the clock hooked to the wall above bay window.

CHAPTER THIRTY

———— ♦♦♦♦♦♦♦ ————

"I'D BETTER GO get the pizza. Do you want to ride with me?" He asked Dan.

"No. I think I'll talk to Claire."

Claire walked into the kitchen, and began to take out plates and bowls from the cupboard. "May I offer you something to drink, Agent Forester?" She offered sodas, low calorie juices, and milk.

"No beer?" He asked and grinned.

"I don't usually buy it." She answered, shaking her head.

"I'll take a Dr. Pepper." He watched as she filled two large glasses with ice and poured Dr. Pepper in one and Diet Coke in the other. "While Mac is picking up the pizza, would you sit down and tell me how you and your friend found him."

Claire sat down across from Dan and took a sip of her drink. "I own an animal hospital. I was working late one Saturday evening, when my friend Suzanne, a Medical Examiner in training or MTE, called me. She asked me to come over and take a look and one of her 'clients'. I asked her why I should come and look at a dead individual, and she said, and I quote. "Don't think he's dead."

"So I drove over to the hospital and the 'undead' individual was Mac. He was in bad shape, He, I'm sure now, had a severe concussion, a bullet had grazed his left shoulder, burns on his arms, and he was very cold. We smuggled him out and took him over to my clinic and put him in the basement."

"Why your clinic, why not this house?" Dan asked.

"Because I had IV bags, a place to put him, and a heater to warm him at the clinic. Some medications that work on dogs, work for humans, too."

"Why not take him to the hospital?"

"Because he rose up and told Suzanne, *'no hospital'*. That's why she called me in the first place."

"So where did you think he came from?" Dan asked.

"Las Vegas. We thought he was a 'wise guy', or a victim of a hit. But then when he woke up, he couldn't remember anything. And about a week later he came down with pneumonia. And I suspected he would."

"Why would you suspect that?" Dan asked.

"Physical and emotional trauma, he suffered." Claire said calmly.

"So as you took care of him, you two 'bonded'?" Dan asked.

"He was sweet and started fixing things around the house. Her voice rose, and she smiled. "And then he began remembering technical things." *I'll let Mac tell Dan about our trip to Cedar City, if he chooses to.*

They both could hear Mac's car drive onto the gravel driveway outside the kitchen door, and stopped talking.

Mac came in with the extra-large pizza, and set it in the middle of the table. He pulled out his new cell phone and continued to talk. "Excuse me, I'll finish this conversation in a minute." A few minutes later he came back and sat down. He glanced at Dan and Claire. "Did you get the story of my rise from the 'ashes'?" Mac stared at Dan.

"Pretty much. The pizza smells great. Do we use these plates, Claire?" Dan opened the large box and took a giant slice.

Dan left about 9 p.m.. He had booked a motel in St. George, and needed to check in. Mac and Claire sat in the den and turned on the evening newscast.

"The phone call I had when I came in, was from Andy." Mac said. "He's changed apartments in his complex and offered me the one he has been living in. "It's semi-furnished, but it only has a queen, not a king sized bed. I think we'll need another king bed to be comfortable, don't you?" He picked up Claire's hand and kissed it.

"You mean there'll be room for me to come down on weekends?" Claire said.

"Well, Suzanne is going to come down some weekends. And I thought- - - - -." Mac shrugged.

"Why are you moving down- - - - -? Okay, I see. You and Dan and the LVPD are going to chase terrorists. Well, Suzy and I will come down, we'll help too."

"I don't want you to become involved. These guys are killers. Think about what could have happened if those three terrorists had made it to Las Vegas with the plastic explosives. Dan and I and some of the police must be super aware of things that don't add up. I'll miss you, and I thought I'd find some furniture to make the apartment more comfortable."

"You forget. I am involved. The minute Suzy and I put you into my animal clinic van, I became involved. Besides I own a gun. I'll just have to go to the gun range and practice."

"You own a weapon? What is it, and where is it?" Mac scowled.

"It's a 3.8 Glock. And I keep it in the sanitary napkin box in my bathroom."

Mac tilted his head and grinned. "Clever, no guy would ever think to look there. Maybe I'll take you to the gun range, and see how well you shoot. I need the practice, too."

"There's a big gun show this weekend at the Dixie Center. We could drive down there, and perhaps you could pick up a weapon of your own." She smiled.

"Good idea. We should get there early, because I should drive down to Las Vegas Sunday afternoon." Mac said and kissed her. "Thanks for being a gracious hostess for Dan Forester. He can sometimes be rather, should I say rude. But when the chips are 'down' he is a very skilled and cool headed man to have on your side."

Mac touched Claire's shoulder. "Are you ready to go to bed? Because, I am." He pulled her to her feet, and kissed her.

"That was a hint? Okay, turn down the heat and lock the door. I'll meet you upstairs."

Thursday evening Zuhdi decided to contact the embedded terrorist cell in California. They explained to him that they had delivered the needed 'items' to Kahlid and the other two comrades on last Sunday morning. That cell had also concluded that Kahlid and his two companions had been the victims of the car crash in California. "Is there no other materials you can send us?" Zuhdi begged.

"No, we must wait for another shipment, and that could take months." One of the nameless men suggested "To carry out your mission, you must improvise."

"We have an American we are sheltering with us. He is talented with computers. He thinks we can find alternative explosive 'recipes' on line." Zuhdi said.

"Then see what he can find, and 'Allah be with you'." The conversation ended.

Zuhdi sat down with Jeremy. "Do you think you can find information about bomb making on the computer?"

"Yes, there are all kinds of crazy websites. You just have to find out who posted them. Most of their 'recipes' use easy to find' materials. It's just the 'how' we must find. I fact, if you could lay your hands on some plutonium, and other special materials. Of course, if you had the expertise, you could build a nuclear device. All of that would take time and money, which we don't have, and I don't really recommend." Jeremy answered.

"Colson controls the money." Jahreal said.

Jeremy feigned surprise. "Really? I'll give him a call. Meanwhile, when do you guys get paid?" Jeremy asked. "What we need is a budget. We must buy another car and food and purchase our *special* materials. I believe I'll shop for the car tomorrow, and Saturday we can shop for 'ingredients' It's a good time, because it will be busy, and no one will give us the any particular notice. Now, what's the plan? Where are these bombs going to be placed?"

"In the shared basement of the three hotels, where we are now employed. Possibly even up on the floors with hotel rooms, put some bombs on those floors, also." Aukmed said. "Think of the destruction."

He smiled and threw up his arms

It was Monday evening and Claire had closed the clinic an hour earlier. She wasn't in any hurry to go home, because Mac had gone to Las Vegas that morning to move into the apartment that Andy had moved from. He decided to take up residence there until the terrorist threat was vanquished. Already she missed Mac, and wouldn't see him until Saturday.

Right now Claire was engrossed in a human anatomy text book. She was studying those areas of the human body most vulnerable to attack. Places where a karate chop, or a bullet would do the most damage. Mac had showed her some areas of where a squeeze, a pinch, or a up word blow would render an individual helpless, at least a few seconds or even longer. Of course, he was describing hand to hand combat. Though she was tall, and in good physical condition, she would quickly lose any advantage against any well trained man.

Just then the clinic phone jangled. *Maybe it's Mac. He may have forgotten something essential to his existence in the Las Vegas apartment.* "Hello?"

"Claire is that you? Of course it is." Her mother answered her own question.

"Hi Mom, how's the pacific coast."

"Oh, rainy, chilly, but not too bad. But a weather report is not why I called."

"Okay, then why did you call?" Claire heard an edge in her own voice, and tried to soften it.

"Now dear, must I have to have a reason to check up on my own daughter? How are you getting along being the owner of the clinic?"

"Fine we're better than breaking even. I can't ask for much more, since we've been open about two months. I have a vet coming in three days a week, and three reliable employees." Claire said.

"Well dear, I had a very strange phone call from Sally Bradshaw. So I needed to talk to you."

"Sally, that bitch." Claire mumbled.

"What did you say, dear? Actually, what I'd like to know. Who is this man that you have taken in? The man who is now living in our house?" Her mother's voice rose into a whine.

Claire grimaced, and phone in hand, walked out of her office. She ran her hand through her hair, and went to the counter when she kept the coffee pot. Mindlessly she poured the last of the cold coffee into a cup. "He's a - - - - - - - - friend. Okay, a boyfriend. Besides, it isn't *your* house, it's mine. I've been making payments to the bank for over two years. So why are fussing about me finally in a romantic relationship?"

"Well, I am glad you finally have a boyfriend, but where did he come from?" And why is he living in our house?" What does he do?"

Mom, if I told you where he came from you'd never believe it. You see mom, I found him in the morgue. Claire's temper spiked into the danger zone, along with her blood pressure. "Who's house it it mother? My house, mine. You were paid by the bank, when I assumed the loan. I have not missed a payment."

"I'm sorry I've upset you, dear. I was just concerned, that's all."

"Don't be." Claire took an audible breath. "Mom, his name is Jonathan. Jonathan David Mackay. He's thirty-four years old and from Kansas. He works for a security firm. He's also an independent investor. Right now he's out of town. When he's here with me, he also cooks, and he even fixed the kitchen door. Right now I'm in the process of locking up the clinic and going home, I'll talk to you later. Bye." Claire returned the phone to her office and grabbed her coat, purse and keys, hit the security lights and walked out the back door locking it carefully. Once she was in her 'new' car, she rested her head against the steering wheel. Talking to her mother always gave her a major headache.

CHAPTER THIRTY-ONE

——— ✦✦✦✦✦✦ ———

M ONDAY EVENING WHEN Jeremy knocked on the door of the house where the Jeep was parked, he met an older woman. She was nicely dressed, but seemed tired or unhappy.

He had bought an outfit of slacks, blue shirt and a leather jacket. He also had Jahreal trim his hair. "Excuse me ma'am, I've driven by your house two or possibly three times and would like to know more about the Jeep Grand Cherokee you have for sale outside?"

"Oh yes, that is actually was my husband's car. He is in the hospital right now, and will be for a while." She took a deep breath and glanced away. "I'm going to need the money from the sale of that car."

"I understand. When I was younger, my mother had to sell our car really fast. My roommate, Jay, he's out in the old car we are driving. We're just looking for something else better to drive to UNLV and travel home for the Holidays. I'm J. A. Sutherland, and I have credit in my account up to one thousand dollars right now. How much would you take for the car? How about, $10,500?"

"I'm Patricia Flake. If you bring me the $1,000, tomorrow, and the rest in the amount of, $12,500. On Wednesday evening, I'll sign over the title to you." She gazed at Jeremy. "What are you studying at UNLV?"

"Computer Science. It's the way the world now communicates. We need to keep up." Jeremy flashed a wide smile.

"Okay, J. A. Sutherland. See you tomorrow." Patricia said and closed the door.

Jeremy climbed back into the Mercedes. *Right now I'm going back to all my roommates, and about four a.m. Jahreal and I are going to check out the construction site I found.*

++++++

Jeremy decided to take Jahreal with him, because he knew the young man would follow orders and work quietly and quickly. They left the other guys sleeping and climbed into the old Mercedes.

The padlock on the gate and fence surrounding the building site gave Jeremy little trouble. They broke into the construction trailer and took blasting caps, wiring, and a box of dynamite and loaded it in the rear of the Mercedes.

Jahreal eased the car down the dirt road while Jeremy broke into the filing cabinet in the trailer. He had trouble picking the lock and was forced to take off his glove to get a better hold on his tool. To his surprise, he found $1,500 in cash in the drawer. He shut the drawer, locked the cabinet, but dropped his glove and had to search around in the dark for it. Once in the car, the two young men didn't bother to take the nights' 'booty' into the apartment, but threw an old blanket over it. Reason? Jeremy and Jahreal had felt that the apartment was too dangerous a place to 'work' on the bombs. They decided it was much better to transport the 'materials' up to the 'safe house'. It was the best place to work. No one would bother them. The group would take the 'materials' up as soon as Jeremy bought the Cherokee.

They two young criminals returned to the apartment, crept off to bed and slept soundly until the light came in through the cheap beige drapes to wake them.

The next morning the Sons of Allah stood around and watched Jeremy make eggs, and place them on bagels with cheese for breakfast. Even Zuhdi, who was usually 'out of sorts' appreciated Jeremy's efforts to feed and clean for the Sons of Allah. Jahreal brought up the dangers of working on the bombs in the apartment. "We really need a safe place to work. Jeremy and I think we should go up to the safe house and work there. Let's go up there and take a look. We have that large table and the bedrooms to hide the materials. Besides Jeremy is going to purchase a car for us, and we can leave the Mercedes up there in the shed."

"Where must we go to find these bomb materials?" Ali asked.

"The local hardware store." Jeremy laughed. "Friday or Saturday is a good time to go. Because it soon will be Christmas, and those stores stock Christmas trees and other decorations. We Americans like to brighten up and decorate our houses this time of year. No one will pay us much attention, to a bunch of guys buying fertilizer, electrical components, and other combustibles."

"Good. Let us make a plan for things we need to take to the safe house. We'll leave as soon as you pick us up from the hotel parking area." Zuhdi said.

"Okay, Jeremy said. "I'll make a list. After all, if we work up there, we have to be comfortable."

That afternoon, Mac sat at the small kitchen table in his new apartment with his computer. But his mind was not on his work. He sat there watching the sun go down through the sliding glass doors. Those doors led to a small deck. The apartment management advertised that each apartment had a 'roomy' private deck and a small gas fireplace.

Mac missed Claire. Being away from her was becoming more and more difficult. He realized he was truly 'in love' with her. The thought of being with her forever, even marrying her shocked him. He never before thought of another human being the way he thought and felt about her.

When he glanced at his wrist watch, he was reminded that she had taken him shopping, and he supposed, she more or less picked the watch out for him.

She would drive down Saturday, but today was only Thursday. Suddenly the doorbell rang. Through the side light next to the front door he could see Dan Forester.

Mac flipped the chain lock on the front door and opened it. "Come in Agent Forester."

Dan strolled in, stood and looked around. "Why didn't you tell me you had moved down here? And why the alias? Why didn't you rent the apartment in your own name?"

"I spoke with Director Velois, and since the Sons of Allah think they have killed me, Velois decided I should keep the alias. If we're going to hunt for the four terrorists who kidnapped me, and even Strickland thinks they are here in 'Vegas, I need to stay hidden."

"Okay, V. L, my boss thinks they are here in Vegas, too. But since the explosion in the desert in California, the terrorists have lost their major source of explosive materials. And since you have a functioning alias, I suppose staying JD Mackay is good for now. Have you come up with anything else?" Dan asked.

"Not really." Mac said.

"We think they have jobs. This time of year thousands part-time people are employed in this town. We believe they have sought work near their destruction target. It's like seeking four needles in countless haystacks.

This is off the subject, but I have to say that getting rid of the red hair and wearing those shaded glasses certainly helps you look less conspicuous. But on to a related subject, we just heard about another 'fly in the ointment'." Dan said.

"We received a report from Director Hafen in the bay area. They have been watching a Professor G. Colson He had a 'gofer' named Jeremy Ardmore. This guy has dropped off the radar. The one thing that may be pertinent about Jeremy's disappearance is that Colson rented a truck a week ago. He drove it to Las Vegas, then turned around and drove back to his teaching job taking a Monday off. A girl who is FBI and a 'plant', is now teaching Jeremy Ardmore's course on Middle Eastern religion and lifestyle." Dan said.

"We need to talk with Andy Freeman. He's an officer with the North Las Vegas PD. He told me about a guy who rented a motel room and disappeared. They found blood stains and the police think there was a possible surgery that took place in the guy's room. I'll give Andy a call right now."

Mac called Andy, and asked him to bring the report about Jeremy Ardmore. "You should meet Dan Forester." Mac glanced over at Dan. "He's with FBI and working on the Sons of Allah case."

"Why don't you bring him up to *Lil's* and we'll grab some dinner. Then we can discuss this situation. I wonder if this Jeremy Ardmore is still in "Vegas?" Andy said.

The three of them met for dinner, and after they had eaten, Andy pushed a large manila envelope toward Dan and Mac.

"This is the latest we have on this Jeremy Ardmore. We have tied him to the shooting in Cedar City, Utah at the university up there. The police there think that he was wounded when he left the Biology Building. Somehow he managed to drive, or was driven to the King of Cards motel. He left bloody sheets and towels, and there was evidence that someone did surgery, possibly on this Ardmore guy. We speculate that he had friends in Las Vegas. He has not returned to the Bay Area in California."

Dan picked up the paperwork. "It says he was working on a masters' degree in computer science. His knowledge and skill with computers would make him useful to any number of criminal types."

"What about this Professor Colson? Are they planning to 'move' on him?" Mac asked.

"That's up to Director Hafen. They believe that he controls at least two of the shore accounts with upwards of a million bucks in one of them." Dan said.

"Interesting." Mac said blandly. "Who managed to hack the accounts?"

"Some computer geek, who works for the Bay Area, FBI." Dan said. "Oh I see that gleam in your eye, Mac. Now you're going to go back to your computer and see what you can find."

"I could give it a try?" Mac shrugged.

"Thank you for this information, Officer Freeman. We'll put this Jeremy Ardmore on out local 'hunt and bring in' list." Dan said.

When Dan and Mac returned to Mac's 'new' apartment, Dan said "I've got to be in court for at least two maybe three days, testifying on a fraud case. I'll fly back to Las Vegas Monday afternoon. Would you be ready to drive up to the mountain and find the old house we checked on and found it on the 'sold' list in Clark County. We should get up there no later than Monday evening." Dan suggested.

Claire sat in her airless little office, with books stacked on her scarred oak desk and studied another anatomy text book. There was no sense hurrying home, because Mac was in Las Vegas. What was there to go home to? The office phone began to jingle. "Southern Dixie Animal Hospital, how may I help you?"

"Claire, when did you get back from 'Vegas?" Suzanne asked.

"About 10 p.m. last night. How about you?"

"Somewhat earlier than that, because I came home to put Justin to bed. I have a question?"

"Okay, about what, exactly?" Claire said.

"Do you still have that little Glock hand gun; you showed me a couple of years ago?"

"Yes, why do you ask?" Claire frowned at the wall and played with a pen.

"Would you like to go for some target practice?" There's a new indoor shooting range, 'just opened Saturday. It's down River Road about 3 miles south."

"When do you want to go?" Claire asked.

"Tonight. I'm working days this week. I'm finished with my shift in twenty minutes." Suzanne said.

"Can you wait another half hour?" I have to go home to pick up my weapon." She whispered, because one of her employees was doing the cleanup.

"Sure, I'll call in for a reservation, and maybe we can pick up some dinner afterward." Suzanne said.

"So you're all for sharpening your and my skills. What weapon do you have anyway?"

"One Andy bought for me about two years ago. You know the situation, the guys are working on, and as I told Andy last night we *are* also involved. They may not approve, but those are the facts, ma'am. Personally, I rather like it." Claire heard a little hitch of excitement in Suzanne's voice.

CHAPTER THIRTY-TWO

———— ✦✦✦✦✦✦ ————

THEY MET AT the gun range, and Suzanne took out a .32 caliber revolver.

"How long have you had that gun?" Claire asked.

"Andy bought it for me when I was working nights at the morgue, and he worked for the sheriff's department here in St. George. How about you? How long have you had that little gun?"

Claire laid the small weapon on the counter in front of the target. "Neil bought it for me, because he worried about me closing up alone, and taking the cash to the night drop at the bank."

"Well let's get to it." Suzanne said, pulled up the target, and set the headphones working them over her mass of curly, blond hair. She hit the lever on the target, sending it down the long tunnel. She stood, and picked up the gun, took aim and fired.

Claire did much the same, checking the target, sighting, firing and checking how well she hit her target.

A half-hour later, Suzanne pulled off her headphones. "That wasn't half bad. Besides, my hand is tired." She set the revolver in its case and shook out her right hand.

"You're a wimp." Claire laughed. "Try lifting an angry dog from the bathing tub and doing that several time a week. You're hands get strong pretty quickly."

"Well, I turn my 'clients' over and examine them every time I work, and pick up forty pound Justin at home."

"In not too many years, Justin will be lifting you. You ready to go? How about *Cafe Rio?* "

As they were eating chicken salads, Claire stopped chewing and turned to her friend. "Have you done any Christmas shopping yet?" What about a tree? Have you decorated it yet?"

"Mom did the tree over the weekend, with Justin's *help*, of course. I heard lots of whining from both of them, because I wasn't there to help."

"Have you discussed your plans of moving in with Andy after Christmas Day with your mother?" Claire asked and studied Suzanne's face.

"Well, not exactly." Suddenly it took all of Suzanne's focus was to 'fish' an olive from her salad. She glanced up. "It's just that she never leaves the subject alone. You know the litany. Las Vegas' AKA, 'sin city' It's a wicked place. It pollutes anyone or anything that goes near it. It will ruin Justin, and he will be a *Juvie at the age of 10."* Suzanne sighed. "I'll come up with a plan. Maybe I'll run it by you. Do you want to meet later on this week? Here, I mean."

"How about Wednesday? Only earlier. Then we can 'run' by the outlets afterward. Christmas is the end of next week. I already sent a Christmas basket to my parents." Claire said.

"Sounds like a plan, because I want to drive down to Las Vegas Friday evening. For an extra night with the 'big guy' in his new bed." Suzanne tilted her head and gave Claire a 'knowing' glance. "Speaking of plans, what does the future hold for you and JD?"

"Well- - - - - - -." Claire's cheeks took on a rosy hue. "He proposed, and wants to take me diamond ring shopping, but lots of plans have to take place before we could get married. It has to be after the terrorist 'caper' is resolved as JD calls it. He now has partnered up with a guy from the Las Vegas FBI office. Meanwhile, you and I need to keep practicing, and not ever be a burden on the guys. That's my plan."

Mac and Dan decided to hunt for the terrorists' 'safe house'. As they drove, clouds blanketed the western sky. The higher in elevation they traveled, the thicker the fog. The road was rutted, and even though Mac drove slowly and carefully, there were dips and pot holes to navigate.

"I'm glad you offered to drive up here. My Mustang would have bottomed out around the last turn." Dan said.

"Yeah, it is rough terrain especially that last 'bump and twist'. There's evidence of some run-off. Hang on, I have to pick our way up this last turn." They bounced and tipped but finally came to the top of a hill. "For a second, the headlights picked up some sort of dwelling." Mac said. He eased his SUV around the side of a ramshackle house, and killed the engine. He reached under the seat for a lock picking kit.

Dan glanced at the kit in Mac's hand. "I see you came prepared, but then so did I." He grinned and pulled out a similar kit. As he climbed out of the car, he checked his shoulder holster for his weapon. He pulled on a set of latex gloves from his pocket and handed another set to Mac.

Mac pulled on the gloves and walked up the sagging porch to the front door, and found a new padlock on it. "Look at this, a shiny new lock." He set to work picking the lock.

They both entered the house, armed with flashlights. "Well what do we have here?" Dan said.

"Looks like fertilizer, blasting caps, wiring and some liquid substance in these jars." Mac took the lid off one of the jars and took a sniff. "Yep, diesel fuel. They're also collecting shoe boxes, and high end shopping bags."

Dan walked to the second table. "Over here, it looks like they've set up shop."

Mac's eyes narrowed, and he shook his head. "Somebody is directing this operation, someone new to the group."

"Why do you think there's a new member involved?" Dan asked.

Mac carefully scanned the room. He walked over to one of the camp tables and lifted a corner of a newspaper covering it. "The price tag is still on this table."

"Okay, but what is your reasoning about a new guy?" Dan bent down and examined the table.

"When we raided them in California and here in Nevada, there was no organization. They were sleeping on the floor, eating fast food, and they left the trash all over. No tables no chairs. Look, a portable heater." Mac walked into the kitchen. "Here, on the counter, a coffee maker." Mac could hear the humming of the fridge, and opened it. "It has been cleaned out, and there is fresh food in it. Hey, do you want a sandwich or a soda?" It's all here." Mac waved his hand at the contents of the refrigerator.

"You think another 'Sons' has been brought in?" Dan asked.

"Either that or a home grown boy, radicalized. What do you know about a professor at UC Berkley named Colson?" Mac said and walked into the smaller bedroom and opened the closet. "Well, I'l be damned: My Kevlar jacket!"

Dan stomped into the bedroom. "Where did you find that?"

"In here." Mac stood in the smaller bedroom and checked the closet, and watched a rat ran back into a hole in the closet floor.

"I wonder why they missed it? Maybe they're afraid of rats." Dan flashed a smile. "Let's see what else there is?" He walked outside." He turned on his flashlight.

Mac followed, and up a little hill they could see another small structure. "This must be what I must have seen in the headlights. It's a shed of some kind. It has double doors." Mac pulled out his lock picking kit and went to work on another padlock.

Dan opened the doors, and let out an explosive breath. "The Mercedes. Hot damn! We could raid the place, just on the fact that we found their car."

Mac went to the broken taillight. "Yeah, I'm sure there dozens of fingerprints inside. But first we've got to catch them to get a solid case in federal court. Besides, how do we know when they work here? We must find them in the city."

Mac turned his flashlight on something else over in the trees. It looked like something covered with a tarp. "Dan, something is over here, large." Mac continued up into the trees. "It's a car under the tarp."

Dan climbed up. "The tarp is taped down." Dan went to one corner and lifted the cloth. "It's a small, older Honda, gray." Dan pointed his light into the back seat of the car. "Looks like blood stains."

As Dan held up the tarp, Mac glanced into the car. "That car could be the one that kid, Jeremy drove and who had a shoot- out with the guard in Cedar City. We need to talk to Andy Freeman. He told me about a connection between the shooting in Cedar City, and blood stained sheets and towels found in a hotel in 'Vegas. In fact he gave me some paper work."

Dan got out his cell phone and began snapping pictures of the interior of the Honda, and the license plate. "I know its dark, but I hope we'll be able to see something."

"It's raining" Mac said as he held up the tarp. "We'd better cover up this little car, the way it was."

"You're right. We don't want them to know we've found their 'safe house', but bring you jacket." Dan turned and sprinted down the hill to Mac's car.

"I've got to lock up. Be down in a minute." By the time Mac slid into his car, the rain had become a down pour. Mac had to do a tricky turn to maneuver the car back down the hill, and to the more stable road.

Dan watched the wind shield wipers whipping back a forth. "Maybe the weather will defeat the "Son of Allah." They won't be able to get up to their 'safe house'."

The next evening Andy Freeman called Mac. "You want to go get some dinner?"

"Sure. Do you want to go back to *Il's* or try another place?" Mac asked.

"We can meet there in an hour or so. I'm something of interest to run by you." Andy said.

"Do you mind if I bring another guy? His name is Dan Forester and he's FBI."

"Hell, no. Is he investigating the terrorists, too?"

"Aren't we all? We'll see you in an hour."

This time, because of rain and wind, the restaurant was not as busy. The three of them were seated at a large table in the back. After the special for the evening: roast chicken dinner, they sat back. Mac turned to Andy. "What interesting news do you have tonight?"

"Early Thursday morning, Atlas Construction's building site was burgled. It was a B and E. The materials that were stolen: blasting caps, wiring, dynamite and the filing cabinet was broken into. The Forman had left a bank deposit of fifteen hundred, and that was taken, too." Andy said.

"I knew it! They had to get the explosive materials from somewhere." Dan said.

"The most interesting fact that came out of the break-in were fingerprints. One of the perps left a fingerprint or two." Andy sat back with a grim smile on his face.

"Fingerprints. Did the department run them?" Mac asked.

"Yes, and we got a hit, and you'll never believe who they belong to." Andy toyed with a spoon, enjoying both his dinner mates wide eyed expression. "One Jeremy Ardmore, of Las Denis, California, A suspect in the attempted murder of the campus guard at the university in Cedar City."

Dan eye's narrowed, and he seemed lost in thought for a moment. "So our new member of the Son's of Allah *is* home grown. Mac and I found their safe house last night. We could tell there was a new member in the group. What is the connection between Jeremy and the "Sons of Allah? Because this new guy, Jeremy, is 'running the show'."

"How did Jeremy 'hook up' with terrorists?" Andy asked.

"It has to be Colson. Angela Biddaugh, Hafen's plant, is teaching Jeremy's class. Now I know where to search on the computer." Mac said. "I'll run a background on Jeremy."

CHAPTER THIRTY-THREE

———— ✦✦✦✦✦ ————

"**D**O WE HAVE a contact in Iron County, Utah police?" Mac asked.

"Yes, his name and number is in the file I gave you." Andy said. "But, if someone asks, you guys found this all on your own. I didn't tell you anything. However I'd like an update on 'what I didn't share with you two." He sat back and grinned.

"Thanks for the information we didn't get, and you'll be informed of the information I never discovered. How's that?" Mac laughed.

"That's what we get from cooperation between the various policing organizations." Dan rolled his eyes.

Mac spent several hours on a computer search for anything available on Jeremy Ardmore. Finally he found Jeremy's background. He was a kid from a broken home with an abusive father. Yet, he became a computer 'geek' and managed to win a scholarship to UC Berkley and now was in a graduate program.

Professor Geoffrey Colson had to be the link. Jeremy had been his graduate assistant for the past fifteen months. Mac found the account of J. A. Sutherland in a Las Vegas Bank. It showed a withdrawal of fifteen thousand the past week. Also there was a debit to *Home Depot* for $278, plus change, this past weekend.

Mac sat back and studied the two debits from the account which had an influx of funds a week ago for nearly $25,000.U.S. dollars. He guessed the first was for another car, and the second for bomb building materials.

With Jeremy's computer expertise, Mac was sure the kid had found 'recipes' for bomb making on the 'dark web'. Now he knew why Colson had sent Jeremy to the find the computer that Mac had used to hack into the off shore accounts.

So Colson controlled the money in these accounts. Some set of circumstances had caused Jeremy to be careless and clumsy. And the result was a shootout with the Gus the guard in the Bio building. Where were the new funds coming from? That would be the next search on Mac's list. Mac rubbed his burning eyes. He could barely see the computer screen. Time for a break. He shut down his laptop and went for a drink of water. The new bed he had bought looked very inviting. He'd just rest for a while. He flopped on the bed and pulled up the new comforter.

The week whizzed by for Suzanne, Claire, and even for Mac and Andy. Friday evening Suzanne opted to drive to Las Vegas and went to pick up Claire. Along with her overnight bag, Claire shoved a large box in the trunk of Suzanne's car. "What's in the box?" Suzanne asked as she moved items around in the trunk of her car to stabilize the box.

"Christmas decorations. Mac and I have been together for over two months, and yet we know so little about each other. I don't know if he has even celebrated Christmas in the past few years. So, I thought we could go out and find a small tree for the apartment." Claire said.

"That's a very thoughtful thing you're doing and it makes me feel guilty. I should do some sort of Holiday Decorations for Andy's place."

"You've already put up a tree for Andy since he's planning to go home with you for Christmas he'll see it then." Claire said.

"It's my mother's house, and her tree, remember. I still need to do something special for Andy. Do you want to go shopping tomorrow? Oh on another subject. I think the best thing we should do: be spies." She grinned over at Claire and picked up speed on the freeway.

"Spies? How can we be spies?"

"You know, while we are shopping, searching for sales. I know a great group of hotels down the 'strip' a ways. These three hotels share a basement. They have snack bars and restaurants and lots of shops in the common basement. We're just innocent young women with our large hand bags. We can wander around, and just watch for unusual behavior of some of the employees in the place, or even if we go into Home Depot, or a store like that. Of course we have to stop for lunch." Suzanne grinned.

"What about your job at the hospital morgue?" Claire asked.

"I'm taking the week off. And I told you, I'm quitting after the first of the year." Suzanne said.

"Where are you going to work?"

"I got a new job at a hospital close to Andy's precinct. I start January fifteenth."

"Great. What about Justin?" Claire asked.

"There is a school close to the apartments where Andy and now JD live."

"I've been thinking that I should close the clinic the week between Christmas and New Year's. Give my employees a week off." Claire said. "I'll open up on January third. I'll move in with Mac that week between Christmas and New Year's"

"We need black clothing if we are going to do surveillance." Suzanne giggled.

"Oh *sure,* Suzy. You'd better a get a ball cap to hide your blond hair. A large one.' Claire laughed. 'We'll be like that old TV show *Charlie's Angels. We work hard for the preservation of our democratic way of life.* Suzanne chanted. "You think we'll need holsters that hug the back of your waist?"

"Oh, we'll get Kevlar vests, and wear a side arm under our jackets. What do you think Andy and Mac we'll think of our plans?" Claire laughed.

Suzanne shook her head. "Andy will say: *Stay out of it. Or get in the car!* We'll just have to be sneaky until we discover something useful."

"I truly believe that this 'caper' in going to need all of us. All the help they can get." Claire said softly

Saturday morning, after cooking Mac a special breakfast, Claire suggested they go shopping for a Christmas tree.

"Why do we need a Christmas tree?" Mac grumped.

"Simply put, it's the Christmas Season. This little apartment needs some *love*. And the best way to do that is to decorate. I brought a box of decorations, and I want to use them." Claire said. She couldn't understand Mac's attitude? What did he have against decorating for Christmas?

Mac made quick work of the tree shopping. He drove into the first store which advertised live trees. Once they returned to the apartment, Mac did go over to Andy's place and borrow some tools to trim the lower branches, and put the tree into the stand they had purchased.

The door swung open and Mac stomped in carrying the little tree. 'Where do you want to put this thing?" He growled, while brushing bits of tree bark and needles from his suede jacket. "Luckily, Andy had the right tools to fix this tree."

"Over here by the sliding glass door. I moved the table and chairs a little more into the living room."

"Whatever." Mac carried the tree to the place Claire indicated, and set it down on the small rug she had brought from home.

Claire stood and quietly with her eyes closed, counted to ten. "Why are you so unenthusiastic about decorating for Christmas?" She fought to clear the irritation from her voice.

"It's just I haven't had time to be bothered with Christmas trappings lately." Mac dropped into a chair and watched as Claire took a string of lights from the box and began to carefully place each light on a branch. "We never had a tree after my mother died." He spoke so softly, that Claire stopped and turned around to stare at him.

"You've never mentioned your family. When did your mother die?"

"I was in my second year in college. She never said anything to me about being ill, to my Dad nor my sister. Eva just called and told me to come home. I barely made it back for the funeral. I remember it was raining when we drove to the family plot. So unusual for January in Kansas." He mused.

"My poor sister tried to make it nice for my father and me the next year, but it didn't work. My father refused to open the gifts Eva and I bought for him. After dinner I went over to a friend's house and Eva went out with one of her friends. It was tough on her, because she was only eighteen when Mom died." Mac stared down at the beige carpet.

"Oh Mac, I'm so sorry. Sorry for your loss and pain." She walked to him and hugged him. For a moment he was stiff, but then he relaxed and wrapped his arms around her. "What about your sister now? Where is she?"

"Eva is married to a good guy, and they live in Nebraska. I talked to her after she had a baby, about three years ago."

"Do you want to send something to them for Christmas? You could get on that computer and send a fruit basket, or something like that. It's not too late to order a gift of some kind." Claire suggested. "What about your father?" Where is he now?"

"I found a retirement place for him in Lawrence, Kansas. I own the farm and from the rent I receive I pay for his little condo. He's a little forgetful."

"So you want to send him something?"

Mac wiped away tears from his face. "I don't know?" He choked out.

She stroked his face, and stepped back. "Well, think about it."

Mac grabbed up his jacket and swung out of the apartment. Claire understood he had to walk off his pain and perhaps come to terms with this relationship with his family.

She took a tissue from her pocket and blew her nose. For several heartbeats she stared at this little tree, a reminder of her Christmases as a child. She bent down and found another string of lights.

Marla Bunker sat at her computer in the field offices of the FBI in Las Vegas. Dan Forester, her now ex-partner, had given her an assignment. She was calling all the used car lots in the 'Vegas area and inquiring if a Jeremy Ardmore had purchased a car in the past week. And if he did, how did he pay for it? She didn't mind doing routine office work, since she was over seven months' pregnant. Dan had been a good partner, and she understood the threat the 'Sons of Allah' posed to the city.

So far she had come up with nothing. If this guy had purchased a vehicle of some kind, he had not bought anything from the thirteen used car lots, she had already called. There were two more to check. Then she would have to start with those in Henderson.

She stood up and stretched, and knocked off the newspapers, and they scattered to the floor. She had begun looking at the weekend advertisements. Then she had an idea. Maybe this Jeremy, guy had found and bought car from a private owner. Maybe there would be a newspaper from last Sunday around here. She searched, but only found today's and yesterday's papers. She knew where she would find last week's papers, at her house.

Forty minutes later she had driven home, grabbed a snack, gathered up a pile of newspapers and was walking into the FBI offices.

Dan walked in fifteen minutes later. He came into her office and said. "Have you found anything of interest?"

"Well, I decided to look for ads in the newspaper for people selling their cars or trucks privately. What kind of a vehicle should I look for?" She asked Dan.

"Something large. They are going to need to transport bomb making materials."

"Like an SUV?" Marla asked. "Okay I'll look for something roomy." She bit into a granola bar and sipped a cup of tea.

Dan went into his cubicle and began going over the file Andy had given him. Then he called Mac. When Mac picked up he asked. "Have you found anything else on this Jeremy Ardmore?"

"Hang on. I just walked into the apartment. Claire drove it down here last night, and now she's decorating a Christmas tree."

Dan heard bits of conversation. Then Mac said. "Let me pull up the file on Jeremy Ardmore. Okay, basically this is what I found: The Kid is from a broken home, abusive father, left the family when Jeremy was six years old. Mother managed to return to college, and get a nursing degree when J. Ardmore was fifteen. Older sister went to college. Jeremy went to Berkley with full scholarship. The tuition there is ridiculous. He would have never made it without a scholarship. You have to give him credit, he's smart and hardworking. I'll bet he's having fun dragging those 'Sons of Allah' around by their noses."

"So those 'not too bright' terrorists have a new, savvier leader." Dan said. "Right now I have Marla going through the newspaper ads looking for a car or for a truck 'for sale' by a private owner. We'll see what she comes up with. Enjoy your Christmas tree. I'll call later if anything 'pops'."

An hour later, Marla stood up from her desk, stretched and walked around. She then stood over her desk and glanced down at an ad she may have missed. *Grand Cherokee must sacrifice. $13,.500 obo.* Below that, a telephone number. Marla sat down and called: A woman answered.

"Ma'am, have you sold the Grand Cherokee yet?" Marla asked.

"Oh I'm sorry, I sold it nearly a week ago."

"I'm from the newspaper where you placed the ad. May I ask who you sold the car to?"

"Well, I don't know- - - - - - - -."

"Oh, I'm sorry. I don't want to invade your privacy. However, our department wants to make sure our customers are served well." Marla said in her best businesslike tone.

"It was a young college man, very pleasant. And he basically paid me cash."

"I'm glad you were able to sell it. How did he pay you in cash? Check credit, cash?" Marla asked.

"He gave me $1,000 in cash, and then the next day he had a cash credit on the account of J. A. Sutherland. I checked it the next day and the money went straight into my personal account."

"May I ask one more question?"

"What color is the Grand Cherokee?"

"The car is white. And in very good condition for vehicle over seven years old."

"Thank you. Have a pleasant afternoon." Marla dropped the phone on her desk. She grabbed the paper and moved with amazing speed for a woman having a baby in in two months. "Dan." She screamed. "I found the car!"

CHAPTER THIRTY-FOUR

I MMEDIATELY, DAN CALLED Mac. "Marla found the car that Jeremy bought. It's a 2013 White Grand Cherokee. So that's the car we should look for."

"Great. How did he pay for it?" Mac asked.

"With an account at a local bank. The name on the account is J. A. Sutherland. You wouldn't mind, ah- - - -checking on it. You know, make a computer search?"

Mac laughed. "I'll get right on it."

Claire and Suzanne had gone shopping, giving Mac time on his computer and he began a search, not on accounts in local banks, but the one he had originally found on the computer in Cedar City. He knew that Colson controlled the funds for the Sons of Allah, but he wanted to find the original source of the money trail. When Claire breezed in, he was deep into his 'hacking' of those offshore accounts.

She came in lugging sacks, and then went back out and carried in another large parcel. Mac jumped up and held the door open for her.

"What did you buy?" He set one of the grocery sacks on the counter.

"Food and some household items for this place." Claire said, and set down a long package that looked like a broom. She began placing items of food in the refrigerator and other cleaning products under the sink and some in the bathroom. Once she had all her purchases put away, she dropped into a chair. "Shopping the week before Christmas is 'combat duty'." She laughed.

"You wouldn't have any sandwich making materials in all of the food you bought?' Mac asked

"Yes, but I bought something just as good. Suzy and I stopped at a Subway Sandwich Shop. There's one in the front of the supermarket we found. Do you want a Pepsi or a Dr. Pepper?"

"Hang on for a minute. I'm building a file." Mac said. He went back to his computer and pulled up a screen, and then another. Five minutes later he turned to Claire. "You said a Subway? Sounds good, I'll have a Dr. Pepper."

Suzanne, Andy, Mac and Claire went to dinner Sunday afternoon at Il's and then the girls had to return to St. George and their jobs. Andy and Mac decided to drive up to Rawley for Christmas Day and then the four of them would return to Las Vegas the day after Christmas.

Christmas Eve, Suzanne's sister, Karen, her husband, and her children came down to Southern Utah for Christmas. She and her family were staying in Suzanne's mother's house. Since Frieda, the sisters' mother had been invited to Ogden for Thanksgiving, Karen and her husband, Victor and the two children still living at home also came down to Rawley for the Christmas Holidays. Their children, a girl aged fourteen Jennifer, and a ten year old boy, Nathan enjoyed playing with Suzanne's son Justin.

On Christmas Eve, when Andy arrived from Las Vegas there was an angry scene when Frieda opened the door and saw Andy standing on the front porch. "What are you doing here? You are not invited to my house on Christmas!"

"Mom he's my husband. I invited him, and I'm going to Las Vegas tomorrow to live with him in Las Vegas." Suzanne said.

Much to Frieda's consternation, Victor was more than 'thrilled' to have Andy there at the house.

Suzanne and Karen soon had a private discussion in the guest room. "Are you and Andy going to live together in Las Vegas?" Karen asked her sister.

"Yes, I've been going down to visit with him the past two weeks."

"What about Justin?" Karen asked.

"I am enrolling Justin in the elementary school near Andy's apartment, on January 15th. That's the day the second semester begins at that school. I am going back to Las Vegas tomorrow whether Mom likes it or not." Suzanne said, with her hands on her hips.

"Okay, this where I think I can help. My kids would love to take Justin back home with us for the rest of Christmas week. Their school starts on January third. I could drive him back here on the day after New Year's."

"That's quite a bit of driving for you to do. Are you sure you want take him with you?" Suzanne asked.

"Yep, and I'll tell you why. Mom's getting a bit confused about things. Especially the trust Dad put all his worldly good in. I need to spend some time with the trust officers at the bank, and go through the Dad's will and trust. It's going to take a few days to set up some safeguards in the trust so that Mom doesn't get herself into a situation financially she shouldn't."

"Wow, I just thought she had become more irritable than usual. Let me know if I can do something to ease things around here." Suzanne said.

"I think the reason she's so against Andy is that she depends on you for so much. You need to have a good marriage and take Justin with you. Let's see if he would like to come up with us the day after Christmas." Karen said.

"Okay that would be good for everyone in the Freeman family right now." Suzanne hugged her sister.

Claire and Mac spent a quiet Christmas together and Claire's house. Mac went over to the animal hospital with Claire to clean and secure it until Claire decided to reopen it after New Year's.

The four terrorists and Jeremy spent Christmas building bombs, and placing some of them in department store bags and boxes. The plan was to wait and then put them in the bottom of trash containers on New Year's Eve. Their plan was to build each bomb with a timer to go off as close to midnight on that last day of the month as possible.

After working most of the day, the five of them left the 'safe house' and drove back to the apartment. Jeremy fixed a chicken casserole, and made a green salad. Only Jehreal would eat much of the salad, because the rest of them called it 'eating weeds'. Jeremy shook his head. "Don't realize that I only fix food that is good for you?"

Aukmed stood up and laughed. "Jeremy we are all going sacrifice ourselves for the great cause of liberation for our Muslim brothers and sisters. I'm afraid we don't worry about eating healthy food."

"Ah, come on. You guys *are* really serious about doing all this for the liberation of other Muslims? I think you guys just enjoy wreaking havoc around world. Your people are liberated as much as your leaders allow them be. I understand that you want to make everybody honor the Muslim religion. But trying to convert people, especially most women to your faith is impossible. At least not here in America. Our whole way of life is based on freedom. It's part of our DNA." Jeremy frowned and shook his head.

"There are more Muslims that Americans. Don't forget that, Jeremy." Zuhdi said.

"Sheer numbers won't do it. Besides you are forgetting all of Europe, Australia, New Zealand. Canada and South America." Jeremy reminded them.

"One thing you people should understand. When you supress and control half your population. As you do to your women. Only half as much progress happens in your countries. Why so you think America is so wealthy. It's because nearly half of its total wealth is brought into the GNP by women."

Jahreal picked up his dishes and dropped them in the sink. He tilted his head and frowned. "Isn't there a football game we can watch Jeremy?"

"Yes, I suppose there is." Jeremy came around and searched the TV for the channel where there was an NFL game in progress. Aukmed, Ali and Jahreal sat down and began to watch the game. Zuhdi stomped to the bedroom and slammed the door.

As soon as Jeremy cleared up their supper, he sat down with them. When the game stopped for a commercial, the advertisement was for a rock band called *Always Detroit*. The band was booked to play two concerts on Fremont Street. One New Year's Eve, and the second on New Year's Day.

"Hey, Jahreal we could cause a little explosive *experience* on Fremont Street. What do ya think?" Jeremy laughed. "I'll bet we could park in the *King of Cards* underground parking. They'll set the band stand up on the corner close to the zip line."

"What if the weather turns bad, won't they bring them into one of the casinos?"

"That's true. But we could still cause a little 'fireworks' for those outside walking around. Jeremy said. "We wouldn't need more than six smaller explosive units."

"What about the band coming to the Tri-hotel corp. Isn't it a retrospective band playing the music of a famous Eighties Rock group. "What is it called now?' Jeremy asked.

"The group call themselves the *Blacksmith's*. We sometimes hear the music with a voice commercial." Jahreal said.

Aukmed turned to Jeremy. "We would like to watch this game of football. This is something new for us to enjoy. We especially like your commentary on the game."

"Okay. Let's watch the game. But also think about a second location to bring some more *excitement* to Las Vegas for the New Year."

CHAPTER THIRTY-FIVE

————— ✦✦✦✦✦✦ —————

CLAIRE, SUZANNE MAC and Andy all returned to Las Vegas the day after Christmas. Claire and Suzanne went shopping for basic foods. They decided it would be easier to cook for four/ Rather than the girls preparing foods for just two people each evening.

After shopping for meals easy to fix, Claire and Suzanne went down to Fremont Street to watch the crowd and look for anything unusual going on. They found a coffee bar, where an individual could sit inside or outside at umbrella shaded tables. They found the crowd entertaining. Especially since the weather cooperated. It was fairly warm and sunny even on this day in late December. They watched the crowd and now and then glanced at the pictures of the five terrorists, which now included Jeremy. Claire had printed them from Mac's computer and gave a copy to Suzanne.

Next they walked into the casinos of the various gambling parlors and even those with hotels. The Fremont Street area was in an older, actually the original section of the city. There were several older hotels above the gambling casinos, and they walked around those, too. Their afternoon surveillance yielded nothing. But they learned one new piece of evidence from listening to Mac and Andy talk. The terrorist group now had a newer car to travel in: A white, fairly new, Grand Cherokee.

The girls could now search for that model of car, too,

The next day the girls went to the Tri-corp hotels and learned that maintenance was constructing a band stand between two of the three wings of the largest hotel. The area they were working on seemed quite large and would hold several rows of seats plus standing room near the rear of the seating. To reach the concert area, people would have to enter the concert venue from the third floor. A fence would be built around the whole stage and seating. There were only a few hotel rooms on that floor.

They watched the employees on the basement level, and then moved up to the main casino and found a Starbucks to sit by and scan the crowd. After a few hours they grew bored and decided to leave.

The terrorists continued to work at the safe house each evening to create more explosive units.

Jeremy drove them up and kept them alert with coffee and snacks. As he watched and helped, he began to plan for his future. *After Jahreal and I 'plant' the devises on Fremont Street, I'm taking that Grand Cherokee and fleeing the state of Nevada. He already had come up with a new name, and knew where he could buy a new identity. Ah, Las Vegas, city of opportunity.*

The local law enforcement and the FBI quietly began checking hotel parking lots and lists of newly hired employees, searching for the four terrorists. It was a daunting job, and all they could hope for was a break.

Finally, the Las Vegas office decided to raid the safe house that Dan and Mac had found. The raid would be in the early morning hours of December thirty-fist, New Years' Eve. Dan and Mac would lead them up, with a backup of at least three agents. The plan came together more easily that an attack on private property. They were forced to find the history of the ownership of the property that the 'safe house' sat on. Finally Dan and Mac went before a federal judge and managed to get a wide spread warrant. They neglected to tell him that they found the safe house by 'hacking' in to public records.

The LVPD also stepped up their surveillance. Everybody was on edge, especially Mac, Claire, Suzanne and Andy. The tension in the apartments rose, especially when they came together for dinner at one or the other's apartment. There seemed to be a 'fifth' individual at the table. Sometimes, late at night, sex seemed to relieve the tension, and would help Mac to sleep. Yet in the morning, the unsaid words, and the guys' warnings to both Suzanne and Claire were to: *stay out of the situation. Let the guys work it out.*

On December 30th. the girls went back to the Tri-hotel-Corp and were wandering around in the basement. It became close to 4 p.m. and Suzanne had planned to roast a chicken for dinner.

"Let's leave. I can't drink another latte, or I'll stark to 'moo'." Suzanne said.

"Okay let's go. We've noticed staff change shifts at around 3:30 p.m. Maybe we can see something or someone interesting." Claire said and the girls began the long walk out to the parking garage. As Suzanne drove out of the lot, around the corner and into the mid-afternoon traffic, she spotted an old blue Mercedes a few car lengths ahead of them. "The blue Mercedes!' She yelled.

"Can you drive any closer to that old Mercedes?" Claire yelled. "Let's follow it."

Traffic would not cooperate. Suzanne slid over into the right lane when the Mercedes did the same. Suzanne tried calling Andy, but got a busy signal.

"I can see the broken tail light, on the left side." Claire yelled. "I'll call Mac." Finally she speed dialed Mac's phone. The phone rang four times before he picked up "Come on Mac answer!'

He finally answered his phone. "Hi Claire."

"We saw them." Claire yelled into her phone." They're driving the old Mercedes. I saw the broken taillight. There are three of them in the car. We're in line to an exit, they are taking. It's the 295 on ramp. We're behind at least five cars. I'm not sure they are getting on to go east of west."

"Get on driving west, and see if you can catch them." Mac ordered. Claire could hear Mac talking to someone, probably Dan Forester.

"We are going west, but can't see them, damn."

"They could have taken the east ramp." Suzanne said.

"Tell Suzanne to turn around and take the ramp going east. And tell her *not* to get a speeding ticket. If you don't spot them, come back to the apartment." Mac ordered.

"But if we see them we're going to find their apartment." Suzanne yelled.

Suzanne roared up the freeway, but neither Claire nor Suzanne could see the car. After driving over ten miles, Suzanne took the off ramp and picked her way back to the apartment.

⁺⁺◆◆◆⁺⁺

"Okay. Explain to me just what these women saw." Dan said as Mac drove into his parking spot at his and Claire's apartment.

"I believe they were hanging out at the Tri-hotels Corp. When they decided to leave and they spotted the old Mercedes with a broken left tail light, a few cars up ahead. That means that the terrorists are working at the Tri-corp and targeting those hotels, and also most likely the concert tomorrow night." Mac said. "They saw the Mercedes that we located in the shed at the safe house?"

"Why did they go get that car? Unless, they need it because they are targeting both Fremont Street, and The tri-hotel corp.' Dan said.

"The girls said they saw three men in the Mercedes. That means that Jeremy and probably Jahreal are targeting Fremont Street."

Soon, Claire and Suzanne parked the car and slowly dragged their big purses upstairs to Mac and Claire's apartment. Claire reached for the door, but before she could, it was yanked open.

Mac grabbed her arm and propelled her inside. "Just what do you think you're doing?" He yelled in her face.

"Let go of my arm, and I'll tell you." She shook off his hand and met his eyes glare for glare.

"Do you realize what a dangerous game you're playing? These terrorists are killers. KILLERS!"

Dan stood back with a grim smile on his face. "Hello ladies. Would you like a soda or something?"

Claire stomped over to the refrigerator. "I'll get my own soda." She pulled two glasses from the cupboard got some ice and opened a diet coke. She handed one to Suzanne and collapsed on the blue denim sofa.

Suzanne had already dropped into the matching blue chair. "I tried to call Andy, but he didn't answer." She flashed a nervous smile at Dan and took a sip of the drink.

"What's so terrible about doing a little surveillance of our own? What's the harm? We look like empty headed shoppers, and today we spotted them. Now we know where they work." Claire scowled up at Mac.

Mac frowned back but turned to Dan. "You want a soda, too?"

"You got anything stronger? Sure, soda's fine. Meanwhile would you two ladies sit down at the table." Now let's start at the top. Just what have you two seen and where have you been?" Dan asked.

He asked several questions, then asked them again with a slightly different twist. "Now why did you decide that these three men were terrorists?"

Claire reached over and pulled out the mug shots that she and Suzanne had in their purses. She laid them on the table. "We've seen them in the basement of the Tri-corp hotels"

"Where did you get these?" Dan frowned, his face grim.

"From Mac's computer." Claire answered. "He's not the only one to know how to retrieve certain- - - - - -files." Claire said. "There was even a picture of the Mercedes on the computer, too. I studied it." Claire said.

Dan asked more questions. Finally Suzanne said. "Okay, it was the left taillight I noticed. So I followed the car. All these questions have made me hungry. I need to go home and put a chicken in the oven. She picked up her purse, jacket and marched to the door. "I'll call you when dinner is ready." She yelled over her shoulder, and slammed the door with a bang.

"Let her go." Mac said. "She's a very smart woman, and if there is anything she recalls, she'll tell us a dinner."

Claire got up and began picking up the soda cans and glasses from the table.

Dan sat back and called FBI headquarters, and talked for several minutes. He turned to Mac. "Tomorrow, 5 a.m. we are going to raid the 'safe house'. We're meeting at the office at 4:15 a. m. See you in the morning. Get some sleep." He stood and put a hand on Mac's shoulder. "Wear your Kevlar jacket." See you in the A.M." He let himself out.

Two hours later the four of them sat down to a tasty supper. At least Mac *decided* it could be tasty. He ate without thinking. As they sat and ate quietly, it was as if there was the 'elephant' in the room. The fifth guest that was not wanted, yet there he was.

They were tense, each thinking about the activities of tomorrow. Finally Mac and Claire walked back to their apartment. The sunny day had morphed into rolling dark clouds, and a north-west breeze had picked up. It looked as if the last day of year was going out as a 'winter lion'.

Mac could not sleep. He tried not to thrash around and not bother Claire, but finally he got up, grabbed a pillow and blanket from the bed and went to the living room sofa. The only comfort the sofa provided was its length. At least he could stretch out. He worked around to get as comfortable as possible, and finally closed his eyes.

Three hours later he woke up in a sweat. He had been dreaming about being in the safe house, and being tortured by one of the terrorists. Somehow he knew it was Zuhdi. Mac rubbed the scar on the inside of his arm, 'compliments' of the Sons of Allah. He staggered up and glanced at the clock over the kitchen stove. 4:00 a.m. He'd better get a move on.

CHAPTER THIRTY-SIX

———————— ✦✦✦✦✦✦ ————————

A S HE DRESSED quietly in the small walk-in closet, he clearly remembered his dream. In his gut he knew that this whole 'caper' would come down to killing Zuhdi, or being killed by him.

Claire was awakened by Mac, trying to be quiet in the closet, and bumping his head on the door frame. She heard him make coffee, and a soft curse as he spilled some of it on the stove.

She wanted to reassure him, to comfort him, but this was not the time. She knew she must help him, and that would happen tonight.

When Mac walked into FBI headquarters: the team consisting of four other members were strapping on Kevlar vests, loading and checking weapons, dropping those weapons in secure holsters. All this activity seemed so familiar and comfortable, it eased Mac's anxiety.

They traveled in two large black SUV's that the team with Mac and Dan in the lead vehicle. They knew the way, and were in the lead car to guide them up the mountain. In the second car were Carl Davidson, Cynthia Carlton, and Jay Alverez. The three agents in the second car had been doing surveillance for weeks, and were anxious to use all the information they had gathered.

The morning was dark and it had rained most of the night. As they reached road that took up into the western mountains, Mac finally spoke. "When you get close to the house, watch that last curve, Dan. This rain has made the road even worse than before."

"I'm ready for it." Dan said. His driving skills helped him stay on the road as it wound up and around the hill and he pulled his car up to the house. He decided to drive around to the rear of the house. There was a flatter more stable area between some trees. The second vehicle went to the right of the house and managed to wedge between two old hulks of half- dead trees. The car bent some branches and they brushed against the rear doors of the large SUV.

Suddenly the doors of the shed were pushed open and the headlights of the Mercedes were angled down. Dan backed up and spun the SUV in front and across the rutted road, blocking the Mercedes path.

The driver of the Mercedes tried to go around Dan's SUV, but the rear wheels of the old blue car came off the ground and dirt and rocks flew down the embankment. The driver slammed on the brakes and the car fishtailed and began to slide sideways down the hill. The wet ground gave way with dirt and rock which began a landslide down the hill. With the rear end pointing down, the car ground to a halt at an outcropping of rock.

The three agents exited the second. car and eased down the soft ground with weapons drawn. "Stop and get away from the car." Davidson yelled.

The driver's door flew open and the agents watched as the man's foot slipped on what was left of the wet dirt and rock. As the ground gave way, he lost his balance and tumbled down and away from the car. He stopped, tried to stand. Then took a step up the steep hill, but the ground gave way under him, and he fell another ten feet or so. He slowed, but kept sliding down the hill. His head hit rocks and debris until a large boulder stopped him. His now limp body hung against the large rock.

With the engine still running in the Mercedes, it tilted and began to roll. "Everyone get down!" Dan yelled. Quickly the five agents hit the ground, Two or three long seconds of nothing

Mac and Dan, further up the hill stood up near to the old house and watched the terrorist hit the boulder. Then Dan saw smoke coming from the rear of the Mercedes. "Take cover!" He yelled.

The gas tank of the Mercedes exploded. The explosion rocked the car and it continued to roll down the hill until a stand of trees stopped. it. A moment later a series of explosions followed, blowing the Mercedes apart.

The agents lay on the rough, cold ground and held their ears. The noise from blast after blast was deafening. Pieces of metal, plastic, upholstery, and even engine parts flew into the air and began to rain down in a wide arc. First was a huge fireball, and then plumes of smoke went high into the sky, throwing an eerie red glow into the winter dawn.

A hot wind blew across the ground. But then a bolt of lightning flashed in the trees higher up the mountain, followed by a clap of thunder. It was as if 'mother nature' was jealous and wanted to compete with the explosion.

The wet, cold ground seeped into the agent's clothing. and one by one they moved. Dan glanced up, and pulled up on his knees from his spot of wet ground. "Anyone hurt?" He yelled over the din of the falling debris. The agents began to come up on their knees, and pushed up to stand. Cynthia was up and began to brush away the leaves and twigs. Then the guys began to brush away to dirt and debris.

Dan stood, picked up his ball cap and jammed it on his head. He made his way stiffly to the SUV, and searched for his cell phone. He called the crime scene unit and gave them the coordinates of the farm house. He watched as Mac stood up and eased his way to the farm house's front door.

When Mac picked the lock and entered the house, his cell phone was ringing. He heard the voice of his boss V.I Strickland.

"What the hell happened up there? The fireball or whatever exploded is now being broadcast from the NBC affiliate helicopter. They are filming and want to know what is going on."

"It was the terrorists' Mercedes. One of the terrorists drove up here, and the car must have been full of homemade bombs. It slid down the hill, because part of the hill fell away. It hit a boulder, and then the gas tank exploded; The explosion took out the bombs with it." Mac took a deep breath. "Tell them whatever you want." Mac waited a beat.

"There was only one of terrorist's in the car. I guess he was sent on an errand to pick up the explosives they planned to use. The other four are still 'in the wind'. Most likely two of them are at the Tri-corp hotels waiting for the bombs that just went up in smoke. Two of them are probably at, or heading for Fremont Street and could have their own explosives devices with them."

"Someone needs to check on the perp." Cynthia yelled. "Never mind I'll try to get over there." She interrupted Mac's phone call from his boss.

"I'll do it." Davidson yelled back."

"Be careful where you put your feet. There may be some stuff ready to explode." She yelled.

A few minutes later Davidson called out. "This guy needs the morgue wagon."

Dan, Mac and Alverez surveyed the interior of the house. "It looks like they finished their projects." Mac said as he opened the fridge. "The fridge is nearly empty."

Dan walked into the bedroom. "Someone has cleaned up the place. The filthy cots are gone as well as the blankets, dirty pillows, and rags, all gone. Yet the new tables remain as well as the folding chairs."

"Hey, they folded them up and stacked against this bedroom wall. "I'll bet someone plans to come up and get this stuff." Alverez said

"I'll lay money on Jeremy. He's no martyr, just an opportunist." Dan turned to Mac. "Do you think all the bombs they built were in the Mercedes?"

"No. I think some of them have already been placed. Or they planned on placing those that went up in smoke on this mountain. Forget the paperwork. I plan on having breakfast in the basement area of the Tri-corp hotels."

Mac walked out on the sagging porch and took one long gaze at the old house. It was if he were saying goodbye to a rather nasty chapter of his life. As he walked off the porch, a cold north wind blew rain in his face.

Alverez yelled at Davidson and Carlton. "Go get in the car. We need to get back."

Dan climbed into the SUV. "Get in the car, Mac. It's damn cold up here."

Mac nodded, and while snapping on his seat belt, and his phone rang. He listened and said "Yes sir." He shook his head, and then jammed the phone into his pocket. "That was V. I., He wants a debriefing. He's ordering breakfast for all of us."

Dan eased the big car down the 'new' trail cut by the Mercedes. All the while the rain pounded down.

Suzanne picked up Claire and they drove over to Fremont Street. This time they couldn't find a place to park. Suzanne tried to sneak into the King of Cars underground parking, but it was blocked off with a chain and large sign that read: FULL.

"Why don't I get out and wander around here and you take my car and go back to the Tri-Corp hotels. There's more parking down there. Call me when you're ready to go back to the apartments."

"Okay. Call me and let me know if you see any terrorists." Claire said.

"Andy was up at the crack of dawn. He had early cruise patrol. Let me tell you, nobody is getting any sleep. It was close to midnight when he came home last night." Suzanne sighed. "I'll be so glad when they catch these terrorists. Then everyone may begin to have a normal life."

"My sentiments exactly. Mac didn't sleep even three hours last night. He finally tried sleeping on the sofa. Today is it. We've got to find them." Suzanne glanced up. "Hey, I'm pulling over there. I'll double park for a moment." Suzanne jumped out and Claire climbed into the driver's seat. She glanced at a car behind honking at her. She sped away giving Suzanne a wave.

Suzanne walked the length of the old Fremont Street acting like any tourist, Even this early in the morning, the street was crowded with them. Though the part of Fremont Street had a mesh covering over the zip line area, the rain seeped through and drizzled on the street.

Suzanne walked down to the band stand. The roadies were checking the sound systems, speakers, and the sound board. One of them unzipped a large canvas bag and took out a base violin and began to pluck the strings into a microphone. He thumped a few strings as the technicians worked with dials and switches on the sound board.

The wind had become a factor, and it was blowing in from the north and scattering dust and debris in gusts. The temperature had dropped. Various flags advertising the rock band snapped in the wind.

Suzanne hunched down into her jacket and pulled up the collar around her face. With her bag wedged tightly under her arm, she walked quickly back to the area of the coffee bar. As she walked into the bar she sighed. At least it was warm, but also crowded. She ordered and finally picked up her beverage. Luckily, a couple that had been sitting in front at a small table offered her their place. She sipped her hot latte' and watched the crowd.

CHAPTER THIRTY-SEVEN

———— ✦✦✦✦✦ ————

A S NOON APPROACHED, the weather continued to intensify: Becoming a true winter storm, Suzanne could see three men in suits, huddled with another man near the band stand talking and gesturing. The cold rain forced people back inside into hotels, shops and restaurants. She had been at this surveillance for nearly a week, and she was bored. She wished she had dropped a magazine or paperback into her large bag. NO! She was here to watch the street. Bus she couldn't stop yawning, and blinking.

She watched as the roadies began to tear down the band stand. She guessed they were moving the concert inside.

There, across the street were two youmg guys, one tall the other shorter. She searched for the copies of the bad guys' pictures she carried in her bag and studied them. They could be Jahreal and Jeremy! She jumped up, threw her coffee in the trash and shot out the door. For a moment she lost sight of them.

As she angled across the street, she fished her phone out from her purse. Then she saw them again, casually walking up a narrow alley between hotels. She hurried back across the street. By the time she reached the alley, they had disappeared. She slowly eased up the alley, but finally spotted a dark green door flush into the wall of the building. She pulled on the handle, and to her surprise it opened allowing her to walk into a stairwell.

There were stairs that went up and some going down. They were metal and painted dark green. She gazed up for a long moment but saw no one. The lighting was poor, and she decided to go up. As she climbed, she took time to speed dial Andy. She walked up to the first floor door. As she opened it, could hear the ring, zing, ka-ching of the myriad of slot machines in the casino. She stood there and stared at her phone. Andy had not answered. She sent a frantic text.

Suzanne glanced around and saw the wide stairs that led to the mezzanine. She walked up and found rest rooms, offices, and bank of sorts with white steel bars across the entrance and a heavy metal door to enter. There were teller windows inside. Walking past the bank, she followed the curve of the level and came to another set of stairs. She took them and climbed up.

This floor had hotel rooms and numbers that began in the three hundreds. She started down the corridor, but behind her she could hear male voices talking softly. She glanced back and she knew it was Jahreal and Jeremy. Sheer panic enveloped her. She took a deep breath and stopped in front of a hotel room door. She fished a credit card from her purse and tried to stick it into the key slot. As the two fugitives walked past, she mumbled. "Damn key, never works right."

One of them laughed, but they kept walking.

She glanced furtively at them and noticed that they both carried sacks that seemed heavy. She was about to turn and run in the opposite direction when the room door suddenly opened. A man in his mid-thirties stood behind the open door with blue eyes blazing, and confronted her.

"Who are you?" His angry stare stopped her.

Marshaling up her courage she answered, hands on her hips, "Well, who are you?" Just then her phone rang. While answering, she pushed by the man and walked into the room. "Andy. I just saw Jahreal and Jeremy. Here in the Fremont Hotel on the third floor, but it's the first floor for the hotel rooms. Yes. I had a good look at them."

The man stood listening to her conversation. "Did you say Jeremy? Jeremy Ardmore? Where is he?"

She pulled the phone from her ear, and nodded. "Out in the hall. They walked past me." She continued to talk into her phone. "Come now or we'll lose them." She yelled.

The man snatched the phone away from her hand." Paul Reston, from Cedar City. Room #318. I'm going after them. Yes I'll call security." He ran to the dresser, and grabbed a gun, slammed it into a holster he wore, snatched up a pair of handcuffs, and ran out of the room and down the hall.

Just then a blond woman walked out of the bathroom. "What in the world is going on?" She asked, while tucking a shirt into her jeans.

"Your husband just ran down the hall after Jeremy Ardmore and another fugitive. Call security." Suzanne said to the woman.

The woman went to her purse and pulled out another gun, handcuffs and a cell phone. She dialed the security number listed on a chart on the inside of the door and talked. Then grabbed Suzanne and dragged her out into the hallway. She asked. "Which way? If there are two of them Paul will need another pair of handcuffs."

"This way, down, around the corner." Suzanne answered, and ran with the woman at her heels. As they turned and entered the second hall, they heard Paul Reston yell. "Freeze both of you. You're under arrest."

Jahreal took a swing at Paul and began a struggle to grab Paul's gun. Jeremy stood against the wall and watched them scuffle.

Suzanne took out her gun and ran up to Jeremy. "Turn around, against the wall."

"Sure little girl, you going to arrest me?" He laughed, and lunged at her gun, but she backed up and flipped the safety off her weapon.

Tammy Reston, who was closer to Claire's size, and weight, kicked and tripped Jeremy. He fell against the wall. As he got up on one knee, she shoved her foot into his back, and she kicked his knee out from under him. Then she stood with her foot on his back. "Hand cuff him." She yelled at Suzanne. "I'll keep my gun on him."

Paul Reston took the opportunity of Tammy's distraction and slammed his fist into Jahreal's mid-section. Jahreal collapsed in a heap.

Paul flipped him over and hand-cuffed him. He then picked up his weapon and dropped it into his holster.

Just then two hotel security guards came running down the hall yelling. "Hotel security. Stop what you're doing!"

Paul faced them and pulled out his identification. "Paul Reston, Iron County Police. These two are wanted by the FBI. And I want him." Paul turned and pointed to Jeremy. "For attempted murder."

One of the security guards pointed to Tammy and Suzanne. "And who do these blond ladies work for?"

The other security guard picked up Jahreal and pushed him down against the wall next to Jeremy. Everyone then turned to see Andy and his partner, Brock Peterson come running down the hall. "Las Vegas Police. He announced. "Officers Freeman and Peterson." He flashed his badge. He turned to Suzanne. "Good, I see you called for back-up."

The first security guard turned to Andy and said. "She's with the LVPD?" He pointed at Suzanne. still holding her gun on Jeremy.

"No she's my wife. She called me when she spotted these two fugitives." He waved at Jeremy and Jahreal.

"And the other blond lady?" He gestured at Tammy.

Paul Reston walked over to Tammy and put a hand on her shoulder. "This is Tammy, my wife."

Security guard number one said. "Are you sure they're not a new secret weapon in law enforcement?" He flashed a grin. "We could use a couple of blond bombshells like these two." He cleared his throat. "What we actually need is an explanation as to what went on here."

Andy was already talking on his shoulder phone to his boss. He turned to the security guards. "Their transportation is on the way." He pointed down at Jeremy and Jahreal. "What we need is an escort down to the 'wagon'. My captain wants us all down at the precinct. I'm referring to Tammy, Paul, Suzanne, Office Peterson and me. We'll send you a report when we finish the paperwork."

Security officer number one said. "Just send it over to our office. You'd better buy these two ladies a good steak dinner, they deserve it." He stepped in an alcove. "Hey, the top of this trash container is sitting on the floor. He glanced down in the trash can. "Their's a bag at the bottom."

'Don't touch it!" Andy yelled "Call the bomb squad."

Walking all through the basement of the tri-corp hotels took Claire most of the morning. Then she moved up to the casino level. She studied the people, especially young men, or those who seemed to be staff. She wandered through shops, but saw no one she recognized or looked suspicious. She checked out the ticket booths, and they were doing a brisk business for the concert tonight.

Outside, maintenance workers were putting up barricades on the sides of the seating area for the people who were planning to attend the rock concert.

Finally, she glanced at her watch. It was 1:15 p.m. She was tired and hungry. She walked out on the long ramp, and took the elevator up to the parking level where she had left Suzanne's car. She tried calling Mac. Her message went to voice mail. She called Suzanne but her friend didn't pick up either.

Claire drove north toward Fremont Street, but the wind and rain slowed down the traffic. As she drove north, she changed direction and went back to the apartment. Inside the apartment, found an apple to eat and took it into the bathroom while she showered and cleaned up.

CHAPTER THIRTY-EIGHT

————— ✦✦✦✦✦✦ —————

M AC HAD BEEN home, because he had thrown damp jeans in the clothes hamper, and left a partially eaten slice of pie and a coffee mug still half- full in the kitchen. The mess he left surprised her. He must have something 'super' heavy weighing on his mind.

She brushed through her damp hair and applied a little makeup: Enough to look like many other women, but not to be memorable. Claire pulled on black jeans and a dark purple turtle-neck. She put her back- of- the- waist holster on and checked her Glock to make sure it carried a full clip. Next, she put on her black hoodie and grabbed her black sneakers. Just before she left the bathroom, she checked her reflection from behind, checking that her weapon was well hidden.

She found the keys to Mac's car on the dresser and decided to drive that car rather than Suzanne's.

Mac must have gone to FBI headquarters with Dan. His keys slipped nicely into the front pocket of her jeans. Before leaving, she made a peanut butter and jam sandwich and drank a glass of milk.

The rain had eased, but the wind had dropped the outside temperature. As she drove into the parking garage at Tri-Corp, she could see maintenance men fastening a heavy mesh roof over the bandstand. It looked quite sturdy, and was anchored into posts in the concrete. Also they were fastening guy wires to places in the building. Because of the wind, they shifted the concert stage tightly between the south- east south -west wings. That helped shelter the concert stage from the north wind.

She could not find parking in the normal Tri-corp parking garages. Everywhere she drove levels were marked as full, so she was forced to drive up into a newly opened section. She took careful note of the numbers and letters on the first of each row of cars, and paid attention to the elevators she had to take to reach the casino.

By moving in the stage, it allowed the band to walk out of a hotel room and directly out to the stage. The over-all security was heavy. Claire stopped and watched maintenance from the parking garage. A security guard came by told everyone to go inside. It felt good to go into the warmth of the hotel. Her phone rang. She glanced at the number.

It was Suzanne. "Suzy, I've been calling you all day. Where have you been, and what have you been up to?"

"Oh Claire, we got them." The bright excitement of Suzanne's voice came into Claire's ear.

"Are you talking about Jeremy and Jahreal?"

"Yes, here at the Fremont. I spotted them and followed them up to the third. floor, all the while calling Andy. Then an amazing thing happened, I tried to get into a hotel room and in there was Lt. Paul Reston, from Cedar City and his wife. The three of us chased them down, plus Andy and Brock, and hotel security. But the bad guys had begun to hide bombs in the trash cans. Luckily there was so much attention going on outside. Because of the weather they moved the bandstand inside. Jeremy and Jahreal couldn't get near it to plant bombs. So they tried to plant some bombs inside."

"Whoa, all this happened at the Fremont Hotel?"

"I know it sounds a bit complicated, and it is. Andy and I are still at the Vegas North precinct. Where are you?"

"I'm back at the Tri-corp Hotels. It looks like I'll be here most of the night." Claire hung up and tried to find a quiet corner to call Mac again. Again the message went to voice-mail. She tried a text, nothing.

The casino level was a pushing and shoving fest. Some of the guests had started to celebrate the New Year early. There were loud conversations, and some minor disputes. She managed to get on the escalator to the basement level. She went to least crowded food shop and bought a diet coke.

Then she saw a maid loading a cleaning cart with towels and rags from the rear of the food shop, Claire decided to follow her. The woman went to the employees' elevator. Then there was a man who hustled into the elevator just before it closed. She stood and watched the overhead LCD readout to see on which floor where they stopped. While she stood there, she searched her bag for the terrorists' picture. The guy looked familiar. Was he Ali Hakim?

The employees' elevator stopped at the third floor. So Claire went back down on the escalator to the casino level. It was crammed with people. She went to the lower bank of elevators and managed to jump on one that went up to the fourteenth floor. She eased off at the fourth floor and walked back down the stairway to the thirdlevel.

Claire had an idea. She would travel around the hotel as would any employee could. She walked from the elevator in the direction to the entrance of the rock concert. There was already a lineup of ticket holders to be let into the seating area. She walked back to the central hub and went in another direction. Each wing was built to accommodate about fifty hotel rooms. She got halfway down the hallway and came to a double room. She slid into the tiny recess between the two doors. She heard "Stop or I'll shoot." A second later she heard a gunshot and then another. Something heavy hit the carpet.

She heard another male voice. "He's down. "I'll check." She eased down about two strides. And then she could see Dan Forester with a semiautomatic in his hands. He bent down and turned over the man that Claire had seen in the basement. "It's Ali, He's dead." Dan stood and immediately pulled out a cell phone and began speaking into it.

A third man, another FBI agent ran back to Dan. "The second guy must have ducked back in the elevator. Mac will tell us if he spots him."

So there's one terrorist still lose, and Mac's after him. Claire dashed across the hub to the stairs next to bank of elevators. After having to fight her way up one flight, because crowds of people were climbing down, she decided there was a better way. She must find Mac, and she decided that he was after Zuhdi. She knew he would need her help.

At the fifth floor she went back to the hub, and went down a wing to find an employees' room. There was a mounted bar on the door: it read. LINEN ROOM. To her surprise, it was open. She perused the room and found the usual: linens, towels, soap, lotion, etc. She tried an employees' elevator, and found it locked. One must have a key to open it. Searching for a key she walked around the room and spotted a cleaning cart. On the top she found a key inside a glass. Another useful item caught her eye. A group of black cotton tops with the Hotel Motif on the pocket. She picked one, took off her hoodie, and slid the top over her turtle neck. She tried the elevator key and door slid open. She crammed the elevator key in her back pocket.

Which way? Up or down? She thought for a minute. The terrorist would want drama. *I'll bet he's planning to throw himself off the top of the building. But which floor is the top?*

Mac chased Zuhdi down the hall, but he ran into an employees' room. Mac tried the door but it would not open. He shook the door, but realized that the terrorist had put something up against inside the door rather than locking it. He pushed and shook it until whatever was against it moved slightly. Mac managed to get his hand inside the door, and pushing his knee against the door moved the block a little more. It was a maid's cart, and finally he moved it enough to slide in the room. It was a maintenance room, but it had an elevator.

The LCD readout on the elevator stopped at level six. Why level six? Mac guessed the man wanted to be as close to the concert as possible. Mac found the elevator door opened and took it up to six. He found that there was a door leading outside from that level. He went out and realized that there were huge air-conditioning vents out there. Mac went to the edge of the roof and looked out. There was the stage below with seating and standing room on level three, and it was brightly lighted. Night had fallen, otherwise it was dark and cold, but the wind had died down. The clouds remained, especially in the western sky. But then a light rain fell, and because it so cold, it turned to sleet.

People began to stream out searching for their seats. Mac could hear voices, chairs scraping and now a recording of the band playing an old song being piped over the sound system.

Zuhdi would go up. Which floors had areas like this one? Mac went to the stairway and started up. He fought that people were going down in a steady stream. He'd take the elevator. Running back he took the elevator up and stopped at level twelve. Another door led outside on the mechanical level. No. Zuhdi.

Because Mac was close to the stage he could feel as much as hear the music. The concert had started. The speakers were blasting out the first song. He went back to the stairs, and pounded up. No more people passed him going down.

Mac ran down the hallway to the stairs. The stair climbing became automatic, just like riding his bike. It kicked him into automatic overdrive. He felt a huge sense of exhilaration, but also combined with a sense of dread.

His phone rang, and he picked up. "We eliminated Ali Hakim." Dan said. "Where are you?"

"Level 12. There is a mechanical room. A door leads out to the air vent level. I can hear and see the band. Zuhdi has to be on one of these levels. I'm going after him." Mac shutdown his phone.

He continued up and stopped at level twenty. He went into the mechanical room. There was no way out to the roof. Back to the stairs, he eased up two more flights until the sign said. ROOF. The door leading outside had a small window, high up on the door. He couldn't see anything but a large air conditioner and a streak of the cloudy sky. He tried the door. It was unlocked and with gun in hand, he eased out into darkness.

As he stepped onto the roof, he saw a slight movement to his right. He moved his body slightly, before Zuhdi's gun slammed down on the side of Mac's head.

He heard the lead singer scream into the mike. *Walk this Way,* as his face and the asphalt collided.

The gloomy, multi-colored light was coming from a giant search light parked on the strip. Everything went black for Mac for a few seconds. A hard kick to his side, and then someone moaned. Was it him?

From faraway, someone yelled at him. "Get up American scum, get up."

CHAPTER THIRTY-NINE

———— ✦✦✦✦✦✦ ————

M AC HEARD SOMEONE kick his semi-automatic hand gun across the rooftop. Through half-open eyes, he pushed up to his elbows and saw the large air conditioning vent near him. He rolled over to it.

"You thought you could stop us! We shall make our revenge, Many of you devil Americans will die tonight, in this most evil of cities." Zuhdi screamed.

When Mac reached the vent he pushed off it and worked to sit up. His head hurt abominably, and he wondered if he would be able to fully open his eyes again. He felt moisture trickle down the side of his head, into his ear and down into his collar.

"Zuhdi. It's only you now. You're alone. All your people are gone. Dead or arrested. We got everyone else." The words came out low, along with a cough.

"You lie, you lie! At midnight all the bombs will go off, and I will go off this roof, and everyone else listening to this devil music will die." He gave a high almost hysterical laugh.

Mac managed to open both eyes, though he saw only a blurred figure. It had to be Zuhdi. His chest was laced with wires and several sticks of dynamite.

"Sorry pal." Mac worked to make his voice low and condescending. "The bomb squad has been neutralizing your bombs all day, one at the time." Mac managed to get his knees under him, and with hand on the top of vent levered himself into a shaky stance. He straightened and leaned on the vent for support.

Finally he opened his eyes and could see Zuhdi clearly. The strobe light and the lights from the stage gave the night a wavy Technicolor glow. The terrorist waved a cell phone in his left hand and a gun in his right. The cell phone must control the dynamite on his chest. The man was a walking time bomb.

The band stopped playing and the crowd clapped and cheered wildly. He watched Zuhdi close his eyes and wince. Now Mac remembered reading Zuhdi's dossier. The man suffered from migraines. Right now he must have one-hell-of-a-headache. Mac managed a grim little smile. He must get that cell phone away from him.

The band now launched into *Dude looks like a Lady.* Zuhdi glanced down at the covering over the stage and scowled.

Mac took a chance and moved to the front of the vent. Glancing at his watch it read 11:52.p.m.

The elevator opened on floor twenty-one, in the linen room. Though only one light burned, Claire could easily see there was no outside door. She left that room and went out into the hallway. Again she went to the hub and down a hall next to the stairway. She galloped up the stairs and found the door marked ROOF. She had to stand on tiptoe to see out of the small window at the top of the door. All she could see was a huge air vent, and she could hear the band play. But she stopped before she opened the door. Anyone outside could see the light from the stairwell. She ran down to the landing and turned off the light. Groping back up the stairs, she slowly eased the door open.

The first thing she heard besides the band winding up the song: *Dude Looks Like a Lady,* and was a competing hoarse voice. Zuhdi began ranting about American food, American clothing, especially about the lack of clothing American women wore. Too bad he didn't know much about the clothing, What he hated was probably made in China. He now complained about the weather. He hated the cold, and now the rain had turned to snow. He stopped talking for a moment because the snow turned into wet snowflakes falling into his hair and on his shoulders. He brushed at his shoulder.

She couldn't see him because of the air conditioning vent. She began to ease around the vent to the right and almost touched Mac's hand clinging to the side. She stepped back and watched him wipe the side of his head with his sleeve. The blood looked almost black dripping down the side of his head.

The song ended, and the lead singer went to the mike and began chatting with the crowd. He started asking the audience to shout out which state or country they were from. That went on for a few minutes. All the while Claire was inching around the huge vent so she could clearly see Zuhdi.

The lead singer then announced the next song would take them up to midnight. The band launched into: *Jamie's Got a Gun.*

Zuhdi had a cell phone in one hand and a gun in the other. When she stared at his chest, she saw the dynamite wired across his chest. She sucked up a shuttering breath.

"Breathe your last, FBI man. At least the air is cold and clear, and it snows. Enjoy your last moments here on earth, before you and these devil people go with you down to hell."

"You first Zuhdi." Mac began to move around the vent to the right.

No Mac. Not yet...Claire thought.

Zuhdi waved the cell phone high into the air, and gave Claire a clear target. She pulled out the Glock and sited it, snapped a bullet into the chamber as she had practiced. This 'nut' case was *not* going to kill anyone else. She took a deep breath.

Okay Claire, next time the cell phone goes up in the air, you must fire. Zuhdi's arm went up clutching the phone. *NOW!* Claire aimed and eased back on the trigger. The bullet went exactly where she had aimed it.

A spurt of blood like a small fountain shot out of Zuhdi's upper left arm. She had severed his brachial artery. As Zuhdi grabbed his left arm, the gun clattered to the roof of the building. His eyes followed the blood running down through his fingers and splashing on the asphalt. "What have you done!?" He screamed

Mac whirled in Claire's direction. "Claire?!"

On shaking legs, Claire managed to walk toward Mac.

The cell phone now slick with blood, fell out of Zuhdi's other hand and thumped to the roof. The pool of blood at Zuhdi's feet reached the size of a large pizza.

Mac grabbed up the gun and scooped the cell phone from the rooftop.

Claire took a deep breath and walked close to Zuhdi. He had dropped to his knees.

"Look, look up at me Zuhdi. I did this. I shot you. A mere woman,- - - - - - *is* the author of your demise."

"NO!.- - - - - - - - - He screamed and reached for her pant leg. She jumped back and he fell on his face. For a moment she felt triumphant. She had managed to put an end to this lunatic. Then she began to shake. *I just shot someone.*

Mac came behind her and put both hands on her shoulders. "How long will he last?"

She took a deep breath, but could not stop shaking. "When his heart doesn't have enough blood left to pump, it will stop beating." She turned around to him. "Don't we have to let the FBI know he's up here?"

"No, we've got to get out of here, off this roof, and as far away as possible." He grabbed her arm.

"Why?"

"Because you're a civilian. We don't want the FBI, the press, anyone finding out you're the one who 'took him out'." Mac stood next to Claire and took one long look at the terrorist, laying very still, his eyes wide open. Blood still dripped from between his fingers clutching his arm. Mac turned away.

"Let's go." He hustled Claire to the roof door and swung it open. "It's dark out here."

"Hold on." Claire inched down the stairs to the landing and switched on the overhead light. "This way." She led him down the hall into the linen room, and the elevator. "I have to go grab my hoodie." Mac grabbed a pillowcase and dropped in the weapons he had gathered up off the roof.

"You need a key." Mac said.

"I know. She fished in her pocket and opened the door with the key she had.

Mac hit the button and they went down to level six. Claire went in and exchanged the blouse for her hoody, and pulled it on. "Hold the elevator." She ran back and put the key where she had found it. The elevator took them all the way down to the casino level.

The New Year revelers noise slammed into them, as they pushed out of the elevator. They fought their way slowly to the ramp leading to the outside elevators. They would take them to the levels in the parking garage.

"I parked on level stratosphere." Claire laughed. As they came out, they could still clearly hear the band playing some old favorites.

"You drove my car?" Mac said, as Claire led him to the Subaru.

"I had to. We went down to Fremont Street in Suzanne's." Claire fished the set of keys from her jeans' pocket and dropped them Mac's hand.

Mac followed by Claire, walked around to the passenger side of the car. Before he opened the door, he pulled her into a long kiss. "You're amazing, you know that?"

"Happy New Year, to you too." She laughed, and reached up to kiss him back.

"Let's get out of here." He glanced around the partially filled parking garage, shook his head and frowned. "We'll celebrate at home," Mac laughed, in relief, with a sense of pure joy. "Now woman, get in the car!"

CHAPTER FORTY

———— ✦✦✦✦✦ ————

M AC'S CELL PHONE rang at least four times. Then the message went to voice mail. He stirred, put his arm out toward the small night table. With eyes still closed, he reached around on the table and grabbed the phone. He held it for several seconds, and managed opened one eye to look at it.

His head ached, both inside and out. A large band aid nestled just above his left ear. He gently touched it and winced. He rolled over on his right side, and still clutching the phone, and dozed again.

Claire opened her eyes to glance at the small clock on her night table. 9:45 a.m. Did it read Utah time or Las Vegas time? She couldn't remember if she had ever changed it when she brought it down from her house in Rawley. How long had they slept?"

When she and Mac had arrived at the apartment, it was after 1:00 a.m. He was hungry, and besides peanut butter and jam, the only thing she had to fix for him was canned soup. He ate, took a shower, then she patched up his head. They went to bed, and hugged for a while, and then he crashed.

Claire knew how much stress he had been in these last few days, and yesterday was an emotional marathon. She slid from the big soft bed, and pulled on some sweats. Next she made coffee, and searched the fridge and found some bread and a box of eggs.

Mac's phone rang again. This time he answered and talked for a few minutes. When he came into the kitchen he was dressed, and grabbed for a mug of coffee. "Believe it or not, we're not expected at FBI headquarters until tomorrow."

"Are you okay? How's your head?" She touched the band aid.

"It hurts, but my vision is clear. Do you have some over -the-counter pain pills?" He asked.

"I think so. I'll search." Claire came back with a tissue of orange pills. "Hold out your hand. "I have to drive back to Rawley tomorrow, because I have to open the clinic on January third. I will leave you the bottle." She said.

"I know." He took his coffee to the kitchen table and sat down. "I'll call you when I can get away from here."

"Are you going to be an official federal employee from now on?" She sat down across from him.

"I don't know. He shook his head. "To be honest, I've not thought about anything past last night. My focus has been on catching the terrorists." He stood up and walked to the sliding glass doors. He opened the drapes, and slid the door open. He went out and stood quietly for several moments.

Claire could feel the cold air from the open door. Her first thought was to ask him to close the door, but she knew the cold air helped his thinking, deciding on his next move.

She searched the fridge and began a mental list of what he would need to have around here when she left. Her world was in St. George. She and Suzanne would drive back to their world tomorrow.

He closed the door, and came over to her. "Are you going to make breakfast? If you don't want to we could- - - - - - - -.""

"I'm just checking to see what you will need when I leave. I can go to the market and pick up some things- - - - - - - -.""

He pulled her up, and held her close. "I don't want you to leave. I know you have a business to run, but I meant it when I told you we need to be together, for the long haul. I love you Claire Talbot, and I want you to be Claire MacCandlass."

"I really don't know what my status is going to be with the FBI. However, I have to report in tomorrow, and they have to officially close the case on eight foreign hostiles, plus one home grown boy. It will depend on the justice department, and how they'll want to pursue this case, or even bury it. I don't interpret the laws. My job is to catch the bad guys and get them off the streets. Tomorrow we'll sit down and review the case. It will depend on many different factors."

"Okay, but I have my life in Rawley, and you will be assigned-- - - - here or back in Southern California?"

"I'll request to be assigned here or in Utah, someplace. We'll just have to see how the investigation goes. Officially it is still open." Mac said.

Claire took inventory of the food in the apartment. She went to the laundry room and washed Mac's clothes, sheets and towels. When she came back with a clean load of clothes, he grabbed her and held her close for a several moments.

"I like the way you take care of me. So- - - - -if you chose to continue to do this, we have to get married. Marry me Claire. I don't care if you want a big traditional wedding or if we pop down to a 'Vegas wedding chapel tonight. You decide." Mac pulled her close and kissed her forehead.

"Don't worry about a big wedding. I've thought about our future, too. We could take Suzanne and Andy with us as witnesses. Suzanne has to go home tonight, too but she'll come back with Justin in two weeks. I'll talk to her." Claire said.

"But first on the list is the wrap- up of the Sons of Allah case. I'm afraid when we get the autopsy on Zudhi, they'll find out he was killed by a .38 caliber bullet. I carry the official .9 mil. semi- atomic weapon.

I'd like you to be in Utah tomorrow when the official FBI meets and goes through the details of this 'caper'. I'm afraid this case will get national attention sooner than we expect."

"I know. I talked to Suzy, and she needs to go shopping for Andy, too. We'll discuss the situation."

Claire walked around the little tree and kissed him. "If you need my gun, I'll leave it with you."

Mac, Dan, and all the other FBI agents involved in the 'Sons of Allah' investigation were in attendance it the FBI headquarters' conference room. Also attending the meeting were representatives from the North precinct of the LVPD.

"Okay." V.I Strickland cleared his throat. "First on the list to discuss is the raid on the terrorists' safe house. Dan, Mac, Cynthia, Carl and Jay were involved in that. We got a lucky break. One of the terrorists was driving the infamous blue Mercedes and apparently it was full of homemade bombs. We surmise that the driver Aukmed had been driven up there to pick them up. We stopped him, with the agents' good, smart driving and help from the rain. As you know the car blew up with the homemade bombs inside. Aukmed was the first loss to the terrorists. An autopsy was done last evening. He died from a head injury.

Second was the capture of Jahreal Hakim and Jeremy Ardmore at the Fremont Hotel. There were fortunate events that involved Police Lt. Paul Reston, from Cedar City, Utah. His wife Tammy, Suzanne Freeman, her husband Office Andrew Freeman, and Officer Brock Peterson. LVPD. All of these individuals helped to capture these two junior bad guys. It will up federal prosecution of these two, because they had bombs in their position.

Third, was the identification of Ali Hakim carrying explosives at the Tri-corp Hotels. on New Year's Eve. Dan Forester stopped him. Autopsy: Death by gunshot."

The last and most dangerous of the group, Zuhdi their supposed leader. His autopsy was most intriguing. Though he had strapped to his body a bomb made of dynamite, wired to a cell phone, his death was caused by one shot with a .38 caliber weapon to high on the inside of his left arm. The individual who shot him knew just where the most damage could be caused. The bullet ruptured his brachial artery causing a complete loss of blood. He died of total blood loss." V. I glanced across the table to Mac. "MacCandlass, do you carry a .38 caliber weapon?"

Mac, ready for this question, answered: "I've been known to carry a backup weapon." Mac pulled out his Smith and Wesson .9 mil. semi-automatic, and laid it on the table, and then Claire's .38 Glock from his boot.

"Did you get that bruise on your head from Zuhdi?" Dan asked. Casually easing back in his chair.

"And how did you know where the brachial artery is even located?" Carl asked.

"One time my girlfriend showed me where it was, and gave me an anatomy book to read." Mac said and rocked back in his chair and folded his arms. "She showed me some other pressure points that could be used to subdue an enemy."

"Well wherever you learned the information, we're glad you could it use it successfully. This is a great victory for us and the city of Las Vegas. There are more arrests to come. The next on the list will be in California. One professor G. Colson. for aiding and sheltering terrorists." V.I said.

He stood. "Go home and relax. We'll see you all on January fourth."

As Dan and Mac took the elevator to parking garage, Dan turned and touched Mac's shoulder. "I noticed you have another abrasion on your head."

"Yeah, Zuhdi saw me come onto the roof and smacked me with his gun." Mac scowled.

"Is that what happened?" Yet you managed to walk off the roof and leave the building?" Dan stared a Mac for several seconds, but then he grinned, and shook his head. "Better not forget to give the Glock back to Claire. If she keeps hanging around with *you*, she may need it again. See you in a couple of days." He saluted Mac and sauntered to his car.

EPILOGUE

CLAIRE ARRIVED AT her house a about midday January second. The house was chilly, and seemed to echo her sadness of being alone again. She sat down with a cup of tea and stared out the kitchen window. She thought back to the early last in October and fateful phone call from Suzanne to come home to St. George, because Neil had died. She had to return home for Neil Bradshaw's funeral. Then Neil, in his will, had left his animal hospital to her. That was at first a shock.

Then a less than two weeks later, she received yet another call from Suzanne. This time her friend sought her expertise, because Suzy had a 'not dead' client at the morgue. That was shock number two.

Since that night, her life had been tilted in the direction of unbelievable events. Culminating in a love from a good man, and these events caused her to take the life of an evil one.

Perhaps she should write all this down in a journal, and leave it for her children to find someday. She now knew she would have children. Now she knew that, because she was definitely going to marry Mac. What would they think of this tale? From this day on, she knew her life would be eventful, filled with adventure. She would meet each day with the sense that she could 'fly' over any hurtle, conquer any challenge with a clear mind, and the hope for the future. All of this would happen with love from a wonderful man by her side.

9 781796 087901